MONSTERLAND
MAYHEM

USA TODAY BESTSELLING AUTHOR
LEXI C. FOSS

Monsterland Mayhem

Editing by: Outthink Editing, LLC

Proofreading by: Katie Schmahl & Jean Bachen

Cover Design: Manuela Serra

Cover Photography: Wander Aguiar & Juliana Andrade

Cover Models: Wander Aguiar, Dina & Jack

Title Page: Susan Gerardi

Illustrated Headers: Ricky Gunawan

Published by: Ninja Newt Publishing, LLC

Digital Edition

ISBN: 978-1-68530-310-5

Print Edition

ISBN: 978-1-68530-312-9

AI Disclaimer: This book does not contain any elements of AI content. All art was designed by real artists, and all of the words were written by the author.

For those who enjoy the chase,
These Alphas will stop at nothing to claim you,
Knot you,
And breed you.
Happy reading, sweet queen…

MONSTERLAND
MAYHEM

A DARK WONDERLAND
RETELLING

One drink. Three maniacal mates.

Drink me.
This is no ordinary task. It's a compatibility test. A way for
the Silver King to find a suitable mate. All because he
needs an *heir*.

Every eligible maiden in the kingdom has to drink.
Including little old me—Ailsa Marvel—a simple mortal
living in a land of magic and wonder.

Never in my wildest dreams did I think *I* would become
the *Chosen Omega*. But the moment I swallow, I find myself
falling *down, down, down* and landing in the middle of
mayhem.

Monsterland is in disarray.
Everyone is hunting the Silver King's salvation. His
intended. The one who can give him an heir. *Me.*

But what if I don't want to be bred? What if all I want to
do is *run*?

Craze offers to help me.
Catum says he'll k*ll for me.
And Krolic says he'll guide me.

But each step toward potential freedom has me
questioning who to trust. Where to go. *How to run.*

My fate has turned into a deadly game.
One where I'm the rabbit and my only salvation is to win
the hearts of those pursuing me.
Otherwise, I'll find myself in the Silver King's breeding
cage.
Or worse, I'll end up dead.

It's time to play, bunny.
You run.
We'll chase.
And when we find you, we'll show you what it means to be the Queen
of Monsterland.

Author's Note: This is a dark standalone paranormal
romance where choosing a mate isn't required. There are
themes of trickery, primal play, and breeding. Check the
trigger warnings in the introduction for more details.

A NOTE FROM LEXI

Monsterland Mayhem is a fast-burn standalone reverse harem romance. It has no relation to any of my other series or worlds. It sits completely on its own.

But it is a fairy-tale retelling.

So you may recognize a few character traits along the way.

However, if ever there was a retelling I would fully butcher and make my own, it's this one. Because what fun would it be to play in a place like Wonderland if all I wanted to do was keep it all the same?

This story is mad. It's chaotic. It's hot. And it's strongly focused on Ailsa and her mates.

Oh, there's a plot as well, one that's twisted and fun. But this book is about being claimed. Owned. *Possessed* by three hot, psychotic men.

Ailsa is an Omega in a world of Alpha-like monsters.

An Omega who is meant to be bred.

An Omega who is destined to be cherished.

An Omega who likes the *chase*.

Will you follow her down to Monsterland and fall into the arms of the Alphas waiting below? Or will you simply… *run*?

Some notes that may interest you regarding content:

✔ Consent (between Ailsa and her mates)
✔ No Other Woman Drama (No Cheating)
✔ Pregnancy/Breeding
✔ No MM, but there are group scenes
✔ Primal Energy

✔ Possessive Over The Top Alpha Males

✔ Touch Her and Die Vibes

✔ Blood Play, Strangulation Play, Rope Play, Knife Play, Wax Play, and Sensual Biting

✔ Knotting, Nesting, Purring, Growling, and Decorative Peens

Enjoy! <3

INTRODUCTION

Once upon a time, a king needed an heir. A *mate*. A breedable Omega capable of taking his seed.

With no available Omegas left in Monsterland, the Silver King devised an edict. One that spread across the realms, creating a mandate for all the inhabitants of this world.

One drink.
On the twenty-first birthday.
It's a requirement for all.

There is no escaping fate.
No denying the Silver King of Monsterland.

Avoiding the drinking ceremony will result in immediate death.
For we cannot risk our relationship with Monsterland kind.

We drink for them. Drink to ensure they continue to support our world. Drink to survive.

Happy birthday, little bunny.
Drink up.
Because it's time to face fate.
And join us...
In Monsterland Mayhem.

AILSA

DRINK ME.

The two words are inscribed in blood-like lettering along the rim of a golden chalice.

Nothing ominous about that.

Nothing at all.

I twist my fingers in front of me, my hands suddenly clammy. I've seen this ceremony performed a thousand times before, but this time I'm the focus of the ritual.

Me. The human servant. *Ailsa Marvel.*

It's no wonder the pews are empty.

No one expects anything from me other than fresh linen and the occasional warm meal.

Yet the Silver King requires everyone—including powerless mortals—to accept this drink on their twenty-first birthday.

"Anyone can be an Omega," his edict claimed. "Therefore, everyone must be tested."

Thus far, no one in my district has ever been an Omega. From what I understand, they're extremely rare. So rare that they may even be extinct.

Hence the requirement to *drink*.

A shiver traverses my spine, the hairs along my neck standing on end. It's eerie here, so chilly and lifeless. Filling it with people didn't seem to matter; this place just exudes *death*.

Yet that has never stopped me from watching the ceremony of others. Some morbid part of me has always been fascinated by this practice, wondering if I'll ever see a true Omega.

That fascination shifted focus when Master Pillar arrived, replacing our old Master of Ceremonies. While he led the ritual in the same way as his predecessor, there was something about his voice that captivated me. His deep and powerful baritone has stayed with me since the first day I heard him speak two years ago.

Sometimes I even hear him in my dreams.

I've looked forward to this day for months, fantasizing about hearing him say my name in that lush voice of his.

Yet now that I'm kneeling before the altar, I'm not all that enthused with the process.

It's usually much faster than this. But, of course, Master Pillar chose today to be late.

Why would he bother being on time for such an unimportant member of society?

Other than me and two sentries, the entire venue is vacant.

My knees ache, the marble floor harsh against my bare skin. My blue-and-white ceremonial dress barely covers the tops of my thighs, leaving my long legs feeling oddly exposed.

It was a dress meant for another woman. A hand-me-down from Baroness Clarice.

"Quick, put it on and make haste," she hissed at me earlier.

There was no pomp and circumstance for my birthday. No glorious gifts or hair updos or makeup. Just a used ritual gown designed for someone five inches shorter than me, and a pair of old blue flats that bit at my heels and scrunched my toes.

I fidget, uncomfortable.

Which causes Sentry Pinka to clear her throat in warning.

It doesn't matter that I've been kneeling here for over an hour. I'm expected to wait here for as long as it takes.

I swallow and bow my head once more.

My morning chores will soon become afternoon chores, which means I'll be working late tonight.

Poor Beast, I think, sighing inside. He's always waiting for me to bring him scraps from dinner.

Usually bones and discarded meats.

He's my pet wolf—if there is such a thing. I met him during one of my many visits to the neighboring forest. At first, I thought he meant to eat me. But all he did was nudge me away from a particularly thorny bush. Then he accompanied me on my trek.

I thought it was a fluke.

Until he met me by the same bush the following night.

And the night after that, too.

By the fifth encounter, I was prepared and brought him food.

That started a little over two years ago, right around my nineteenth birthday. Now I visit him every night.

I hoped to spend a few extra hours with him tonight, to celebrate my birthday.

Alas…

"Where is she?" a deep voice booms, causing me to stiffen.

Master Pillar.

An air of smoky tendrils curls around me, preceding his arrival. I pick up on that scent every time he enters this chapel, his presence an intoxicating claim to my senses.

3

"She's here, sire," Sentry Pinka says, her voice breathy.

Everyone in our district reacts this way to Master Pillar. He's seen as a deity, his fiery magic palpable even to me. But I don't dare look upon his face. I've heard it's quite beautiful, almost impossibly so. Baroness Clarice and her daughters often discuss it.

"Right, let's get this over with," Master Pillar murmurs as he comes to stand at the altar holding the sacred drink.

All I can see is his boots—the fine leather soft and expensive.

"Ailsa Marvel?" he asks.

"Yes, Master Pillar," I reply without lifting my head.

He says nothing for a moment, then clears his throat and the ritual begins.

"We're gathered here on this momentous occasion to celebrate Ailsa Marvel's twenty-first birthday."

While his words are positive in nature—and echo the thousands of ceremonies I've heard before—his tone indicates his boredom.

"She was born to mortal parents, Janice and Ralph Marvel. She has shown no remarkable traits or magical abilities. However, as with the edict set forth by our beloved Silver King, all maidens and gentlemen are required to drink from the enchanted chalice on their twenty-first birthday."

I fight the urge to tremble, my mind more than aware of what comes next.

At least it'll be quick, I think.

"Rise, Ailsa Marvel of Hatter District," he commands. "Rise and taste the bespelled elixir."

It takes effort to stand like he's demanded, my knees shaking in pain at having been pressed into the marble for so long.

And without an escort to assist me, it's even harder.

However, it would be a disgrace to place my hands on the ground.

Gritting my teeth, I slowly manage to stumble to my feet, my toes instantly screaming at me for wearing the too-tight flats.

But at least the dress manages to cling to my ass. Not that there is anyone to flash, anyway.

Still, I want to retain what's left of my dignity.

Master Pillar clears his throat, causing me to glance at him.

And sure enough, the rumors are right. This male has a remarkably symmetrical face.

However, his eyes… his eyes hold a touch of violence to them. One that has me wondering what kind of sins this male has committed.

Such a strange fascination, but nothing in my life has ever been deemed normal.

Most beings in the Hatter District have some semblance of magic. But not me. Never me.

Yet this being possesses intoxicating power, the wickedness of it flashing in his alluring eyes.

Like warm chocolate, I think, losing myself in his stare.

He raises a single brown brow, the dark color similar to his elegantly messy hair.

"Miss Marvel?" he prompts, drawing my focus to his full lips.

This is why I've never dared to look upon him, I think. *I always knew he would be extraordinary.*

His voice warned me of his appeal.

His presence cautioned me to submit and look away.

Yet a single clearing of his throat prompted my disobedience, and now… now I can't stop staring at this beautiful male.

"Focus, Miss Marvel," he tells me, his tone edged with dominance. "Drink."

I blink as though yanked out of a daze, my surroundings settling around me in a flourish of chilling reality.

Master Pillar's knuckles are white as he holds the chalice before me. *Drink me*, it says.

"Yes, right. I mean, yes, Master Pillar." Wow, I'm fumbling this up spectacularly.

Just accept the drink and be done, I think with a mental shake.

Stepping forward, I instantly wince as pain shoots up my leg.

Ignore it, I growl at myself. *Ignore it, take the chalice, and finish this.*

I've not yet eaten today, or really drunk anything at all. Yet my stomach revolts at the sickly sweet scent wafting from the golden cup.

Still, I reach for the stem while Master Pillar observes me from beneath his long, thick eyelashes.

I wrap my fingers around his and the chalice he's still holding, then lose myself in his gaze once more.

There's a hint of malice dancing in his dark eyes, a hint of malice that has my insides churning once more.

Yet it's not fear I feel. It's intrigue.

Something is very wrong with me.

But what else is new?

I've always been drawn to the shadows, to *danger*.

That was how I met Beast, why I always wandered the forest after dark, and why I can't seem to stop myself from holding Master Pillar's intense gaze now.

His nostrils flare as I press the chalice to my lips.

Then I tilt my head backward and tip the contents into my mouth.

I instantly wince at the saccharine taste. It's like swallowing a spoonful of liquified sugar.

Too sweet, I think, fighting a gag and wishing someone were here with me to hand me a glass of water.

Alas, I'm alone. Like always.

Janice and Ralph—I don't dare refer to them as Mom and Dad—work in a different home. I see them once every few months. It's been that way since I turned twelve.

The day Baroness Clarice purchased me from the Farmington household.

I push the memory from my mind and take a deep breath, then I steel my spine, ready to complete the ritual. A simple look will lead to a quick dismissal, and I'll be on my way.

Only, Master Pillar doesn't say a word.

He's staring down at me with a feral expression, his dark irises rimmed with violence.

I swallow, suddenly wishing I hadn't been so bold. Because this male—this *powerful* man—looks like he's about to teach me my place. And I'm not sure I'm going to enjoy that lesson.

An apology lingers on my lips, yet I'm not quite sure what to apologize for. Maintaining eye contact? Delaying the ritual? Something else entirely?

The sentries are staring at me as well, only with widened gazes that project surprise with a hint of fear.

How bizarre, I think. Most superiors barely look my way. But these two are acting as though I've shocked them.

Except they're running their gazes over my body, not staring at my face.

My brow furrows as I glance down, half expecting to find that my gown has ripped.

But no.

The fabric still clings to me like a second skin. However, it's *glowing*.

Wait, no, that's not my dress.

It's… it's me.

My eyes widen.

I'm the source of the glowing.

I lift my arms to see the golden shimmer dancing across my skin to my fingertips, and instinctively drop the chalice. It falls to the floor and shatters against the marble, Master Pillar having released it at the same time.

Yet I barely hear the crash.

There's a roaring in my ears, one that sounds like a wind tunnel but might be the approach of a speed train.

I…

I don't understand what's happening.

Master Pillar finally says something, the word "Omega" leaving his mouth. But I can't understand the rest. It's too far away. It's too foreign. It's too *wrong*.

This can't be happening.

There is no way I, Ailsa Marvel, am an Omega. "This is a mistake," I manage to say. "It has to be a mistake."

Hands clasp my arms, the touch hot and unexpected. I glance to my right to find a male with horns dragging me forward. Another man—this one with tusks—appears on my left.

"What are you doing?" I ask, my voice sounding shrill to my ears. Unnatural. Like it's not even my voice uttering those words.

The men—*monsters*—don't reply.

"Where are you taking me?" I try again.

Nothing.

They just continue marching me toward a dark hallway, one that leads to… to… I don't know where. But I don't want to find out.

This is all wrong.

I can't be an Omega.

I'm human.

I'm *nothing*.

"Don't bruise her," a voice says from the void ahead. "The Silver King will want her unharmed and ready for breeding."

Breeding? I echo in my mind, knowing exactly what that term means, but not how it could possibly apply to me.

Oh, no, no, I think. *Absolutely not!*

"We really should change her clothes," that voice continues, the source of it neither feminine nor masculine. "Although, I suppose it won't matter. He'll remove them as soon as he sees her anyway."

The hairs along my still-glowing arms stand on end, a shock seeming to go through my body.

A hiss leaves the horned guy's mouth as his grip loosens.

I have no idea what I just did, but I very much want to do it again.

Because I do *not* want to go into that hallway or to the infamous *Silver King*.

He'll break me. I'm sure of it.

This is all a misunderstanding. I am not an Omega. The moment he realizes that, he'll kill me.

Another electric current flows across my skin, drawing dual growls from the males holding me.

The horned one barks out a curse, releasing me in an instant, while the other flies into the wall beside me like I've just pushed him.

A magnetic pulse? I wonder. *A wave?*

Oh, who cares! I tell myself. *Run!*

CRAZE

SUCH A PRETTY LITTLE RABBIT, I muse, watching Ailsa Marvel freeze as my power runs through her. *Time to run, sweetheart.*

Her big blue eyes dart around, terror rippling through her athletic limbs.

Then she bolts, just like I desire.

I follow her with my gaze, aware of her every movement. Her sweet scent curls around me in a welcome kiss, that elixir already working its magic.

First, she'll glow.

Then, she'll burn.

And finally, we'll *chase*.

Graves, I can't fucking wait to hunt her.

Our Omega.

Our future queen.

I've dreamt of this moment for centuries, of when our

circle would finally claim our intended. Of when we would finally be *complete.*

Krolic discovered Ailsa two years ago, but she wasn't ready then.

Oh, but she is absolutely ready now, I think, smiling as she runs.

Ailsa's the salvation we've been searching for. The Omega who can give our true king an heir.

Welcome to Monsterland, my sweet girl, I whisper to her. *But watch your step. It's a long… way… down.*

I slip back into the shadows and wander into the mist between our realms.

It's time to prepare. That elixir will work quickly, giving us a handful of days to convince her to be ours. Because while we may be Alphas, we still value consent.

Mostly, anyway.

Seduction is an art form.

And sometimes all an Omega needs is a little taste of oblivion to willingly fall into the illustrious pit of eroticism and carnal pleasure.

Tempt you, we will, I think. *Beg us, you will.*

Because an Alpha's touch is all that will save her now.

The elixir has awoken her dormant spirit.

In one week's time, she'll be screaming with need. Demanding satisfaction. And it will take all three of us to please her. Fuck her. *Claim her.*

Catum meets me in the darkness, his eyes lit up like twin flames in the night. "The androgynous voice was a bit much," he says conversationally.

My lips curl. "It worked, though, didn't it?"

"I think your comments on breeding are what set her off," he returns.

"Hmm." He has a point. "I thought Omegas were

supposed to supplicate and beg to be fucked. The notion of breeding should have excited her, not scared her."

"I don't think Ailsa Marvel is an ordinary Omega," he murmurs, a hint of admiration underlining her name.

"Is anything in our world ordinary?" I ask him.

He shrugs. "I suppose that depends on your definition of *strange*."

As though to punctuate that point, the dark hole around us begins to spin, stirring the hairs along my nape. In a blink, a land of color appears, the purple-rooted trees a stark contrast to the evergreens of the realm we just left behind.

"Fires, it feels good to be home," Catum says as a flurry of vibrant red fireflies swirl around his hand.

I grunt. "This isn't our home." But it will be again soon. Thanks to our beautiful little rabbit.

Flames play over Catum's fingertips, exciting the fireflies dancing around him. His gaze glows with triumph, yet his voice is bored as he says, "I need a pipe."

I scoff at that. "You always need a pipe. Personally, I would prefer a violet tea."

"Says the Mad Hatter," he murmurs.

I roll my eyes. "I hate that nickname."

"Yet it suits you so well," he muses.

I hum noncommittally and shift my attention to the rainbowlike horizon. A new day is approaching. A rebirth of sorts. "The kingdom knows."

"The kingdom knows," Catum echoes.

"Everyone is going to be hunting her now." I can't help the hint of excitement in my voice. I should be concerned. Yet the notion of impending death has my blood heating with expectation.

All that blood.

All those screams.

All for her.

"She's ours to claim," my best friend states. "They just don't know it yet."

"They will," I say, smiling. "And soon, she will, too."

"That she will." Catum's voice deepens with the words, his expression bordering on feral. "Let the fun begin."

My smile grows. "See you in the caves?"

He nods as ash-like tendrils swirl around his legs, his power igniting. "You know just where I'll be."

"And you know just where I'm going," I return.

"Happy hunting, de Hatte."

"Happy nesting, Pillar," I tell him as he disappears into a cloud of smoke.

We all have roles in this courting game.

And mine has finally been activated.

I pull out a deck of cards, my fingers instantly shuffling them while avoiding their sharp ends.

The clock starts now.

Tick, tock.

Tick, tock.

Tick… tock.

AILSA

SHOUTS AND GROWLS trail behind me as I sprint through the courtyard.

I can no longer feel my feet, my shoes cutting off the circulation to my toes. But I can't stop—*won't* stop—running.

At least my dress feels looser, I think, not bothering to determine why. There isn't time. All I can do is *go*.

If they catch me, I'll end up in Monsterland. Where the Silver King will *breed* me.

A shiver runs through me despite the heat assaulting my veins.

I do *not* want to be bred.

I just… I just want to be free. To be in the woods. To run with Beast. To live a carefree existence.

"Ailsa! Stop!"

I ignore the voice and keep running. Faster. Harder. With no real direction in mind, just… forward. Away. Anywhere but here.

Gods, this is bad. Very, very bad.

Something hisses near my ear, a sizzling sound that seems to echo all around me.

I gasp as another shock wave ripples through the air, resulting in grunts and shrieks all around.

What is happening to me? Since when do I have electrical

14

powers? It feels foreign, like the gift isn't actually mine, just covering me from head to toe.

An impossible sensation.

And yet, it zaps again when someone nears me. Like a protective shield.

I shiver and stumble, then shoot forward in an effort to reach the district gates. Pounding follows in my wake. I'm not sure if those boots belong to sentries or monsters. I don't care. I simply *run.*

More of that static energy hums over me as I pass through the iron gates, creating a current in my wake. Or I assume that's the cause of the buzzing I hear.

Screams echo behind me. I don't turn to see the reason for them; I'm too focused on the trees ahead.

The forest.

My home.

My favorite place to hide.

Every step closer relieves a weight from my back, allowing me to push myself even more as I approach the edge of the trees.

I duck beneath the overgrown branches, then swerve toward the path I know by heart. Only, just before I find it, a giant white wolf jumps in my way.

A yelp catches in my throat as I stumble, trying not to land on Beast, but it's too late. I fall into his soft fur with an *Oomph*, then roll to the side toward a nearby evergreen.

Oh, no… I look to the edge of the forest, expecting to see my many pursuers. However, no one is there. At least not until Beast blocks my view with his gorgeous face. He leans down to scent my neck, something he's done since our very first meeting.

A subtle rumble touches his chest, the sound more purr than growl, then he slowly backs up and cocks his head in a "follow me" sort of way.

He's done this before, but I'm not sure now is the time for another of our adventures.

I'm about to say as much when a trumpet sounds nearby, sending a chill down my spine.

Because that loud noise is swiftly followed by my name, demanding my immediate return.

Beast nuzzles me with his snout and repeats the motion.

"I—"

He growls, cutting off my protest before I can even utter it. Then he tilts his head once more with an irritated little huff.

I blink at him.

Where else am I going to go? I wonder.

"Fi—"

Another growl silences my acceptance.

Narrowing my gaze, I push up off the ground and wave toward the path, saying, *Go on, then,* without speaking.

His eyes hold mine for a beat, almost like he's challenging me. Then he slowly turns in the direction he kept gesturing and leads me deeper into the woods.

Every so often, he checks over his shoulder to make sure I'm following. And each time he sees me, he seems to pick up speed.

I have no idea where we're going, but the blaring horn behind us grows quieter with every step, suggesting this is the right way. At least for now.

Minutes pass, maybe even close to an hour, before Beast finally slows near a cave deep in the forest. He glances back at me, that purring rumble coming from his chest.

"Is this your den?" I ask him.

He shakes out his fur coat, leaving me uncertain if that's a *yes* or a *no*. Then he trots inside.

My lips twist, uncertain if I should follow.

His big head pops out a moment later, and I swear I see exasperation in his light green eyes. When I don't immediately move, he comes all the way out and takes my dress between his teeth to give it a tug.

I yelp as it rips, the too-tight fabric barely holding on after my sprint to the forest edge. I didn't realize it before, but the dress had torn all the way up from my thighs to my hips.

No wonder it felt looser, I think, glancing down at the tatters of blue and white. My white underwear and matching bra are completely exposed. Not that Beast seems to care. He's too busy trying to drag me into the cave.

"Okay, okay!" I say. "I'll follow you."

He doesn't let go, just yanks backward, causing me to stumble forward after him.

"Stop that," I hiss at him.

He grumbles in response, still pulling.

"You're going to tear my dress off, Beast!"

I swear he grunts.

Then he goes absolutely still, his pointy ears twitching. His green eyes find mine, and he releases a low warning growl.

"What is it?" I ask, instinctively whispering.

He does that strange head tilt thing again, and when I don't immediately move, he walks around me to nudge my ass with his nose, shoving me toward the cave.

"Impatient much?" I mutter at him.

The wolf snorts in response.

Sometimes I swear he understands me.

Perhaps he does.

I'm about to comment on it when that blaring horn

suddenly echoes off the surrounding trees, sending a chill down my spine.

I don't think; I move, nearly jumping into the cave to duck out of sight.

Beast follows, then passes me to dart deeper into the cavern. I follow, but the uneven rocks beneath my thin shoes seem to reawaken the sharp pangs in my feet. Every step has me cringing, the pain growing stronger until I debate kicking off the flats and going barefoot instead.

Beast must notice my slow pace because he bounds back to me, his eyes glowing somewhat eerily in the dark. He glances over me, a snarl in his lip.

Then his attention goes over my shoulder, toward the sound of scuffles behind me.

"I found—"

The words die as Beast lunges forward and tackles the owner of that male voice to the floor. A sharp crunch echoes around me, then a gurgling sound that has me scurrying away from the skirmish.

Because Beast didn't make that noise. He *caused* it.

I have no idea what kind of being he just took down— a monster? A human? A fae? The choices were endless.

But he did it with unerring precision, confirming what I've always known about him—he's deadly.

Yet as he returns to me, he simply rubs against my side with that purring rumble again and nudges me forward once more.

I should be mortified by what he just did, especially since the evidence of it lingers around his snout. But all I feel is relief.

He's keeping me safe.

Beast *always* keeps me safe.

It's been this way for two years.

And even though I probably shouldn't, I… I trust him.

He's been my only friend here. The only one who seems to look out for me as much as I do him.

In a world of chaos, befriend the wolf, I think. *His intentions are always clear.*

Except right now as he pauses by an unexpected watering hole.

He stares at it like he's conflicted about whether to swim through it or try to balance on the rocky edge to go around it.

I creep forward and kneel to test the water, curious about its temperature and potential depth.

My fingers graze the top, only the substance doesn't move like liquid.

It… it feels like glue.

I jerk my hand back, and the darkness comes with me. Yelping, I try to dislodge the sticky glob.

"Oh!" I cry out as the inky texture starts *crawling* up my arm. "What is this?!"

I attempt to stand, to jump backward.

And scream as the thick substance yanks me into the obsidian pool.

My face meets the strange liquid, muffling my protests. Panic surges through my limbs, my arms instantly trying to right myself, to bring my head back up for air.

But I only seem to be going down.

Sinking.

Drowning.

My heart beats faster in my chest, creating a thrumming in my ears that sounds ominous and chilling.

I can't breathe.

I can't swim.

I can't do anything other than allow the black glue to take me down, down, *down.*

I hope Beast doesn't follow me or try to help. There's

no escaping this bizarre fate. It's so dark. And heavy. And... and...

My brow furrows. *And gone*, I realize as my hand suddenly meets air.

I wave my arms and kick my legs, surprised to find them free.

What...?

Another shriek escapes me as air whips around me, my long hair tangling in the wind as the sensation of *falling* spikes through my veins.

"Oh!" My limbs pinwheel as I try to grab something—*anything*—to stop my fall.

But there's nothing here.

Just more darkness.

Light air.

And whooshing sounds.

My dress flaps around me, my shoes long gone thanks to the bizarre liquid. I'm not too upset by that last part. But I wish I knew what was—

Blinding light has my arms flying up to meet my face, my palms instantly covering my eyes.

Then everything stops on a violent splash.

Gasping, I struggle, the icy water an unwelcome sensation against my skin. I know how to swim, but this... this has all been so jarring. So overwhelming. So *impossible* that I... I can't... I just...

My lungs scream with the need for oxygen, my mouth threatening to open. But I'm submerged. I'm lost in this chilly sea of unfamiliarity. Drown—

Something grabs my wrist, jerking me out of the waves as a sturdy band encircles my lower back.

I gasp as fresh air hits my face, my chest instantly filling on a much-needed inhale.

"You're all right, sweetheart," a deep voice murmurs near my ear. "I've got you."

I freeze.

It wasn't a *something* that grabbed my wrist, but a *someone*. And that sturdy band was a muscular arm.

My eyelashes flutter as I try to focus—*to see*—but all I end up doing is slamming them shut as water drips into my eyes.

"Shh," he hushes.

I will not *shh*. I have no idea who is touching me, how I ended up here, or where *here* even is!

I flail in his arms, earning me a grunt from my captor.

Or… or *savior*, I guess. He saved me. Sort of. Maybe.

And he's *very* strong because those bands—*arms*—of his wrap even more securely around me as he drags me through the water.

I don't stop squirming until he pins me to the sandy beach, his athletic form easily dwarfing mine despite my five-foot-seven height.

"Ailsa," he says, my name a caress with that soothing baritone.

I blink. *What…?*

My lashes flutter once more as I finally focus on the man above me.

Or rather… *creature*.

Monster?

His face… it's… it's covered in skull makeup. Black ink. Black irises. Long black lashes. Thick black hair. Everything is *black*.

Except the hollows around his eyes are white.

And his lips… his lips are white, too.

A scream bubbles up inside me, only to be smothered by his palm covering my mouth. "Ailsa," he says again, his knowledge of my name only making my heart beat that much faster. "You're safe. Or you will be. But I need you to be quiet. You landed in an unexpected place."

That's an understatement.

Nothing about this is *expected*.

First, I found out I'm an Omega—something I'm convinced is a mistake.

Then I ran through the forest after a wolf and stupidly followed him into a cave.

Where I fell into a black pit.

That turned into sky.

That eventually became *this*.

My gaze darts around as I try to define what *this* is, and I realize the *beach* I'm on isn't a beach at all. It's... it's a cloud.

No, that's not right.

It's just white like a cloud. Soft. Squishy. *Like cotton*.

And the water we just escaped is bright red. Not blue. Not translucent. Not even turquoise. But *red*. Like blood.

My gaze flies to the trees dotting the cotton-like beach. They're all pink with flowers instead of leaves.

"I'm going to remove my palm from your mouth," the male above me says. "But I need you to be a good girl and stay quiet for me, okay?"

My lids flutter again, the blinking instinctual as I stare up at this skull-faced madman. Beneath the makeup, I can see defined cheekbones and a square jaw, his features clearly handsome even with the paint. Or perhaps, made even more handsome *because* of the paint.

I have serious issues, I decide.

His dark eyes narrow like he heard that. "Are you going to be a good girl for me or a naughty little rabbit?" he asks.

I'm not sure I like that question, something I convey by arching a brow.

"I see," he murmurs. "Well, you should know, the

louder you scream, the more punishments you'll earn. I happen to like my cards, and I would hate to waste them on the blossom gremlins."

Now I just… stare. Because what? Cards? Blossom gremlins?

He smirks and removes his hand, only to replace it with a quick and unexpected kiss against my lips. "Hold that thought, darling," he murmurs, rolling off of me and onto his feet in a fluid motion that leaves no question as to his inhuman status.

Definitely something other.

He whistles, a deck of cards appearing in his palm as he shuffles the item between his hands. I frown at him, not understanding what he's doing or why. But clearly this has something to do with his comment regarding his—

A card sails through the air so fast I jump.

Only to nearly scream as it slices right through the neck of an approaching creature with very sharp teeth.

"What—"

Another appears, this one taken down in a blink by a flick of the madman's wrist.

Chattering begins, causing the skull-faced male to sigh. "You realize I have fifty more of these, yes?" He renews his shuffling and starts sending cards all over the beach, knocking down the two-foot-tall beings with a precision that is borderline insane.

He whistles the whole time, then pauses as the ground begins to shake.

"Ah, fuck," he mutters. "Tattletales." He spins toward me. "Time to go, gorgeous."

"I'm not going anywhere with you," I tell him, scooting backward along the sand—*cloud*—and freezing when my hand meets the water's edge.

He arches a single dark brow, the movement causing

the white paint around his eye to widen slightly. "I'm not sure you understand the choice you're making, darling rabbit." His gaze skates down my body. "You're practically naked, and a very deadly, very *horny* bull is about to part those trees. And while I'm good at a lot of things, taming a bull-man isn't one of them. You feel me?"

I blink at him. *Practically naked?* I glance down, my lips parting at the state of my dress. It's... it's basically no longer there. All I'm left in is my panties, which are translucent thanks to my time in the water.

If only the red color had soaked into my white garments, too.

Alas, no.

I... Yeah, I'm practically naked, just like he said. *Great.*

"So what's it going to be, darlin'?" he drawls, adopting a strange sort of Southern twang. "Me or that?" He points to the trees as a giant being with large horns breaks through the forest's edge. His feet are hooved, his legs hairy, but his upper body is all athletic male. At least until I reach his face, which has a large snout and two fiery red eyes.

Those eyes take in the massacre along the cotton-like beach before finding me near the water.

Steam billows out from his nose as he looks at me.

"Tick, tock, sweet rabbit," the skull-faced man singsongs. "Tick, tock."

KROLIC

I GLANCE down at my wristwatch, my teeth gritting together. *Come on, Craze.*

He's showing off.

Trying to impress our future mate.

But he's wasting precious minutes. The longer he keeps Ailsa on this beach, the less time we have to secure her future in Monsterland.

"Tick, tock," Craze says, probably because he can sense me lurking in the shadows with my watch.

Tick, tock indeed, I think at him.

Unfortunately, he can't hear me. Oh, but he can sense me. Just like he can sense the other approaching predators.

The bull-man, as Craze so lovingly refers to Brandt, is only one of the incoming problems.

Ailsa's alluring scent will travel far and wide, marking her as a beacon for trouble. All because the Imposter King —I won't call that bastard by his real name—is cheating the system.

The elixir edict is bullshit. Especially since that elixir causes Omegas to go into a forced heat.

I suppose it's one way to ensure an Omega is found, but a real king creates a mate-circle and *hunts* for potential mates.

Real kings don't cheat.

And they don't take over the palace while the kingdom's true monarch is out searching for a queen.

Alas, here we are.

If the imposter on my throne catches Ailsa, he'll forcibly breed her and solidify his rule over Monsterland.

I can't allow that to happen. *We* can't allow it to happen.

Which is why I need you to fucking move, Craze, I growl in my mind.

He cants his head. "What'll it be, princess?" he asks our intended.

He's gone through about a dozen pet names since meeting her, each one seeming to call to one of his varying personalities.

"Do you——"

Brandt roars, cutting off whatever Craze was about to say. He glances back just as the fiery bull takes off toward them, his red eyes focused on my best friend.

"Rude," he drawls. "I was giving the lady a choice, but now you're forcing me to act."

He casts a series of his rigged cards through the air, each one perfectly catching on Brandt's torso and exploding a second later.

"Such a waste of fire power," Craze mutters. "I'm going to need another deck."

He's talking about his cards, but Ailsa doesn't appear to be listening. She's too busy gaping at the bloody beach.

Just pick her up and run, I want to demand.

Alas, we agreed this part would be played by Craze. He's the only one who hasn't spent any time with Ailsa yet. Not that Catum has been around her much, but he's at least been able to observe her from afar.

Meanwhile, Craze stayed here to spy on the Imposter

King. He's a literal jack of all trades. His primary skill set centers around survival, thus making him the obvious pick to play hide-and-seek with the fake monarchy.

"Ailsa," he murmurs, his voice softening as one of his rarer, more tender personalities comes out to say hello.

She finally looks at him, her expression wary.

"I realize this is a lot to take in," he says. "But your scent marks you as bait for a very dangerous game. So we need to run, as I can't properly protect you here."

Oh, he can protect her anywhere.

But staying here will require him to reveal one of his more violent sides, something Ailsa isn't ready to experience.

Those parts of Craze's nature also weren't meant for her.

Our diamond needs love and affection. Protection and patience. Pleasure and understanding.

We have a long road ahead, one we need to quickly maneuver down if we have any chance at all of safely reaching the finish line.

Speaking of… I glance at my watch again. *We are definitely going to be late. Fuck.*

"I don't even know your name," Ailsa whispers, blinking those beautiful eyes up at my best friend.

He gives her a playful grin, one that pulls at the white paint around his mouth. "Craze de Hatte, at your service." He bows and then straightens as the sound of rustling grows in the trees.

Orange orcs. I can smell them, their citrusy aroma underscored by the scent of rotting fruit.

Two of them are notoriously known for supporting the Imposter King. *The Tweedle brothers.*

Word is already spreading of Ailsa's arrival. We knew this would happen. We expected it. We *wanted* it.

Claiming her must be a public event. It's the only way to resecure the throne and prove once and for all that the current king is unfit to rule.

He's a lone wolf.

I have an Alpha-circle.

And soon, my Alpha-circle will have a mate. Then we'll have a whole kingdom, too.

"Please," Craze says to Ailsa, drawing my attention back to them. "Please let me escort you."

I smirk. Craze never begs. But he knows he'll have to use up several more explosive cards to take down the two massive orcs. And Craze hates wasting his toys.

Ailsa sighs. "Damn it, Beast."

My eyebrow inches upward as Craze cocks his head to the side.

"That's an intriguing nickname," he tells her. "I much prefer it to 'Mad Hatter.'"

She stares at him. "What?"

"The nickname you just gave me; I said I preferred it." He frowns. "Are you hard of hearing, love? Is that why we're still here instead of running?"

"I... *No.* I can hear just fine. And I wasn't talking to you. *You* are not my Beast."

My inner wolf purrs at the possession underscoring those two final words. *That's right, little mate. I am your beast in more ways than you realize.*

"I can become a beast for you, if that's your preference," Craze offers.

"You can turn into a wolf?" she asks.

He stares at her. "No, sweet rabbit. I'm a different beast entirely."

I nearly snort. He's not wrong. But he's not talking about physical forms so much as his sexual prowess.

Which, of course, goes over her head.

Because she frowns and asks, "Should I be afraid of you?"

He chuckles. "Probably, but not in the way you think." He winks and glances over his shoulder again as the scent of rotting citrus grows stronger. "I really don't want to play with the Tweedle brothers, Ailsa. Can we please run now?"

"How do you know my name?" she asks, ignoring the urgency in his tone.

"How about a game?" he counters. "For every direction that you follow, I'll answer a question. Starting with the one you just asked in exchange for you running."

She studies him for a moment. "You're saying you'll tell me how you know my name if I agree to run?"

He smiles, but I don't. Because I recognize the devious twinkle in her gaze. I've spent the last two years getting to know her in my alternate form. And that look isn't one of obedience. It's one of defiance.

"Okay, I'll run," she adds as she stands.

Then she bolts down the beach.

Craze's amusement dies. "That's not what I meant," he mutters, chasing after her.

Naturally, she's chosen the worst path imaginable.

Growling under my breath, I shift back into my wolf form and take off in their direction.

There's only one way to distract her now.

I sprint through the woods to the beach and release a howl that has her stumbling forward to an abrupt halt.

She spins around just as I reach the edge of the forest, her eyes going wide. "Beast!"

I cock my head in the way I know she thinks is cute and wait for her to start running toward me.

That's it, little mate. Come get me.

She bypasses Craze—who is glaring in my direction

and no doubt thinking he had this handled when he obviously didn't—and darts straight for me.

I wait until she's about fifteen feet away to turn back around and bound into the woods.

"Wait!" she shouts.

I do, but just enough to string her along and get her moving in the right direction this time.

"What are you doing?" Craze demands.

His words are more for me than for Ailsa.

Yet she replies with, "Following my pet!"

"Pet?" Craze echoes.

Then laughs.

Because of course he finds the term fucking hilarious.

I'm a king. The *rightful* king of all the Alphas and Betas in this kingdom. And this adorable little Omega considers me her pet.

I don't mind.

I'll be anyone she wants me to be so long as she chooses me. Chooses *us*.

It's not just what she is but who she is, and that distinction is what the Imposter King has failed to understand.

He'll take Ailsa by force, knot her until she's pregnant with his heir, and then present her in front of Monsterland like his prized broodmare.

But this connection is much deeper than breeding. It's about mutual respect. Winning her heart. *Marrying her soul.*

That's the lesson Monsterland needs to relearn.

That's why we let her take that elixir.

That's the reason we're playing this game now.

Her acceptance will remind Monsterland of our past.

And her choice will define the future.

I trot along a little more for her, glance over my

shoulder to see that she's well and truly on the correct path now, and take off at full speed.

"Beast!" she yells for me, making me smile inside.

I love that fucking nickname.

She has no idea how *beastly* I can be.

But she will soon.

Very. Fucking. Soon.

AILSA

THERE ARE PURPLE TREES EVERYWHERE, their leaves decorated in a crimson shade. I've never seen anything like this, and I don't have time to evaluate their strangeness. Because I'm trying to find Beast.

He ran off a few minutes ago, disappearing into this area of the woods. Yet now I can't see him anywhere. I push myself harder and faster, trying to find him, all while that strange skull-faced man—*Craze*—follows.

Monsterland, I think, passing mushroom-like clouds hovering between the abnormal trees. *I'm definitely in Monsterland.*

Beast must have followed me through that portal hole. However, his stark white fur wasn't red from the water. He hadn't been wet at all.

Just like me and my dress, I realize, frowning.

I shake my head.

None of this makes sense. But then, it's not supposed to.

I've always been fascinated by the Monsterland realm, just in a morbid kind of way. The others often spoke about it with reverence, hoping to one day be invited into the Silver King's court.

That was never my desire. I simply wanted to experience something different.

And, well, I've experienced enough.

I'm ready to go home now, I think. *I just need to find Beast and—*

The ground falls out from beneath me, drawing a yelp from me as I start spinning down, down, *down.*

My hair whips around my face, making it hard to see and breathe. My arms and legs pinwheel, much like they did when I went through that strange portal. *Oh, not again!*

Everything moves faster, the air swirling all around me until everything stops.

And I find myself suspended in… in… *Gods, what even is this?* It's sticky, like that glue substance from before, except it's… it's stringier. My limbs are all tangled in it, like some sort of weird, gooey web.

Ever so slowly it begins to stretch, my weight pulling me toward the black ground below.

Where Craze is standing with his hands on his hips, legs braced, expression bored. "While you're hanging there, let's chat," he drawls. "You've landed in Monsterland, sweetheart. Nothing is what it seems. Everything's a trick. And you, my darling rabbit, are a beacon for trouble."

I glare at him. "I'm not your *sweetheart* or your *darling rabbit* or any of the other nicknames you've given me," I inform him. "And the only trouble I seem to be in is related to… to… well, I don't know. But I'm not your anything. I'm just me. Ailsa. Human. And ohhh, let me go!"

That last part is for whatever has a grasp on me, my complaint coming out winded as I struggle against the elastic holding me captive in the air. All that does is stretch it a little more, but not nearly enough to reach the ground.

This is ludicrous, I think angrily. *Absolutely mad!*

"You're definitely my something, Ailsa," he replies, his

voice the epitome of calmness. Which is so unfair, given the situation. Because I am definitely *not* calm.

"I don't even know you," I tell him.

"No, you don't," he says. "But you will."

"I won't."

"You will," he counters. "Because we're playing a game."

"What game?" I say through my teeth as I once again struggle to release myself. It's useless, but I can't just hang here. It's… it's too much like defeat.

And I will not be defeated.

I've lived through too much to accept that fate.

"You obey my commands and I answer a question, remember?"

"Obey?" I echo. "I don't recall agreeing to *obey* anything."

He grins. "I may be altering the phrasing a bit. Regardless, I owe you an answer."

I blink at him. "What?"

"I asked you to run and you did. Albeit not in the direction or the manner in which I intended, but you did run. And therefore, I need to tell you how I know your name."

Oh. I… I don't know what to say to that, so I just stare at him. I honestly didn't expect him to tell me anything. Supernaturals typically act as though I don't exist, and the humans I've known haven't been much better.

"Your *pet* told me your name," he says with a lopsided grin.

Right. That's on par with the type of condescending response I'm used to. I roll my eyes and return to fidgeting with the glue-like substance holding me captive.

"It's highly amusing, by the way," the unhelpful male continues. "You calling Krolic a *pet*, I mean. There's no one else in all the realms who could ever refer to him as such and remain living. But you're not just anyone, are you?"

"Krolic?" I echo, stilling once more.

"Your Beast," Craze murmurs, drawing my gaze down to him again. "His name is Krolic."

My brow furrows. "Is he… your pet wolf, too?" Did Beast often travel back and forth between Monsterland and my realm? Is that why he took me to the cave, to help me escape?

Or… or did he lead me there to take me to my fate?

Did Beast betray me?

Craze laughs, the sound skittering down my spine. It's not an unpleasant sound, but it is slightly unsettling. Perhaps because I don't find anything funny about this situation.

I'm half naked and hanging upside down in Monsterland, of all places, after finding out I've been wrongly marked as an Omega.

Oh, and my one friend—a wolf—may have betrayed my trust.

Definitely *not* humorous.

"Krolic is my best friend," Craze says, still chuckling. "And his wolf is most certainly *not* my pet."

"His wolf?" I repeat. "Beast is your best friend's pet?"

Meaning he belongs to Krolic?

Why…? Why did he visit me, then? If he already had a home?

"I suppose that's accurate," Craze utters slowly, then shakes his head. "Nevertheless, I answered your question regarding how I learned your name. So what's next, Ailsa? What else do you want to know?"

I frown at him. "What are you going to ask me to do in exchange for an answer? Because I'm a little stuck up here."

"Yeah, that's usually what happens when you run into a Gum Tree."

"A Gum Tree?" I look at the strands holding me in the air. They're pink, and I suppose they resemble branches, only rubbery. *And sticky like… gum.*

"Yes. I took the cloud slide." He points to a fog off to the right. "That's a much faster route when running off a cliff."

Running off a….? I glance up and realize the "tree" I'm hanging in is rooted maybe a hundred or so feet *above* me.

Gods… "I didn't even see it," I whisper aloud.

"I know." Craze's voice draws my attention back to him as he folds his athletic arms across his chest. "Want to know how to get down from there?"

"I… yes. Yes, I do."

He smiles. "Excellent. Laugh."

I stare at him. "What?"

"Laugh," he says again.

"I don't understand."

"It's an action typically inspired by something funny," he explains, like I'm some sort of idiot. Although, he doesn't say it condescendingly, just matter-of-factly.

"No, I know what laughing is; I don't understand how that'll help me get down," I tell him, somewhat exasperated. Not necessarily by him—well, maybe a *little* because of him —but mostly from this whole wild experience.

"Try it," he tells me. "Try laughing and see what happens."

"I'm not sure I'm in a laughing mood," I return through my teeth.

"Hmm." He taps his chin. "Well, a song might do. Can you sing?"

"Are you serious?"

"Typically? No. Right now, though, yes." He gifts me with a quick grin. "Want me to sing to you instead?"

This man is insane, I decide, just gaping at him.

"I'll take your silence as a yes," he murmurs, then tilts his head back and… and begins to *sing*.

My lips part as the haunting melody reaches my ears, his voice deep and borderline hypnotic. I'm so mesmerized by him that I don't even realize I'm moving until I feel the sticky branch slither against my wrist.

Startled, I glance at it, then gasp when I realize it's *releasing* me. But I'm still a good twenty feet in the air.

"Craze…"

He doesn't acknowledge me, too lost in his song to hear me. I can't understand a word he's saying. It's some language I don't speak.

"Craze!" I try again, louder this time.

He ignores me, his voice seeming to grow louder.

I quiver, the dark tune weaving some sort of enchantment over my being. I'm practically transfixed by the male below, his voice stirring an unhealthy fascination inside me.

"Craze," I manage as the Gum Tree releases one of my arms. My left leg almost immediately follows, leaving me hanging haphazardly in the air. "I'm going to fall!" Which I know is the point, but not from this height!

I shriek as my other arm goes free, the branch only loosely around one ankle now.

Shit, shit, shit!

I cover my head as the sticky substance lets go of my final limb, sending me straight toward the ground.

And into a pair of waiting arms.

I startle, surprised to feel Craze's hold around me again. It's different from when I was in the water, mainly because I'm aware of him now. Of his voice. His smile. *His violent cards.*

But as he smirks down at me, I don't feel fear. I just feel... relieved.

Because I didn't break my neck.

I'm still alive.

And for a moment, I simply breathe.

"Hey there, beautiful," he says with a twinkle in his dark eyes. Then he winces. "Sorry, I mean, *Ailsa*." He frowns. "But you really are beautiful." A note of reverence underlines his words, his gaze tracking over my features.

"Thank you." The two words just sort of tumble from my mouth. I'm not sure if I'm thanking him for the compliment or for catching me or for everything thus far. But I... I mean the sentiment.

"No need to thank me, Ailsa. I'll always catch you," he promises me, his declaration eliciting a shiver from deep inside. Because that almost sounds like a vow of protection.

Although, I suppose that may also be a threat.

The dark glitter in his irises makes it impossible to tell.

"Why are you helping me?" I ask, studying his expression for any tells. But all I see is the skull makeup, his features utterly masked.

Although, I do catch a slight hint of dimples as he grins at me. "How about a new game, hmm?" He starts walking while he speaks, carrying me as though I weigh nothing at all. "Quid pro quo—I answer one of your questions and you answer one of mine. *And* you let me lead for a bit."

I frown. "Lead for a bit in what way?"

"I want to carry you for a while," he clarifies. "The Hot Chocolate Fields are dangerous, and I don't want to risk you stepping on a fudge bomb."

"A...?" I almost repeat that last part but shake my head. Because what's the use? If I keep echoing every strange thing he says, I'll simply become a parrot. So rather than ask what the heck a Hot Chocolate Field is, I opt for a different path. "Where are we going?"

"That's two questions," he murmurs. "Agree to my game first and I'll answer one."

"Why does it have to be a game?"

"That's now three, but I'll answer this one as a freebie," he says, glancing around before taking a large step.

I don't bother looking down to see what he's doing. I keep my focus on him and not the subtle tic in his jaw.

"Games are enjoyable," he tells me. "But honestly, I want to play this one so I can get to know you better."

"Why?" I ask, baffled by this man. "Why me?"

"That's another question, Ailsa. I believe you owe me an answer first."

"I haven't agreed to your game," I point out.

"Which is why I'm not obligated to respond to any of your inquiries," he returns with another smile. "So the choice is yours. Do you want to play a game with me or not?"

CRAZE

THE LITTLE RABBIT stares up at me, her blue eyes a swirl of confusion and exhaustion. It's been a chaotic day for her, and unfortunately, that sense of chaos will only continue.

She's in Monsterland now. Nothing will ever be the same for her again.

I step over another fudge bomb while waiting for Ailsa to make her choice. She seems to have a knack for picking the most dangerous paths imaginable, first by heading straight toward the Tweedle brothers instead of running away from them.

And then by bolting straight into a Gum Tree that landed her in the Hot Chocolate Fields.

Our goal with the elixir was to allow her presence to finally be known, and now it was my job to parade her around just enough for word to spread of her true nature.

But not too much to where she ended up hurt or taken by one of the Silver King's minions.

A tightrope, honestly. One I'm used to skating along. However, this little rabbit seems to have a propensity for hopping off on her own trails.

Hence, I'm carrying her now so she doesn't actually create a chocolate mudslide.

The poor thing is already barely dressed. Hot fudge against her skin would be… bad. Very, very bad.

"Fine," she says, drawing my gaze to her mouth. "I'll play your game. Now it's my turn to ask you something."

I pause mid-step to arch a brow at her. Technically, she just answered my question, which did in fact make it her turn.

"That's the second time you used my words against me," I muse, noting the first time being her running earlier after I said I would address her inquiry if she agreed to do what I requested first. Which was to run, and run she did. "You're very clever."

I like that trait.

It'll suit her well here.

"Ask away, Ailsa," I say, careful not to call her *rabbit* or anything else. Apparently, she doesn't like endearments or nicknames. That's a shame, as I have several brewing for her in my mind, each one suited to my varying moods.

Little rabbit for playtime.

Gorgeous or *beautiful* for moments of affection.

Pet for sex.

Maybe if I seduce her properly, she'll allow me to use that last one. *Sweetheart* and *princess* would do as well. *My queen*. Mmm, the names are truly endless.

"Why are you helping me?" she asks as I resume walking again.

"Because you're the key to everything," I tell her. "And I wanted an opportunity to get to know you."

"Why? And what do you mean by 'key to everything'?"

"That's two more questions," I point out. "Tell me your favorite fruit, and I'll answer one of them for you."

She blinks at me. "My favorite fruit?"

"Yes, Ailsa. What's your favorite fruit?"

Her confusion is cute. I like that it's distracting her from everything else and keeping her attention on me while I focus on safely escaping this field. If she had any idea where she landed, she would probably have frozen in fear.

Instead, she's just staring at me with a look I'm very familiar with—the one that says she thinks I'm insane.

Welcome to the party, little rabbit, I muse, waiting for her response.

"Cherries," she finally blurts out. "My favorite fruit… it's cherries. Although, I've only ever had them once. So I guess… I guess I also really like pears. Specifically the ones that grew back near Baroness Clarice's estate."

Baroness, I nearly echo aloud but instead just snort inside.

Ailsa is going to think my world is strange, but honestly, I find hers even more bizarre. The disparity of wealth, the favoring of magical talents, the belittling of pure humans… None of it makes any sense to me.

Humans are rare.

Just like Omegas.

They should be cherished. Protected. *Respected*.

Alas, that's a conversation for another day, perhaps. Because I now owe my little rabbit an answer.

"You asked why I want to get to know you," I say slowly, mostly to give her an opportunity to protest and rephrase. When she doesn't, I add, "I want to know my potential mate."

"Potential…" Her eyes widen. "*What*?"

I smirk, not at all surprised by her response. "Is that another question? Because you'll need to tell me your favorite flower for me to answer."

"Are you serious?" she sputters.

"I believe I answered that question before," I drawl.

"I don't…" She shakes her head. "Okay, whatever. Sunflowers. The kind found out in the meadows. They're yellow and they smell nice."

Sunshine flowers, I note, aware that they're not exactly the same in this realm as in her home, but close enough. *Sunshine* would also be a good nickname for my little rabbit. Her long white-blonde hair definitely reminds me of the sun.

Alas, nicknames are not allowed.

Not yet, anyway.

"What do you mean by *potential mate*?" she demands.

I don't answer her right away, the edge of the field requiring my complete focus as I navigate us toward a path clear of electric vines.

Definitely don't want to touch any of those dangerous writhing ropes dangling from the nearby cacti.

Ailsa really did take us off course down here, but once we cross through this fiery desert, we'll be back on track to reach the caves by nightfall.

Then the fun will begin.

"What…?" Ailsa's unfinished question has me glancing at her. She's no longer looking at me, but at the currents buzzing between the vines. "Are those… electrical lines?"

"Sort of," I tell her. "But not quite. They're alive. And they like to zap."

One of them stirs as we near it, the mouth along the

end of a rope opening in a hiss that has Ailsa wrapping her arms more tightly around my neck.

"Yeah, they're not friendly," I mutter, avoiding the now-slithering ropelike creature. "Most of the fiery desert is like this, but we need to go through it to reach the mushrooms on the other side."

She swallows. "I... I don't want to be here. This is all a mistake. I'm... I'm just a human."

"You're not," I promise her. "You're an Omega. Krolic found you two years ago. We've just been waiting for you to take that elixir so that everyone else would know, too."

She's shaking her head before I finish. "I can't be an Omega."

"Why not?" I ask as we duck under a red rock arch to officially enter the desert.

"Because I'm *human*."

"Humans can be Omegas," I tell her. "That's why the Crimson King's edict applied to all beings. It's about the soul, not the species classification."

That'll become evident as she learns more about Monsterland.

I'm an Alpha, as are Catum and Krolic. But we're all different species.

"Crimson King?" Her nose scrunches. "You mean the Silver King?"

"No, I definitely meant Crimson," I mutter as I maneuver us around a particularly large cactus. It's the size of a small house and probably has a spiker inside it. If it comes out to bother us, I'll be forced to set Ailsa down and waste another card. Both actions would displease me immensely.

"The Silver King issued the edict."

"No, the Crimson King issued it while masquerading as the Silver King," I correct her. "It's a common

44

misconception. One that you're going to help clear up someday soon."

"Me?"

"Yes, you," I murmur as the hairs along the back of my neck dance in warning.

Fucking hell, I sigh.

"Now really isn't a good time for me," I inform the spiker attempting to sneak up on us from behind.

Ailsa frowns.

I don't give her a chance to question me, just gently lower her feet to the ground and say, "Stay right here, please."

Then I spin around to handle the spiker.

Nope.

Scratch that.

Spikers—plural.

My cards fall into my hands, my fingers automatically shuffling. "I don't suppose you three like magic tricks?" I offer. "Because I have some up my sleeves that you might find entertaining."

Or, well, I'll find it entertaining, anyway.

They snort, their piglike noses flat and large on their otherwise small heads.

One of them drags a hoofed foot across the ground as another flexes the spikes decorating his arms.

"I guess that's a no," I drawl. "All right, then."

I release one card and watch as it slices right through one of the spiker's chests.

"See, this is the problem with Alpha, Beta, and Omega distinctions," I tell Ailsa conversationally. "In our world, it doesn't matter what monster type you are; you'll end up falling into one of three categories. And compatibility is about category, not species."

I throw another card, stopping the second spiker.

"So, as an Omega, human or not, you're capable of being claimed by any Alpha in Monsterland. Which is why"—I flick a third and final card, this one lodging in the spiker's thick neck—"you're being hunted now."

I turn to face my potential mate and narrow my gaze when I find the space vacant.

Of course she ran.

I scour the desert to see her not even twenty yards away and running straight for the Mushroom Jungle.

"You're a bad little rabbit," I singsong after her, my voice easily carrying on the wind. "Better be careful, Ailsa darling, or you might awaken my inner predator."

An inner predator that likes to chase, I think, taking off after her.

"Run to your heart's content," I tell her. "Because when I catch you—and I will catch you, Ailsa—I'm going to teach you a little lesson on proper manners."

AILSA

OH, Gods, where am I even going?

I shouldn't have run away. But seeing how casually Craze killed those… those *piglike men*…

I shudder.

He didn't even flinch. Just tossed a few knives at them. Or were they cards?

I don't know.

I don't care.

I just need to escape.

To where, I have no idea. The strange orange sand beneath my bare feet is *hot*. And I'm practically naked. Not the best attire for this desertlike area.

But I can see something green in the distance. That has to be promising.

My stomach rumbles in agreement, reminding me that I haven't eaten today. At all.

I'm not even sure *today* is the same day I drank from the chalice.

Everything has happened so quickly.

None of this should be possible for me.

And yet… here I am.

Craze's statements start rolling through my mind.

"Humans can be Omegas. It's about the soul, not the species classification."

"Alpha, Beta, or Omega."

"Compatibility is about category, not species."

"As an Omega, human or not, you're capable of being claimed by any Alpha in Monsterland."

I shiver at that last part. I heard him say it after I'd already started running. It almost gave me pause. But then I realized he might be one of those Alphas since he called me a potential mate.

I... I don't know how to feel about that. He seems... a little strange. But he's been informative. Protective, too. However, I just met him. I can't be his mate. Or potential mate. Or his anything.

Because I'm running.

To...

To...

I don't know.

Just running!

I can sense him pursuing me, hear his soft chuckles, and practically smell his spicy cinnamon scent.

Gods, why do I like his cologne?

And why does it seem like it's swirling around me? *Claiming* me?

Is he right behind me? I wonder. I swear I can feel his hot breath on my nape, his fingers brushing my hair.

I spin around, wanting to face him.

But he's not there.

He's nowhere.

Yet I can *hear* him. *Smell* him. "What's happening to me?" I whisper, turning around again and jolting as I run into a wall of masculine heat.

Yelping, I stumble back but find my hips caught in an unyielding grip.

Smoke taunts my nostrils as I jerk my face upward.

48

And find a pair of alluring brown eyes staring down at me.

Eyes I know.

Eyes I saw right before my entire world was turned upside down.

"Master Pillar," I breathe.

"Hello, Miss Marvel," he replies, his voice a low purr that makes me feel dizzy. "Where are you running off to, hmm?"

"I…" I swallow. "What are you…? How are you…?" I shake my head, trying to clear it.

Because he shouldn't be here.

I shouldn't be here.

But we're both standing in this too-hot desert. And he's dressed in an all-black suit.

Which makes about as much sense as Craze's jeans and leather jacket in this heat.

Thinking of Craze has me glancing around for him, only to suddenly feel him against my back.

"Looking for me, little rabbit?" he whispers, his lips so close to my ear that I can feel his warm breath.

I can't even complain about the nickname this time. I'm too speechless to fathom words. Too lightheaded to properly inhale and exhale.

"I thought we were meeting in the caves?" he adds as his arm encircles my waist.

Master Piller doesn't release me, just continues to grasp my hips with his hands while Craze holds me from behind.

Being between them is *intoxicating*. Overwhelming. And oddly soothing.

I no longer feel the blistering heat, not even against my bare feet. Which is strange, considering the environment and my exposed skin.

"There's been a change in plans," a third voice says,

snapping my attention to a man with thick silver-white hair.

He's older than Master Pillar and Craze, maybe by twenty years or so, but the ripple of muscles flexing beneath his tight white shirt tells me he's just as fit as the two men holding me.

"Obviously," Craze drawls. "And I assume it's not related to our little rabbit's desire to be chased down like prey?"

The silver-haired man smirks, his pale green eyes meeting mine. "No, but we can table that activity for later." There's a growl in his voice that makes my tummy flip.

But it's his eyes that captivate me.

They… they remind me of… *"Beast."*

He steps forward, his gaze intense. "Instantly recognizing me in my human form only proves how right I am about you, Ailsa," he says, his palm cupping my cheek as his thumb drags a hot path along my lower lip.

I shiver, not just from his touch but also from the realization that Beast is a man. A shifter. *A monster.*

I always knew he wasn't a standard wolf, his size too massive to be anything but spectacular.

But this…

I never considered *this* outcome.

Oh, Gods. Maybe I'm dreaming? I think, dizzy all over again.

I'm surrounded by three men, all of them exuding a masculine prowess that's making it hard to breathe. Every inhale is a mixture of their scents—smoke, pine, and spice. It… I…

Why am I suddenly so sensitive to smell? And why do their aromas make me want to lay them down across the ground and roll all over them?

Beast's thumb leaves my mouth, only to be replaced by his lips.

His *lips*.

All luscious and plump and soft, yet hard and demanding as well. It's a conundrum that stirs conflict inside me. Shock, too.

Because what is happening?

Why is this man kissing me?

And why… why am I just allowing it?

It's quick. Too quick. And only his lips. But I swear he leaves a brand behind, the burning touch searing me to my soul.

What is happening to me? I should be screaming. Trying to wake up. *Anything* other than standing here, staring into his beautiful green eyes while two other men hold me like I'm theirs.

"I need you to be a good girl for us and do what we tell you to do," Beast says. "Can you do that, Ailsa? Can you be our good girl?"

I blink at him. His words should come off as condescending, but they don't. It's… it's the purr in his voice. Something growly. Something I can't define. It makes me want to obey him, to *please* him.

Which is how I find myself nodding in response.

He smiles, the sight of it so stunning that I can barely think.

And then he kisses me again. Briefly. Just a brush of his lips against mine.

I melt in response.

This is insane, I think. *Utterly… insane.*

Yet my knees feel weak, and my brain resembles mush.

This place is messing with my mind.

Or I really am dreaming.

Gods, I hope this is a dream.

But do I? Do I really want this to end?

I... I don't know.

"Catum is going to cloak you," Beast tells me. "Don't fight him."

Catum? I repeat to myself, borderline delirious. *Who is Catum?*

Master Pillar's hands roam up my sides, over Craze's arm, until his palms are cupping my face. "Look at me, Miss Marvel."

I swallow and do what he says, completely hypnotized by his voice and his presence. Beast has stepped back, yet I can still feel his eyes on me.

And Craze is against my back, his chest solid and hard as he softly vibrates behind me. I don't even know how he's making that sound or why he's making it, but it's comforting.

"Such an obedient little Omega," Master Pillar murmurs. "I'm proud of you, Miss Marvel."

"Wait until she runs," Craze mutters.

"She won't run from me," Master Pillar returns. "Right, sweet one? You'll do exactly what I say."

My chin nearly dips down, my instinct to nod overriding all rational thought.

"Because you're cheating," Craze drawls.

"I'm *charming*," Master Pillar returns.

Craze snorts. "If that's what you want to call it."

"Stop," Beast interjects. "We don't have time for games. Cloak her, Catum."

Master Pillar sighs, his thumbs drawing a line beneath my eyes. "It'll be a shame to cover all this beauty, but alas..." Energy warms my skin as his palms move again to my neck and down over my shoulders.

Craze releases me, allowing Master Pillar's hands to

roam along my arms and then over to my abdomen and up my sides.

I seem to stop breathing, my body no longer my own.

Because I can't believe he's touching me like this.

I've dreamt of it. Fantasized about it. All because of his voice. It's a forbidden obsession, one I told myself would never become a reality. It was also a silly desire, one born of a presence I barely knew.

But now that I've seen his face, experienced his touch, my mind has short-circuited. This all feels very real. *Too* real.

He crouches before me as his palms go to my hips, then down my exposed legs to my ankles. Craze grabs my sides, pulling me back as Master Pillar lifts one foot to run his finger from my heel to my toes.

I shiver as he switches limbs, repeating the action while Craze holds me from behind.

This is madness, I marvel, my lungs demanding air. *Utter madness. This whole place, this scene, this* everything. *I've... I've lost my mind.*

We're still standing in the orange-colored desert, yet I can't feel any of the residual heat. Just a cool mist against my skin.

I lift my arm to examine it, startled by the inky fabric covering me all the way to my wrist. It's... it's translucent.

Glancing down, I see that the garment flows all the way to my feet in a gown of sorts, reminding me a bit of smoke. It actually feels like air against my skin, yet it moves as though it's a dress. And it completely masks my white undergarments.

Master Pillar lifts the skirt to show me a pair of flats that actually fit my feet. "How...?" I trail off, unsure of what I even want to ask.

There are a dozen competing questions in my head.

And a dozen more statements.

"She's ready," Master Pillar says as he stands.

"Ready for what?" I blurt out.

"Dinner," he replies with a wink before stepping away and holding out an arm. "Shall we, Miss Marvel?"

"I..." I blink from him to Beast. "No. I'm not going anywhere with you."

Craze chuckles behind me. "I see the surprise has finally worn off. That took a little longer than I expected."

I bristle at his words and spin around to face him. "Excuse me for being a little flabbergasted by... by..." I gesture to Beast, then to Master Pillar, and finally to the damn world. "It's a lot."

"It is," he agrees. "Thankfully, you have the three of us to see you through it."

"See me through what, exactly?" I demand, my voice borderline shrill. I can't seem to stop it. All I want to do is... is... *scream*. Run. Hide. *Wake up.*

"You're the first Omega to enter Monsterland in over a thousand years," Beast says. "The realm is full of hungry Alphas and bored Betas. Now, they're all intrigued by your presence."

"I'm not an Omega," I grit out. "I'm a human."

Craze just shakes his head. "I've already explained that species don't matter, but..." He waves a hand at me, similar to how I just gestured at Beast and Master Pillar.

"You're not just any Omega," Beast continues like Craze and I didn't just speak. "You're *our* Omega. The one we've been hunting for the last several hundred years. And you are going to help us reclaim the Monsterland court."

CATUM

AILSA'S SCENT is like a drug. I want to lean into her neck, inhale, and *bite*.

But I hold myself back—just barely—and watch the emotions playing out across her pretty face.

She has no idea how important she is to us, how valuable, how *rare*.

Denial is written across her features, drowning out all of the competing reactions. At least until curiosity starts to peek through, causing her full lips to curl slightly downward. "What's the Monsterland court?" she asks in a breathy voice, one that reminds me of sex.

Flames, I want her. I want to strip off that cloak I just wrapped her up in, remove the remains of her blue-and-white dress, and devour every inch of her with my tongue.

It's a visceral need that's been begging to be released for two fucking years. Since I took over as *Master Pillar*.

I should correct her, give her my first name, but I love the way *master* sounds on her tongue.

"Monster royalty," Krolic tells her. "It's tradition for the king and his mate-circle to hunt for an Omega mate. The royal court is supposed to be protected in the king's absence. But an imposter stepped in during our absence. And with your help, we're going to expose his real identity."

"I don't…" She shakes her head. "I don't understand. How am I going to help you expose…? What are we exposing exactly? I mean, who?"

"We're going to take back the Silver King's throne," Krolic says, trying a new route. "And we're going to make you the Monsterland Queen."

"*Me?*" She gapes at him. "Did you miss the part about me being human?"

Krolic catches her chin between his thumb and forefinger, then crowds her personal space. "You say that like there's something wrong with being human, Ailsa."

"I'm… I'm nothing," she sputters. "No powers. No… no anything."

"You have no idea what you're capable of, little mate," he murmurs. "But we're going to show you. We're going to help you. And we're going to protect you."

"I don't even know you!" she shouts back, clearly at her wits' end. I can't really blame her. This is a lot of change for one day.

"You've spent the last two years getting to know me," Krolic reminds her. "Just in my wolf form. Craze might be new to you, but we both know Catum isn't. You've been dreaming about him for two years."

She sputters, her cheeks pinkening. "I have not."

"Little liar," I murmur, my lips curling. "You have quite the wicked little mind, Miss Marvel." I know because I've witnessed some of those dreams, and perhaps influenced them a little, too. "You've been ours since Krolic first scented you. Now we're going to ensure all of Monsterland knows."

"This is insane," she whispers. "*Insane.*"

"Welcome to the mayhem, little rabbit," Craze says with a wink. "Sorry, *Ailsa*."

I frown. "What's wrong with *little rabbit*?"

"Our mate doesn't like nicknames," he tells me.

"Well, that's too bad," I reply, looking at her again. "Because I can think of a lot of things I'd like to call you, Miss Marvel." Starting with *mine*.

A pretty red shade steals over her cheeks again. "I… I don't mind nicknames. But I don't… I don't know you. Any of you. Not, not really. And why are we even having this conversation? I'm not anything important. Let alone a *queen*. I'm human. Ailsa Marvel. Nothing else. Simply me."

"You're everything," Krolic counters, still holding her chin. "I realize your world didn't respect you or make you feel like a queen, but I promise we will. Just give us some time to show you, Ailsa."

She swallows, her gaze searching his before glancing at me and then at Craze. "This is insane," she says again. I suspect she's been repeating that phrase a lot in her mind as well.

"As I said, welcome to the mayhem," Craze murmurs with a wink. "You're in Monsterland now, Ailsa."

"Where you will become queen," Krolic adds. "*Our* queen."

She shakes her head again but doesn't speak. It's like she's utterly flummoxed and unable to fathom what to say next.

Which means it's officially time for us to go.

"Remember what Krolic said about being a good girl for us," I say as I call a portal with a flick of my wrist. "The Tea Village isn't a place for Omegas to wander around alone."

"We're going to the Tavern?" Craze asks, his dark eyebrow arching upward.

I nod. "As Krolic said, there's been a change in plans."

Craze doesn't ask questions, just shrugs. "I guess I'll be getting that violet tea after all."

"You and that damn tea," Krolic mutters, his hand dropping away from Ailsa's face.

Craze merely grins. "It's excellent."

"It's a psychedelic trip," Krolic tells him.

"Hence the reason it's excellent," Craze replies.

Krolic's head sways from side to side. "Just keep your cards handy. We're probably going to need them."

"My cards are always ready, K," Craze drawls, pulling the deck out of thin air to run them through his fingers.

Ailsa flinches, telling me she's become quite familiar with those sharp little weapons. I have no idea who Craze has taken down in the last few hours since arriving in Monsterland, but I would guess it's been more than a few creatures.

Things have not gone according to plan.

Well, that's not true.

We wanted Ailsa's presence to be known, and we accomplished that. What we didn't desire, however, was the Crimson King's quick response in dispatching his minions.

It's a damn shame how gullible some of the beings of this world have become. They've all fallen for the imposter's charm and truly believe he's their leader.

Ridiculous.

The eldest of our world know how the kingdom should work—a real king hunts his prey.

This imposter simply sends others to do his bidding.

It's fucking insulting that they actually believe he's the Silver King.

I meet the gaze of the actual Silver King now and give him a nod. "It's your show, Your Majesty."

He grunts. "Fuck you, Second."

My lips curl. "You hear that, Craze? I'm the second-in-command."

Craze folds his arms. "Only because he prefers me as his Enforcer."

"You're both children," Krolic growls, his gaze going to Ailsa. "Come with me, my queen. I'll escort you to the Tavern."

She looks ready to protest.

But all Krolic does is lift a single silver brow, his gaze burning into hers, and her head bows slightly in submission.

I suppress a sigh. This is the side of her I've known for two very long years. I want the fiery female beneath. The one who expressed dissent just moments ago.

Reaching forward, I catch her chin in a fashion similar to Krolic's previous hold and gently guide her eyes back up. "You submit to no one, Miss Marvel," I tell her softly. "You're a queen—*our* queen."

She blinks. "But... but you all keep telling me to *obey* you."

My lips curl. "There's a difference between willing obedience and outright submission, sweet one. The former earns rewards. The latter... the latter will never apply to you."

"He's right," Krolic says, his hand still outstretched for hers. "I've asked you to be a good girl and do what we say because we want to keep you safe, not control you. There's a difference."

"But how can I even trust you?" she sputters out. "You... you're... *Beast.*"

"I'm Krolic," he corrects her. "And also your Beast, yes."

"So you... you *lied* to me," she accuses him. "I thought you were a wolf!"

"I am a wolf, Ailsa. A shifter, to be precise. And I'm also the rightful Silver King."

She gapes at him. "You..." She swallows. "Oh, Gods, you want to *breed* me." She takes a step back from the portal I created.

I share a look with Craze. "I told you it was too much."

"And I told you that I don't understand this reaction." He folds his arms. "That elixir is supposed to make her insatiable and begging for our knots, not afraid of them."

"Kn-knots?" she repeats. "What... what's a knot?"

"Neither of you are helping," Krolic informs us.

"I'm not sure there's much that can be helped," Craze tosses back. "She's terrified of us."

"*Terrified* is a strong word," she snaps at him. "*Confused* and *overwhelmed* would be better. Now what's a knot? And why did you lie about being a wolf?"

"Two very different questions," Craze drawls unhelpfully. "Give us your favorite color first."

I stare at him, baffled by his comments. But that's nothing new. Craze frequently loses me with his chaotic statements and word choices.

He uses his hand to create a "hand it over" gesture as he stares her down.

"Oh my Gods, you're impossible," she says to him. "*Purple*, okay? I love purple. Now tell me what a knot is!"

"I would much rather show you," he says softly.

"Craze," Krolic warns.

"I'm just being honest," he replies.

Perhaps a little too honest, I think.

"I didn't lie about being a wolf," Krolic says, ignoring Craze and focusing on our intended. "I *am* a wolf. A shifter. There's no lie. And I didn't try to trick you, either. I just wanted to get to know you, and it was safest for me to do so in my animal form."

"Just like I took over as the master of your district so I could also be close to you," I insert. "As to what a knot is, it's something you'll learn more about later. Something sexual." I reach for her chin again, dragging her focus to me. "And no one will be *breeding* you without your consent. Okay?"

She blinks at me. "I... But that voice said the king wants to *breed* me."

"And I do," Krolic admits. "However, only with your permission."

"That *voice*"—I cut a glare at a grinning Craze before returning my attention to Ailsa—"was referring to the imposter on the throne. The Crimson King wants to force you to carry his heir. That's how he'll solidify his claim over the kingdom."

Krolic winces at the formal name for the jackass who took over the monarchy. He was from a rival bloodline. A supposedly dead one.

Alas, we discovered the hard way that it was very much alive.

Rather than steal the throne back, we continued hunting for our mate. We just didn't expect it to take hundreds of years to find her.

Now our home is nothing like it was before.

So many weak inhabitants, all of them under the Crimson King's spell.

"I have no intention of forcing you to do anything," Krolic adds softly. "The last two years are proof of that. I only ever followed you in the woods to keep you company. Your realm may not be as mad as this one, but there are dangers everywhere. Especially for a rare Omega."

"If you knew what I was—and that's assuming I believe you at all—why make me take the elixir?" she asks.

"The imposter is the one who issued the edict regarding the elixir," he says. "And we needed to be certain."

"As well as ensuring that others found out about your existence," I add. "Which brings me back to the portal." I point to the swirling darkness. "We are expected at the Tavern."

Krolic checks his watch with a curse. "Yes, and we're very late."

Craze simply stuffs his hands into his jeans pockets and rocks on the heels of his boots. "What's it going to be, Ailsa?" he asks her. "Portal or more running in the Orange Desert?"

My nose curls at the formal name for this area of Monsterland. Primarily because it's a misnomer.

Oh, the color is orange.

But it certainly doesn't smell all that citrusy out here.

It's more swamp-like, reminding me of mold and musk. I'm tempted to take a step toward Ailsa just to inhale her sweet perfume again.

The moment she swallowed that elixir, her alluring aroma sprang to life, nearly knocking me on my ass. I was speechless and starving at the same time. It took serious restraint not to grab her and bring one of those naughty fantasies of hers to life.

Ailsa glances between the three of us, her expression conflicted as she looks down at the dress I've fashioned for her. It's a cloak that masks her scent. At least to everyone but us.

Enough inhabitants have picked up on her fragrant presence. They know she's here. Now it's time to make her harder to find.

Which means hiding her in plain sight.

No one will expect her to be staying at the Tea Village.

Not after we've left so many clues in the caves.

That's the key to surviving in Monsterland—always having a plan A, B, C, D, and Z.

Ailsa will learn. We'll teach her. And we'll protect her in the interim.

Krolic holds out his hand once more. "Please, my queen?"

"I'm not your queen," she tells him.

"See? She doesn't like nicknames," Craze says in his usual singsong voice, making it impossible to know which of his personalities is in charge right now. It could be a playful one or a deadly one. Fortunately, most of his personalities like us.

Most being the operative phrase there.

"No *princess*. No *rabbit*. No *gorgeous*, even though she's fucking beautiful," he continues, shaking his head. "A damn shame, really. I have so many nicknames. So many."

She gapes at him. "There's something seriously wrong with you."

"Well, obviously," he drawls, giving her a lopsided grin. "But at least I have decent hearing, unlike you."

Her eyes widen even more. "My hearing is fine."

"Then why are we still standing here?" he counters.

"Because I have no idea what's really going on here or why I should trust you."

"Well, I saved you from the Blood Ocean, then helped you out of the Gum Tree, carried you through the Hot Chocolate Fields so you wouldn't accidentally be burned alive by a fudge bomb, and I knocked out those spikers back there so they wouldn't drag you into their cactus house. What more do I need to do to earn your trust, Ailsa?"

Ah, fuck. I know this side of Craze. It's his grumpier personality, the one who lacks patience and doesn't appreciate being spoken down to. He usually only rears his head when he's feeling frustrated or incredibly bored. I suspect now is a result of a mixture of the two.

"You're a bit of a brat, aren't you?" Craze goes on, causing Krolic's head to fall back on a loud sigh. Because he knows there's no stopping the man now.

"A bit of a brat?" Ailsa echoes. "I literally *fell* into this realm because of one of those portal things, and everything's been trying to kill me since."

"Nothing wants to kill you, Ailsa. Just fuck you. You're an Omega who is about to go into heat. Everything here wants to *knot* you." He folds his arms, his dark eyes glittering with flecks of gold.

It's a warning.

A tell that says a much more violent part of Craze's wild personality has come out to play.

Both Krolic and I take a step forward, but Craze throws up a hand. "Stay out of this."

"We really need to go," Krolic says.

"No shit," Craze fires back. "Tell that to the ungrateful Omega who keeps questioning our intentions."

"I think I'm well within my rights to question everything," she snaps at him. "It's not my fault you keep wasting your questions on frivolous details like flowers and colors."

His eyebrows lift. "There's nothing *frivolous* about my questions, Ailsa."

She takes a step back as he moves toward her.

But he catches her by the hip, preventing her from running.

"I want to know what fruit to feed you in the morning,

and now I know you enjoy cherries," he says, clearly startling her.

"I—"

"I wanted to know what flowers to get you when I've upset you," he goes on, cutting her off. "And now I know you like sunshine flowers, or sunflowers, as you call them. *And* I know what color shirt to wear tomorrow since you like purple. Those are called important details, darling. Not *frivolous* ones."

Her lips part, no words leaving her.

"And further, I answered your questions with honesty and integrity. Yet you still have the audacity to say you can't trust me?" He blows out his breath and shakes his head. "You certainly know how to make an Alpha work for it, Ailsa. I'm trying. We're all trying. But a little understanding would go a long way."

While he's not wrong, he's not exactly going easy on her.

However, a glimmer of comprehension shines in her gaze, dismantling the shock in her features. "You're… right."

"I know I am, but thank you for acknowledging it," he replies. "Now can we go, please?"

CRAZE

I'M BEING hard on her. I know I am. However, there's a time for patience, and now isn't it. Those spikers will be waking up soon, my cards having slayed them temporarily.

The only one I truly injured was Brandt, but even he'll survive.

And then he'll start hunting for Ailsa.

Just like every other creature in the kingdom.

There's a reason Krolic and Catum changed the game. We were supposed to play in the caves. The Tavern was a backup choice.

If they want her in plain sight, that means the Crimson King reacted with more power than we hoped.

That's fine. We have our own tricks. Also, the Crimson King relies on minions. We rely on mutual loyalty.

I would die for Krolic and Catum.

Just as they would die for me.

And now, the three of us will do everything in our power to protect Ailsa.

Including being harsh when needed.

Her blue eyes hold mine, her long blonde hair seeming to wave in the invisible wind. She's so ethereal and doesn't even realize it, a true goddess walking amongst us.

One day, she'll understand.

If I could go back to kill every single person who made her feel small for *simply being human*, I would. I would cut off their heads and deliver them on a fucking platter.

Because this female is so much more than she realizes.

And I'm going to spend eternity proving that to her.

"Please?" I echo, aware that it's a word I rarely use. Most women, hell, most *men*, do whatever I ask the moment I speak.

But not Ailsa.

She's been a challenge since the moment she dropped into our realm.

I hope she continues to be a challenge. It's fun trying to win her over, even if it is a bit exhausting.

"All right," she says, defeat etched into her features. "Let's… go through the swirling black hole thing."

"Portal," I correct her. "And it's just going to take us to the Tea Village."

"You say that like I know what it is," she mutters.

"It's a village of Betas who serve Alphas," I explain. "The highlight is the Tavern. It's both an eatery and a hotel of sorts."

It also serves as a center of information, a way to hear Monsterland rumors and learn more about the royal court.

With Catum's cloak covering Ailsa's identity, no one will know who she is or even care. It's the same magic Catum has used on himself and Krolic whenever visiting the realm.

The three of us have spent many hours, days, and weeks at the Tavern.

We're well known there.

But not as who we really are.

Just a trio of Alphas. And now they'll see us as a trio of Alphas who have found a pretty little Beta to entertain us for the week.

At least that'll help chase off the other Betas who have shown interest in joining our nest.

Oh, we've played.

But not since discovering Ailsa's existence.

She's been our only desire for two years. Even mine, despite not seeing her or knowing her in the mortal world. However, Krolic and Catum told me enough about her to pique my interest.

And now that I've met her, I have no doubt that she's meant to be ours.

Our alluring rabbit is the perfect mix of feisty energy and submission.

"So it's… it's like my district?" she asks, drawing me back to our conversation about the Tea Village.

"It's nothing like your home," Krolic interjects. "This is Monsterland. Everything is going to feel extraordinary to you until you learn more about it."

"And… going home isn't an option." She voices it as a statement, not a question.

However, I nod in confirmation anyway. "This is your home now, Ailsa. You've always been destined to come here. We just altered the way you arrived."

"So you wouldn't end up in the palace," Catum adds. "I wasn't lying about the Crimson King's intentions—he'll take you without consent, Ailsa."

"You all took me here without my consent," she throws back.

"He means *fuck* you without consent," I interject. "The Imposter King will cage you until you go into a proper heat, then growl to force your slick, and knot you until you're carrying his heir." It's a graphic depiction of events, but a truthful one.

Alas, she just gapes at me like I'm the monster here, not the one trying to save her from the monster.

"This isn't a kind place," I go on. "But it is meant to be yours to rule. The Imposter King won't see it that way. He'll parade you around like a glorified pet on a leash. We'll carry you and bow to you as our queen. Just give us a chance to prove it, Ailsa."

"I already said I'll go through the portal," she mutters, a hint of exasperation in her tone. "I can't give you anything else. Not... not yet."

"That's a fair compromise," I decide, my mood instantly lifting as a smile tugs at my mouth. "Let me know when you're ready to compromise on nicknames."

She shoots me a look that says that's not going to happen.

Which only improves my mood even more and makes me grin that much wider. "Oh, I like you," I tell her. "How do you feel about *kitten* instead of *rabbit*?"

She scowls.

"So that's neither, then?" I sigh. "At least let me call you *gorgeous*, Ailsa. It's just a description. An accurate one at that."

"You're very..." She trails off like she's trying to find the right word.

"Mad?" I offer her, smirking. "I get that one a lot."

"Are you done flirting yet?" Catum asks me. "Because this portal is wasting a lot of energy."

"You could have tamed it while we discussed options," I tell him. "But you wanted to impress our intended with

LEXI C. FOSS

your powers. That's not a *me* problem, C. That's a *you* problem."

"I'm starting to agree with Ailsa on you being impossible," he informs me flatly.

"*Impossible* is such a permanent term," I drawl. "I much prefer *mercurial*. Or *surprising*. Or even *intriguing*." I waggle my brows at him and then at Ailsa. "Thoughts?"

"Crazy," she offers. "I think I'll call you *crazy*."

Amusement warms my insides. "You don't know the half of it, gorgeous." I try the nickname primarily to see if she'll turn me down again.

When she doesn't, I grin.

"Gorgeous it is, then."

She sighs. "Can we go now?"

"We could always go," I tell her. "The portal is right there."

The beautiful female throws her hands up and stomps off toward it, only for Krolic to enter her path. "Please allow me to escort you," he says, holding out his arm. "It'll be easier. And I want to make sure Catum's charm works."

"It works," he says without missing a beat.

Krolic ignores him. "Please, my queen?"

She blows out another breath and accepts his arm. "Yeah. Fine. Okay, *Beast.*"

His green eyes light up with the pet name, his power seeming to ripple off him in energetic waves.

Someone likes being her beast, I muse.

He can't hear me.

But he doesn't need to.

He can feel my amusement, and the cocky look he throws back at me says he doesn't even care that I'm entertained by this development.

Without another word, he escorts our intended through Catum's portal.

"I don't understand why he can call her *queen*, but I can't," I say conversationally.

"You're not her king," Catum points out.

"That doesn't mean she's not my queen," I mutter.

"Our queen," he corrects. Then he shrugs. "She's a puzzle, one that'll be fun to solve."

"If that's a euphemism for sex, then yes, I agree. *Solving* her will be quite fun."

He snorts. "She has your knot all tied up, doesn't she? All you can think about is sex."

"Are you telling me yours isn't strung tight?" I ask him, both of my eyebrows raised.

"My knot has been pulsing for her for two very long years," he returns. "Every night she dreamt of me, it took physical restraint not to shadow into her room and turn those fantasies into a reality."

"You're lucky you had those two years," I mutter. "I've had a few hours, and she doesn't seem to like me very much."

"She's struggling with the change," he tells me. "Just give her time."

"I wish I could," I reply. "I really wish I could."

But time is not on our side.

Tick, tock.

"We should follow them," Catum says.

I nod, agreeing.

Then I slip through the portal to join Krolic and our queen in the Tea Village.

Tick, tock.

That looming countdown echoes in my head.

It must be playing in Krolic's thoughts as well because he's busy checking his watch again as I step onto the cobblestone street. Catum is right behind me, the portal dissipating in his wake.

"Well?" he prompts.

Krolic grins. "Time to play."

My own lips curl in response. Those three words are music to my ears.

Because playing, I can do. And playing, I do very, very well.

I pull out my cards to shuffle the deck. "Lead the way, K."

AILSA

THUS FAR, the Tea Village is the most normal place I've seen in Monsterland. I mean, apart from the fact that we are sitting inside a teacup that's bigger than Baroness Clarice's mansion.

I gaze up at the colorful ceiling, noting the way it gathers together at a point... just like the cap of a teacup.

And naturally, we're all drinking out of teacups, too.

The theme is clear.

Only it's not at all what it seems.

I pick up the muffin sitting on my plate, my lips twisting to the side. Because it's not a muffin at all. It just looks like one. But it tastes like spaghetti.

And my tea? Yeah, it's not tea. It's something bubbly and a little too sweet for my taste buds.

Beast—*Krolic*—gave me some water, probably the only "normal" item on the table. They all have varying degrees of strangeness on their own plates.

Well, Master Pillar has nothing. He's just leaning back in the shadows lurking along the wall behind him, smoking a pipe.

Craze is nursing a cup of something that makes him hiccup every few seconds.

And Krolic... has a plate of dirt. Or what looks like

dirt, anyway. He said it's actually a kind of meat and offered a spoonful for me to try. I declined.

"Hey, handsome," a female with long red hair murmurs as she approaches Craze. At some point, he changed his skull makeup to reflect a white mask with black around his eyes.

He arches a single brow at her, causing the paint to stretch along his forehead. "Do I look like I'm shopping, darlin'?" he drawls, the Southern twang different from his usual accent. It's the second time he's used it, making me wonder what it means.

Craze referred to himself as *mercurial* earlier. It definitely seems like an accurate adjective.

The slender woman shrugs. "Maybe I'm the one shopping."

"Hmm," he hums, setting his cup on the table and leaning toward her. "And what are you looking for?"

My gaze narrows. Craze has said I'm his intended mate all day, and he has the audacity to flirt with this female in front of me?

Rude, I decide.

"A good time," she purrs at him.

"Define 'a good time' for me," he says, his card deck appearing in his hands. The sight of it sends a chill down my spine. I've learned what those cards do. And it's nothing good.

Master Pillar puffs out a cloud of smoke as he says, "Silence is my idea of a good time."

"I wasn't asking you," Craze murmurs. "I was talking to the lady shopping for some fun."

Krolic snorts, leaning back to drape his arm along the top of my chair. He's next to me, leaving me sandwiched between him and Master Pillar.

Which places Craze directly across from me, giving me

a perfect view of his flirtatious *fun*.

The redhead leans into him, her long nails meeting his sternum as her fingers begin walking a path upward while her pouty lips move over words I'm no longer hearing.

Because she's touching Craze.

Touching him.

Some part of me, one I've never met before, springs to life. A part of me that suddenly wants to rip that woman's hand off and feed it to her.

I blink. *What the hell is that?*

Why is she still touching him? I think in the next second. *He's not hers to touch.*

He's not mine either, I remind myself, causing some part of me to growl.

All three men look at me.

Oh. Okay. So I made that sound… out loud.

Craze cocks his head, his dark eyes glittering sinfully in the low lighting. "Would you like to know my definition of 'a good time'?" he asks as he shuffles his card deck.

"Yes, I would," the redhead tells him. "I really, *really* would."

But he doesn't answer her.

Instead, his gaze is on me, his eyebrow cocking upward again.

He wasn't asking her about the good time. He was asking *me* if I wanted to know his definition.

Do I?

No. No, I do not.

Because he isn't mine.

And my reaction is… ludicrous.

But it's been a really long day. Week. I don't even know. It's just… this is a lot. I'm exhausted. I don't want to play whatever game he's dragging me into now.

I nearly say that when the female traces her nail across his jaw, heading straight for his mouth.

His jaw clenches in response, telling me he didn't appreciate that move at all. However, the woman is oblivious because she tries to touch his lips again.

Craze moves so quickly that I barely understand what's happened until the woman is cradling her fingerless hand against her chest and screaming.

Krolic shakes his head.

Master Pillar simply puffs on his pipe, the epitome of boredom.

And Craze looks directly at me as he says, "My idea of a good time involves anything that pleases you, gorgeous. As for the things that displease you, well, let's just say I have no problem handling those items for you."

He wipes his bladed card on a napkin, cleaning the blood from the edges. Once he's finished, he discards the napkin in the direction of the furious redhead.

"You're insane," she seethes.

"Why are you still here?" he asks her. "I think I made my rejection pretty fucking clear."

She snarls at him.

He merely arches a brow right back.

"Mad fucking Hatter," she growls, then stomps off.

"I really hate that nickname," he mutters, picking up his teacup again.

"And yet, it's so very accurate," Krolic drawls.

"Fuck you, K." Craze finishes his tea and signals for another.

A wisp of enchanted air swirls around the table as his cup is magically refilled.

I don't fully understand the process or how it works; Krolic ordered for me earlier. But I'm a bit intrigued by it. Particularly as the sensation of magic feels pleasing. Like it makes me happy. Which is strange, as I've never actually felt magic before.

However, I'm learning not to be surprised by what happens in Monsterland.

Nothing is what it seems here.

Including these men, I think, sizing the three of them up.

They want me to trust them, and thus far, they've given me a few reasons to. But that doesn't mean I'm ready to put all my faith in these three *Alphas*.

Gods, just thinking of the term stirs a tremble from deep within.

Between everything Craze has said and the few things Krolic mentioned when we first arrived in the village, I've gathered that they're an Alpha-circle. I don't quite understand what that means, but it seems they fully intend to share me as their Omega mate.

The notion of it makes me shiver. Or maybe that's the lingering magic.

I… I don't know.

So I just… eat my spaghetti-muffin.

Krolic whispers something with a wave of his hand, causing a tray of round doughlike items to appear. They all have holes right through the center.

I frown at them, but Craze perks up. "Pizza donuts. Oh, brilliant choice."

"I thought A might like them," he says.

A is my nickname here.

Just like *K* seems to stand for Krolic.

They haven't explained the reason behind these code names, but I suspect it has to do with the Silver King. Or *Crimson King,* as Craze and Master Pillar have called him.

"Try one," Craze says, drawing my attention back to the platter.

I pinch my lips, considering saying no. But I'm still

77

hungry, and the spaghetti muffin isn't satisfying my rumbling stomach.

Craze nudges the plate toward me with an indulgent look. "Come on, gorgeous. Trust me. You'll love it."

"How do you know?" I ask him. "The only foods I've mentioned that I like are cherries and pears."

"Hmm, true," he concedes. "So tell me how you feel about pizza, then."

"I…" I've tried it a few times, typically cold slices left over from Baroness Clarice's daughters. "It's okay." I prefer spaghetti, as it's easier to reheat and not nearly as chewy.

However, I pick up a donut to pacify him.

And also, maybe, to satisfy my own curiosity.

Flavor explodes across my tongue as I take a bite, causing me to moan in delight. Because *wow*, that's good. I quickly stuff more into my mouth and close my eyes, reveling in the taste of this delicious treat.

All too soon, it's gone, and I instantly grab another.

Which is when I realize all three men are staring at me again.

Warmth creeps up my neck as I set the donut down in front of me. "Um." I clear my throat. "These are good."

They say nothing for a long moment, the tension around the table seeming to grow.

"I can't decide if I prefer the growl or the moan," Craze murmurs. "Both certainly have their appeals."

My cheeks heat even more. "I… I did not mean to growl." The moan, I can't really take back. That donut thing is worthy of the moans.

"That's all right, gorgeous. I didn't mind your possessive growling. In fact, I rather enjoyed it."

I narrow my gaze. "It was *not* a possessive growl. It… it just sort of came out." And I really don't want to explain why, so I grasp at the first thing I can think of to slightly alter the subject. "Did you really need to slice her fingers off? You could have just told her to stop touching you."

Okay, that came out a little possessive again.

Which isn't what I meant at all.

He's not mine. None of these men are. Hell, I *just* met them.

Clearing my throat once more, I attempt to clarify by saying, "I mean—"

"It was a possessive growl," he interjects. "And yes, Ailsa, I did need to cut her fingers off. She touched something that belongs to my queen, which is highly fucking disrespectful and won't be tolerated."

I blink at him. "I… I have no idea how to respond to that."

"There's nothing to say to that," he tells me. "I'm yours, Ailsa. Anyone who attempts to consider otherwise will meet a similar, if not worse, fate."

I gape at him. He can't be serious.

But if I say that aloud, he'll tell me what he's said the two or three times I've asked that before—*not normally*. Or something to that effect.

Because this male is insane.

Certifiably mad.

No wonder that redhead called him a mad fucking hatter.

"And besides," he goes on while waving a flippant hand through the air, "she's a black-widow shifter. Those fingers will grow back in a matter of hours, faster if she shifts. Honestly, I should have done worse. But I didn't want to frighten you."

"He's right," Krolic murmurs from beside me. "He should have done worse."

Master Pillar puffs out a ring of smoke from the shadows, adding, "Yes."

I have no idea how to respond to any of that.

So instead, I watch the smoke ring float away, then frown as it starts to circle our little table in the Tavern's corner. Mist glitters around it, falling down to the floor to create a strange translucent barrier, one I reach out to poke with my finger.

Energy hums back in response, sending a jolt down my arm. I yank my hand away and look up to see the mist gathering over our heads as well.

"What…?" I trail off, a shiver traversing my spine. This magic feels hot. Intentional. *Protective.*

How do I even know that? I wonder, suddenly feeling lightheaded again.

This was all too much for one day.

Too exhausting.

Too overwhelming.

Too *chaotic.*

"We're shielded," Master Pillar says with a sigh. "We can speak freely now. Just be mindful that we can still be seen."

Craze nods, leaning forward. "What happened with the caves?"

AILSA

I LISTEN as Master Pillar and Krolic fill Craze in, talking about *minions* and the *Crimson King* and how he sent said minions into the caves earlier than expected.

"There wasn't time to properly secure the lair," Krolic goes on. "So we spread various pieces of her clothing throughout the caverns to keep them busy."

"Once Brandt and the others wake up, though, they'll say where she really was," Craze points out.

"We're counting on that," Master Pillar drawls around his glowing pipe. "It'll force Crimson's minions to scatter, sending them in various directions while we remain here."

"Plan B it is," Craze drawls.

"Plan B indeed," Krolic echoes, lifting his drink. "May we not need to engage plan C."

"Or D or Z," Craze murmurs, knocking the contents of his tea back into his throat before fixing his dark eyes on me. "What questions do you have, Ailsa? Because I'm certain there are dozens of them."

"What are you going to want to know in exchange?" I ask him, unable to hold back the bite of sarcasm in my voice. "My favorite vegetable, perhaps?"

He chuckles. "How about your favorite position?"

I frown. "My favorite position for what?"

He merely smiles. "I guess we'll determine that together, hmm?"

"I have no idea what you're talking about."

"Which makes this even more fun, gorgeous," he muses. "But go ahead and ask your questions. No games. No requirements. Just... ask."

I'm tempted to point out that I did just ask him something, and he sidestepped it completely.

But I really don't care about his *positions*. I care a lot more about everything else they were just discussing with their plans and the Crimson King.

"I don't understand how he took over," I blurt out. "Or why I should... believe... it." That last part is more stuttered, my frown deepening with the words.

I... I'm not wrong to question what to believe here.

Yet it feels wrong to do so.

Especially when I see Krolic's nostrils flare.

"I-I'm sorry," I say, swallowing. "It's just—"

"You don't need to apologize, Ailsa," he interjects, catching my chin and keeping my focus on him. "You have every right to question us."

His thumb traces my lower lip, his gaze intense.

"How about a story?" he offers. "I'll tell you what happened, and then I'll clarify anything you need afterward."

"I... I think that might help," I admit, a little transfixed by his touch. Because he hasn't released my chin. He's just... stroking me. All while his gaze tracks the movement, like he's mesmerized by my mouth.

I feel pretty similarly about his features.

Those alluring eyes. Long silver lashes. Thick hair. The subtle age lines decorating his handsome face. He doesn't look old. Just sophisticated. Masculine. *Powerful.*

"Once upon a time," he starts, the phrasing drawing a

laugh from Craze and a huff from Master Pillar. But all I can do is watch his mouth while he speaks.

Because the more he says, the more drawn into his story I become.

It begins with him as a younger ruler. "I didn't exactly inherit the title," he's telling me. "That's not how things work in Monsterland. But my birthright certainly set me up for the position."

"It's all about being the strongest Alpha," Craze drawls. "Who has the biggest knot."

Master Pillar snorts. "If that were the case, I would be king."

Krolic ignores both of them. "It's about power, Ailsa. Alphas are all strong by nature. However, one of us will always be the strongest. My father was part of the royal mate-circle, but he wasn't the king. My mother, though, was the queen. Hence the reason my birthright set me up for the role."

I nod, understanding so far.

"But I wasn't the only child," he goes on. "I have two brothers and a sister. All of us are powerful in our own right, as is expected with our parental lines. However, I've always been the more dominant of my siblings. And everyone else, too. Which is how the kingdom became mine to rule."

"He met us later," Craze inserts, causing Krolic to glance at him. Craze puts his hands up. "Sorry. I'm just trying to get to the interesting part."

Krolic's expression doesn't change. "Would you like to tell the story?"

"Of how Catum handed you your ass in a fight?" Craze asks. "Yes. Yes, I really would."

"I wouldn't say I handed him his ass," Master Pillar murmurs. "Just… proved a point."

"By kicking his ass," Craze says. "Catum wanted our king to know that just because he hadn't been challenged didn't necessarily mean he was the strongest."

"That's not why I fought him, de Hatte."

Craze rolls his eyes. "Yes, it was, Pillar. You wanted to take that stick out of his ass and beat him with it. Those were your words."

"A poor summarization of them," Master Pillar mutters. "I just wanted some respect. That's all."

"And you earned it," Krolic cut in. "Unlike other Alphas at the table."

Craze snorts. "I earned my respect when I returned your precious stones."

"They were lava rocks," Krolic says through his teeth. "And we've entirely derailed this conversation."

Craze leans forward, his gaze on me. "I broke into his royal chambers and took some of his prized possessions. I, too, was making a point."

"That he wanted a place in the king's bed," Master Pillar drawls.

Krolic shakes his head as Craze grins. "That's not exactly what I wanted." He looks at me again. "I wanted a mate. A *female* mate. As nice as I'm sure Krolic's knot is, I've never been all that interested in experiencing it. I have my own to play with, and it'll fit nicely in an Omega's—"

"Enough," Krolic interjects. "She needs to know the history of our kingdom before we discuss our mate-circle and what it means."

Craze gives him a look. "Then get to the part about Heart."

The name makes Krolic flinch and Master Pillar curse. "Flames, Craze," Master Pillar mutters.

"Heart is my sister," Krolic says through his teeth, his gaze on me once more. He stopped touching my chin a while ago, which I think is a good thing since both his hands are fisted on the table now. "She's an Alpha, too. But not as strong physically as me or our brothers. Therefore, she always felt… neglected. Like a lesser."

"Now you're just giving her excuses for becoming a psychotic bitch," Craze tells him. A flicker of fire travels across the table, causing Craze to bat it away as he glares at Master Pillar. "Careful or our shield will go up in smoke."

"Stop being an ass and let Krolic finish his tale."

Krolic ignores them both and continues his story by telling me how his sister orchestrated several violent events, including the one that killed his parents and their mate-circle.

"She was imprisoned," he says, swallowing. "Or so we thought."

He goes on to tell me how he became king after the loss of the existing monarchy, how he met Craze and Catum— a name that's hard for me to think, let alone say, since I've spent two years calling him *Master Pillar*—and how they became a mate-circle.

"What is a mate-circle?" I interject, wanting to make sure I understand. They keep tossing that term around, along with several others, and I'm not sure I understand it.

"Alphas form a mate-circle to best protect their mate," he explains. "There are a lot more Alphas than there are Omegas."

"An understatement," Craze inserts.

Krolic doesn't acknowledge him and continues with, "Most Alphas band together with others who have similar skill sets or power levels. The stronger the mate-circle, the better. Especially for a king. Which is why Catum is often referred to as my Second, while Craze is my Enforcer."

"Or that used to be the case before everyone assumed

we died," Master Pillar murmurs. "K, we need to make this a little more interesting. A few too many crows are glancing our way."

My brow furrows at the word *crows*, but Krolic seems to understand because his jaw tightens. "Damn voyeurs. Suggestions?"

Master Pillar leans forward, finally allowing me to see his face outside of the shadows. His handsome features are etched into harsh lines, his thick hair elegantly tousled. But it's his eyes that captivate me. Those warm brown irises swirl with dark intensity. Focus. *Promise.*

"I need you to straddle me, Miss Marvel," he says.

I blink at him. "What?"

"Get in my lap and straddle me. I'm going to pretend to kiss you while Krolic continues his story."

"Oh, I like where this is going," Craze drawls.

Master Pillar stretches his hand out toward me. "Now, Miss Marvel."

I shiver, his command rumbling through me in a purr of sound. "Why?" I ask in a whisper as I take his palm.

He helps me to my feet and draws me closer to him but doesn't respond until he's pulled me between his sprawled thighs. "Because I created the barrier to mask our conversation. Typically, that's only done here when certain arrangements are being made—arrangements that one doesn't wish for anyone else to overhear."

His palms go to my hips as he lifts me in the air.

"Part your legs, Miss Marvel," he says, sending another tremble through my body.

I do what he asks and jolt when cool air touches my skin, the smoky fabric of my dress seeming to part all around my lower limbs.

He settles me against him in an intimate position that has my thighs automatically clenching in response, sending a wave of warmth through my veins. If he notices, he doesn't show it, just continues explaining his bizarre actions.

"We've been too casual for too long, and the patrons are starting to notice." His voice is soft, very unlike his demanding hands that are pulling me impossibly closer. "So you and I are going to give them something else to focus on while Krolic finishes his tale."

His palm slides from my hip to my spine and up to my nape, where he tangles his fingers in my hair.

I grab his shoulders, mostly to hold on, as his opposite arm encircles my waist.

"From their view, it looks like I'm kissing you now," he says, tilting my head ever so slightly to the side. "We'll do this for ten or so minutes, then venture up to our room to continue the charade."

His grip tightens, his breath fanning across my now-parted lips.

"When I tell you to move your hips a little, do it," he adds, his nose bumping mine. "Otherwise, be a good girl and listen to Krolic."

I'm not sure how he expects me to concentrate like this.

I'm in his lap.

Clutching his muscular shoulders.

With my mouth half an inch from his.

And he wants me to *move* my hips soon, too?

This… this is… *Oh my Gods*… It's like my dreams. Only somehow hotter because there are other people watching.

Including Krolic and Craze.

The former clears his throat, or I assume it's Krolic who does because suddenly he's speaking, picking up where Master Pillar left off regarding the perceived *death* of their circle.

"It became clear something was going on around the time my eldest brother died," Krolic says. "It was too coincidental. But by the time I realized who the culprit was, it was too late. My sister had escaped her imprisonment, or was perhaps never completely imprisoned, and was creating all sorts of problems around the kingdom."

Master Pillar's mouth brushes mine as he moves his touch to my cheek, his lips trailing a hot path to my ear. "Focus on our king, Miss Marvel."

I really want to tell him how difficult it is to obey that demand. Especially when I can feel his body heat seeping into mine.

"Heart created her own mate-circle of a sort, just with one other Alpha. One from a rival bloodline. A monster known as Crimson." I can hear Krolic grating his teeth over that name but can't quite see him since Master Pillar has my face angled toward his.

And his mouth is… trailing kisses down my neck.

Gods, why does that feel so good?

"But I wasn't aware of any of this because we were out hunting for an Omega," Krolic continues. "I was only called back after my eldest brother, Spaten, died. Which, as I said, is when I realized something was going on. It quickly became apparent that our family was under attack, something my sister punctuated by killing our other brother. Leaving me as her last mark."

I still, listening intently now.

Only for Master Pillar's mouth to return to mine and actually kiss me this time.

Softly.

A brush of lips.

But with just enough pressure to leave me breathless against him.

"Relax, Miss Marvel," he whispers, his thumb tracing my nape as his hold in my hair loosens a little. "You need to be seen as enjoying this."

"I don't know—she looks pretty into it from where I'm sitting," Craze says, his voice lower than usual. "But perhaps that's because I can smell her."

Krolic doesn't respond to either comment, instead saying, "After realizing my sister was responsible, we feigned a retreat to regroup and observe."

He falls quiet for a moment, something Master Pillar seems to take advantage of by saying, "I need you to move against me, Miss Marvel."

"Move against you?" I repeat, swallowing.

His arm tightens around my lower half, then he shifts his hold to lower his hand to my ass. "Ride me."

I start, nearly pushing away, but his grip on me resembles steel as he easily holds me against him.

"Do what he says, Ailsa," Krolic murmurs, his voice lowering an octave.

I have no idea what these men are trying to do to me or what they want to accomplish, yet I feel my body obeying.

Which is… *terrifying*. Yet it feels so good. Too good. Like I'm trying to achieve something, only I don't exactly know what I need.

"Good girl," Krolic praises me, stirring goose bumps along my neck.

Because he's watching.

Everyone is watching.

And Master Pillar's mouth is ghosting across mine again, a grin forming on his full lips. "You feel amazing like this, Miss Marvel."

I shudder, unable to respond. Unable to *think*.

And then Krolic is talking again.

Something about his sister.

The kingdom.

When *Heart* made her move.

"We waited her out to see what she would do because I suspected there was someone else involved, and I was right," Krolic is saying, his words swirling around me.

I can hear him.

Understand him.

But focusing is… is a challenge.

Especially as Master Pillar pulls my bottom lip into his mouth to gently bite down with his teeth.

"Her partner revealed himself when he stole the throne. That's when I found out about her new mate-circle with Crimson." Krolic sounds gruffer than before, and I can't tell if he's angry or feeling something else entirely.

"Crimson assumed the throne under the guise of being the true Silver King," Master Pillar says against my mouth. "And Monsterland simply accepted his claim."

I start to shake my head, confused by what he's saying.

But his grip tightens, holding me against him as he forces my hips to move once more.

Craze groans. "*Blades*, with her billowing skirt, it looks like you're fucking her."

"Maybe I am," Master Pillar returns, his lips curling. "How jealous would you be?"

"So fucking jealous," Craze says, sounding pained. "I'm already fucking jealous, you asshole."

"Good," Master Pillar replies before sucking my lip into his mouth again. "We need to move upstairs."

"Yes," Krolic agrees. "We'll continue this in our room."

Our room, I think dizzily. *Why is that singular?*

KR⊖LIC

Discussing my family history has put me in a mood.

Or maybe it was watching my queen grind all over my best friend's lap that provoked my irritation.

Because *I* want to be the one she's straddling and pretending to fuck.

Moons, she's fucking glorious. All that long blonde hair taunts my fingers, making me want to grab hold, yank her head toward me, and claim that luscious mouth of hers.

Just like Catum was just doing moments ago downstairs.

Now he just has his palm against her lower back as he guides her down the hallway to our room.

We're up in the clouds here, not that she's noticed. The windows are all darkened up here, indicating the late hour.

She'll see the view in the morning.

I'm sure it'll confuse her, like everything else has thus far.

Fuck. There's still so much for us to discuss, but I can feel Ailsa's exhaustion. Other than the one donut and some sips of water, she barely ate downstairs, too. I've already ordered some evening snacks to be sent up to the room. Hopefully, she'll indulge in a few, then sleep.

And in the morning, we'll continue our discussions.

Talk about how her choice could impact the fate of the kingdom.

Because if she opts to go to the Imposter King, to join his mate-circle with my sister, it'll solidify his claim.

Omegas mean everything in this world, and we've been without one for so long. My mother was the last one. A diamond of her kind.

I suspect the Omegas are actually in hiding, a way to punish Monsterland for what was done to my mother. The Imposter King's edict likely didn't help matters. That he's pretending to be me while doing it… is a whole secondary layer of fucked up.

He never shows his face.

Only chooses to be seen in public as his wolf half— which is white-furred just like me.

I could have ousted him centuries ago, but if there's one thing I learned from my sister's antics, it's that leaving the throne unattended puts the entire kingdom at risk.

It made more sense to observe from afar while hunting for an Omega so we could retake the kingdom as a complete circle.

I just didn't expect it to take this long.

It all feels like an elaborate test, a way for Monsterland kind to prove themselves worthy of cherishing Omegas once more.

Which is why we've played this very carefully, ensuring we woo our mate properly, not take her by force.

Unlike the Imposter King.

And Heart, I think darkly. I rarely refer to her as my sister. Just *Heart.*

Though, she prefers to be called *Queen Heart.* She always has, even though she's never been the Monsterland Queen.

Craze enters a code to open the door to our suite, then steps inside to do a security check while the three of us wait in the hall.

Ailsa glances around with a frown creasing her forehead, but she doesn't speak. Catum warned her before he took down the veil that she needed to be quiet and just stick close to his side.

Thus far, she's done exactly that.

Fortunately, his cloak masked her identity; otherwise, they all would have smelled her delicious slick.

Unfortunately, I'm immune to his magic because he intentionally wove it in a way that allowed the three of us to be very aware of Ailsa's scent.

Which means I'm practically salivating now.

Because our Omega *enjoyed* being on top of Catum.

She might not realize just how much she enjoyed it, but we definitely do. Her sensual aroma is like a drug. All I want to do is kneel before her, lift those translucent skirts, and feast on her sweet cunt.

Craze reappears in the doorway and nods his chin, giving us the all clear.

Catum uses his palm against Ailsa's back to lead her inside, then quickly begins weaving his smokelike enchantments throughout the room.

He's incredibly powerful, his Shadow heritage underscored in dark magic and exceptionally unique. The moment he's done creating a veil, he turns to me to begin undoing the cloak woven into my white shirt and jeans.

A sensation of lightness overcomes me as he frees me from my mask, one that changes my appearance to everyone else in this realm except for those in this room.

He wears a similar one, just like Ailsa does now as well.

The only one not covered in his magic is Craze.

But that's because Craze has his own form of *masks*. Hence the skull makeup smothering his features.

Rather than go wash it off, he leans against the master bedroom door frame and folds his arms. "Ailsa, do you want to take a shower?" he asks her.

She blinks those big blue eyes at him. "What?"

"It's a contraption you use to clean yourself," he drawls.

"I know what a shower is."

"Then why are you confused?" he counters.

"I don't..." She shakes her head like she's trying to clear it. "Why would I shower?"

He shrugs. "To wash off remnants from the Blood Ocean, the Gum Tree, the Hot Chocolate Fields, and the Orange Desert? To have a few minutes to yourself? To shampoo your hair?" His eyes travel over her. "To shave, perhaps?"

Her lips part. "*What?*"

He frowns. "You know, I really am starting to worry about your hearing." He pushes off the door frame to saunter toward her. "Do you want assistance in the shower? Perhaps with the razor?"

"*No*," she bites at him. "And my hearing is fine. You... you just..." She scowls. "You know what? Never mind. I think I will take a shower. To wash *you* off my skin."

His lips curl. "Are you suggesting I marked you, gorgeous?"

She makes a furious sound that reminds me a bit of a growling pup and stomps off toward the kitchen. I'm about to correct her when she freezes on the threshold and starts toward the living area.

"*Ugh!*" She throws her hands up and spins around. "Where is the shower?"

Craze smiles. "Through the main bedroom, Ailsa."

Before she can ask him to elaborate, he gestures to the door frame he was originally leaning against. "Just hang a right. You can't miss it."

She looks ready to argue but bites her tongue instead and marches into the bedroom.

The door slams in her wake, making me shake my head.

"Why are you goading her?" I ask Craze. Then I hold up my hand to stop him before he can respond. "Don't answer that." I'm not interested in his explanation. It won't make any sense to me anyway.

It's a miracle we ever connected as an Alpha-circle. His approach to life is vastly different from mine.

Which, I suppose, is actually why we're compatible. He's constantly thinking outside of the box, while I'm the voice of reason.

And Catum is the observant one.

"There are quite a few crows down there," he states flatly, ignoring everything Craze and I were just saying to one another. "Vultures, too."

Crows and *vultures* are slang terms for court sycophants and royal spies.

"That's what the Tavern is known for," Craze points out. "Why do you think I have such a high tab?"

"Because you're obsessed with violet tea," Catum responds.

Craze lifts a shoulder. "That, too."

"Regardless, Catum's right. There were too many eyes downstairs. We'll need to remain vigilant tonight," I say.

"Are you suggesting shifts?" Catum asks.

I nod. "Perhaps even having one of us go—"

The bedroom door opens, revealing a flustered Ailsa. "This smoke—*dress*—won't come off." She utters the words through her teeth, her frustration palpable and bordering on hysteria.

"Catum, take off her cloak," I say without missing a beat. "I'm going to go fix her a bath. Craze—"

"I'll report back with anything I learn," he tells me, already anticipating my order and heading toward the door.

"Thank you," I call after him.

He just gives a wave and leaves.

By the time the door shuts, Ailsa's gown is all but gone. Catum typically weaves his magic into the fabric of our clothes, but she was practically naked in the Orange Desert. Hence the need for her enchanted gown.

But removing the cloaking spell now means disrobing her.

If her nearly nude state bothers her, she doesn't show it. Or maybe she just doesn't notice.

Because she looks a little lost.

"Ailsa," I say softly, stepping closer.

She just blinks up at me, that sense of despair seeming to grow.

"I'll get the bath," Catum offers, slipping around her.

I nod, even though his back is already to me, and move closer to Ailsa.

When she doesn't startle or jump away, I slowly pull her into my arms. She buries her face against my chest, her body seeming to melt into mine.

I purr in response, the sound one I know she's familiar with, as I've done it many times around her in wolf form.

She grabs my shirt and clings to me, her shoulders shaking as she fights the emotions rolling through her.

"Today was a lot," I whisper. "I'm sorry, baby girl."

It's a nickname I've used hundreds of times in my head, but never out loud.

She doesn't react to it other than to cling to me even more.

"I wanted to reveal myself to you so many times," I admit. "But I had to wait. We had to do this the right way."

"I don't even know what that means," she mumbles.

"I know." I kiss the top of her head. "There's so much more we need to explain, but it's been a long day. You need to eat and rest. Will you let Catum and me take care of you, Ailsa?"

She doesn't answer. It's almost like she's too exhausted to make a decision.

However, I wait.

Because it's the right thing to do.

She shivers against me. "Beast," she whispers, nuzzling my chest as I purr.

She's fallen asleep with me in the forest before, typically with her head on my shoulder. I always wanted to carry her back, but I couldn't risk her waking with me in human form.

Plus, I would've been naked.

And that probably would have intimidated her.

"Bath is ready," Catum tells me several minutes later.

I nod and lift Ailsa into the air to carry her into the bedroom. "Can you grab the tea tray when it arrives?" I ask Catum, aware that it should be here any second now.

"Yes," he confirms.

Ailsa lays her head on my shoulder, her eyes closed. "You need to be awake for your bath."

She hums noncommittally.

"If you can't stay awake, then I'll be taking one with you."

Another hum.

"Hmm, I see." I enter the bathroom, familiar with the

magically enhanced amenities. We're frequent Tavern guests.

Or we were until I found Ailsa.

It's been a bit since I last stayed here. But nothing has changed.

The shower is fully stocked with necessary items, as are the sink drawers. Catum already filled the tub with salts, the scent of smoky embers definitely his aroma of choice. I would have chosen something a little more woodsy. Alas…

I set Ailsa on the marble counter, then catch her chin to draw her gaze up to mine. "I'm going to get in that tub with you." It's not a threat or a question, just a statement of fact.

She doesn't say anything, just stares sleepily at me.

At least until I take a step back and remove my shirt.

Then her gaze widens, her eyes instantly taking a tour of my exposed physique.

When I unbutton my jeans, she licks her lips.

I'm not even sure she's aware of how she's reacting, her exhausted state likely altering her perception of reality and fantasy.

I unzip my pants and push them down, then kick the fabric off with my shoes and bend to remove my socks.

Wearing just black boxer shorts, I step forward to gently peel off the remainders of her ripped bra and underwear.

She swallows. "I've never done this before."

"Done what, little one?"

"This." She gestures between us. "You… you and Master Pillar were my first kisses. Craze, too."

I smile. "First and last," I tell her. "Or that's the hope, anyway." I brush her hair back behind her ears. "And we're not going to do more of it tonight. I'm just going to bathe you."

Her hands land on my shoulders as I lift her again, then she shivers as I take her to the bath.

Distrust shines in her gaze, the sight of it hurting my heart. It's deserved, but I hate that it exists. I'm going to do everything in my power to remove that look.

I walk up the steps to the tub platform, then down a similar set of stairs into the massive bath. It could easily fit all four of us, the benches around it providing seats for five or six Alphas.

I choose one near the controls and sit with Ailsa in my lap.

The water is warm with magic, the oversized tub having been filled by one of the Tavern's many enchantments. All Catum did to fill it was flip a few switches and set the temperature before adding the salts.

Ailsa shouldn't be surprised by any of this. While she may not have firsthand experience with this kind of magic, she's known it to exist her whole life.

Her employer—if Baroness Clarice could even be called that—was a supernatural. So were her children. Ailsa worked in their home, thus exposing her to all sorts of enchanted enhancements.

Alas, she remains stiff.

Although, I suspect her rigid posture has nothing to do with the bespelled bath and everything to do with her unexpected trip to Monsterland.

"Try to relax," I tell her softly, then opt for an offhanded comment in an attempt to lighten the conversation. "We've cuddled before."

"With you as a wolf," she mutters.

"Do you want me to shift?" I offer. "It'll be hard to help you wash your hair, but I'll do it if it makes you more comfortable."

She glances up at me. "This is a little deep for a wolf to sit comfortably in."

"I'm a big wolf, sweetheart."

She snorts, then shakes her head. "This is… fine."

"Fine?" I repeat. "Do you want the jets on?"

"Maybe do that after eating something," Catum interjects as he carries the tray into the bathroom. His gaze instantly goes to our Omega's breasts, causing him to swallow as hunger no doubt ignites inside him.

I'm hungry for her myself.

Something she can probably feel against her ass.

Because I'm hard as a fucking rock.

Catum sets the tray down on the side of the tub.

Then he begins to disrobe, his intentions clear.

Ailsa straightens even more, her back practically glued to my chest as she watches Catum remove his cuff links and jacket. His black vest is next. Followed by his tie. And it isn't until he begins unfastening the buttons of his obsidian dress shirt that Ailsa remembers to breathe.

I chuckle against her ear, amused by her reaction to my Second. "Like what you see, Ailsa?"

Her resulting tremble shudders through me, causing my lips to curl.

"It's okay to find him desirable," I whisper before placing a kiss against her now-raging pulse. "It's okay to crave any of us."

"Or all of us," Catum adds as he unfastens his belt.

Ailsa grabs her thighs, her whole body vibrating now.

"I know this feeling is intense," I tell her. "Your Omega instincts are coming out to play." I kiss her neck again. "Just as our Alpha drives are awakening for you."

I can feel that drive pulsing in my throbbing knot.

I've never been inside an Omega before, never properly *fucked*.

Oh, we've all experimented.

But only a true Omega can take our knots.

This will be a first for all of us in so many ways.

However, I meant what I said about tonight. We just want to take care of her, a directive Catum clearly understands as he disrobes only to his boxers.

And joins us in the water.

CATUM

THE EMOTIONS PLAYING through Ailsa's features vary from shocked to aroused to terrified.

That final emotion grates on my nerves.

She has nothing to fear from us. We'll never force her. It will always be her choice.

Rather than touch her the way I'm dying to, I take a seat across from her and Krolic and focus on the tray. "I think you'll like these mushrooms," I tell her.

Her nose scrunches. "I don't really like mushrooms."

My lips curl. "Trust me, these are no ordinary shrooms. Just try one for me, Miss Marvel. You'll see."

I pick one up from the tray and hold it out for her. She stares at the purple item, then leans forward to take it with her mouth, not her hand.

The sight of her lips wrapped around the violet head has my groin tightening with interest. It's such an innocent move on her part yet so underlaid with sensuality that I nearly grab a fistful of her hair and yank her into my lap.

Alas, she remains on Krolic's thighs.

Which is no doubt killing him even more than it's killing me because now our intended is moaning.

Flames, the way she responds to food is so fucking erotic.

"That's really good," she says, eyeing the tray. "They taste like cherries but… different."

"Chocolate-covered cherries," I murmur, selecting another one for her. "As you can see, nothing here is what it seems."

While her world also has magic, it's not like Monsterland magic.

We're just one of many realms that all interconnect. It's a confusing mess of chaos made worse by our Alpha, Beta, and Omega distinctions.

I feed her another shroom, my thumb brushing her lip with the movement.

Then I pick up a glass of water from the tray. That item is at least normal. By her standards, anyway. Here, water is seen as abnormal.

Our darling Omega has so much to learn.

I, for one, can't wait to teach her.

She moans again when I feed her a third treat, her eyes falling closed as she tips her head back to meet Krolic's shoulder. His lips ghost across her cheek, his arm banding around her waist.

Ailsa just shudders in response, her expression bordering on drunk.

The shrooms possess no drug-like qualities. It's just food. But I suspect our Omega is feeling some of the effects of her future heat.

I diluted the impact of the elixir before giving it to her. Had I given her what the Crimson King prepared, her estrus would have struck within hours of her first swallow.

But we wanted time to obtain her consent first. To seduce her. To *worship* her.

To give her a chance to say no.

If she denies us, we'll simply protect her through the cycle. It won't be easy. In fact, it'll fucking suck. However, it'll be worth it knowing she's safe and making her own choices.

But we won't make it easy on her to say no, something I demonstrate now by feeding her a fourth and fifth mushroom.

We want to love her. And we're going to do everything in our power to ensure she knows that.

After her sixth shroom—an item Krolic no doubt chose after learning her favorite fruit at home was cherries—I give her more water, then smile as she lounges fully on our king's lap.

He kisses her temple, his hold securing her as his palm begins to trace up her side.

I spread my arms out across the side of the tub and enjoy the view. Specifically the peek at her full breasts beneath the water. Her rosy nipples are hard, the stiff points begging for a man's mouth to taste them.

Flames, she'll be a delectable treat.

Maybe she'll let us devour her for dessert before bed.

"Can you hand me the sprayer?" Krolic asks, his words for me, not for our intended. Yet she startles like she forgot he was there.

I chuckle at her blissed-out state and reach for the item in question, clicking the On button along the way.

Krolic takes it with his free hand, his opposite arm still wrapped around her belly.

Ailsa looks at the sprinkler head with distrust as he brings it toward her head. Then she stills when he uses it to dampen her long blonde hair. The color darkens beneath the water, her thick strands absorbing the liquid with ease.

I anticipate Krolic's next move and grab the shampoo for him before he asks for it.

He massages it into her hair, eliciting a groan from Ailsa when he starts combing his fingers through her strands.

Magic flares to life around us, the water naturally filtering itself as he rinses the shampoo from her head.

The process repeats with the conditioner, then again with the soap he uses on her neck and arms.

"Straddle me," he tells her, the words making my dick throb with the reminder of earlier.

Ailsa felt so fucking good in the Tavern, her warmth a brand against my cock.

She was such a natural. A sensual beauty without even realizing it.

And she proves it again now as she follows Krolic's command without hesitation.

Our girl isn't shy. It's a miracle, given her lack of sexual experience. But she's clearly embracing her inner needs, just following her instincts the way an Omega should.

Fuck, I can't believe she's finally here. *Naked*. And sharing a bath with us.

It's like a dream, one of the many I've shared with her over the last two years.

I never provoked her fantasies, simply reveled in them after they started. She reacted so viscerally to my presence, only further proving her Omega classification.

What the Imposter King fails to grasp is that an elixir isn't needed to identify a true Omega. The right Alpha will bring out an Omega's traits.

Or, in our case, the right circle.

Craze may not have been there, his presence required elsewhere, but it was our shared dynamic that stoked Ailsa's inner fire.

Krolic holds her gaze as he brings the soap back to her neck and starts a path downward to her tits—tits that are fully exposed to him because she's kneeling across his lap and hasn't sat down.

Fuck, I can't see what he's doing, but I *know* what he's doing, and that's almost even more of a turn-on. Because she's not stopping him. She's not even flinching.

No. She's fucking *arching*. Giving him more access. Letting him explore her under the guise of bathing her.

He eventually leaves her breasts to travel downward to her navel, then his hands disappear beneath the water, where he grabs her hips and pulls her into him.

The soap automatically dissolves, magic thickening the air as the water auto-filters once more. I feel it roaming down my spine like a live wire, the sensation sizzling through my veins.

Intoxicating, I muse, absorbing the power and keeping it as my own.

"You're fucking perfection, Ailsa," he says, one palm sliding up her spine to her nape as he guides her mouth to his.

She goes to him without hesitation, her body seeming to fit perfectly with his.

My abdomen tightens as I watch them, my insides aflame with need.

A need that's been growing for two fucking years.

Ever since the first moment I saw Ailsa Marvel. All that white-blonde hair reminded me of an angel, then I caught sight of her stunning features and decided she was more of a succubus than a heavenly being.

A sensual creature in an angelic disguise.

Not so angelic now, I muse as her head tips to the side to grant Krolic access to her neck. His green eyes meet mine as he nibbles her pulse. There's a sense of triumph in his gaze, yet it's underscored by reverence. Because he knows what a gift this is, how precious our Omega's attentions truly are.

She's exhausted.

Overwhelmed.

Yet giving him—*us*—this moment. Perhaps as a way to escape her reality. Or maybe because it just feels right.

Regardless, we won't take advantage of her. We'll just make her feel good, show her what life will be like with her Alphas taking care of her.

"I don't know what I'm doing," Ailsa breathes.

"You're existing," Krolic replies. "You're *learning*."

He captures her mouth before she can speak again and rotates them on the seat to give me a better view of their kiss.

Fuck, it's hot watching him devour her like that.

Krolic and I have never been intimate together, both of us preferring to share women between us rather than fuck each other. Craze is the same way. But that doesn't mean I can't enjoy watching my two bond-mates play.

Especially with Ailsa.

It just increases the burn in my veins, making me want her that much more.

Krolic parts her lips with his tongue, drawing a shocked little gasp from our intended. She's very clearly never been kissed or even touched, her innocence an attribute we fully intend to tarnish.

Because none of us are innocent.

We're monsters.

Creatures with wicked imaginations and savage needs.

And it's been over two years since any of us have indulged in our baser instincts.

This beautiful woman is ours to devour. Ours to mark. Ours to *fuck*.

But Krolic goes easy on her, his mouth gentle as he

teaches her how to kiss. Shows her what to do with her lips, her tongue, her *teeth*.

My hands grip the marble siding of the tub, the urge to stroke myself growing with every passing second.

I'm so fucking hard I can barely think.

However, for Ailsa, I maintain control. For her, I force myself to exude a calmness I don't quite feel. One look at my hands will betray my true intentions, but she's so focused on Krolic that she doesn't seem to notice I'm here.

As though she hears my inner musings, she opens her eyes and glances my way, proving everything I just thought wrong.

She very much knows I'm here.

And she likes that I'm watching her with Krolic.

It reminds me of earlier when I played with her at the table—she enjoyed being seen then, too.

"I think our Omega is a bit of an exhibitionist," I muse. "That's good, Miss Marvel. Because I'm a bit of a voyeur myself."

She shivers. "I don't know what that means."

No, I imagine she's not familiar with a lot of things. "It means watching you kiss Krolic turns me on, just like it's making you wet knowing that I'm here, too."

"Wet?" Her brow furrows. "We're in a bathtub."

Krolic chuckles. "He's talking about your pussy, baby girl. You're wet between your thighs."

Her cheeks flame with a beautiful shade of pink. "*Oh.*" She tries to squirm off of his lap, which he only allows because I move in to grab her from behind and pull her into mine. "*Oh!*"

I catch her nape, my opposite arm banding around her as she straddles me. "I wonder if you taste like chocolate cherries," I say, my grip tightening when she tries to move again. "Will you indulge me, Miss Marvel?"

Her pupils dilate, her gaze falling to my mouth as she stops trying to swim away. "This has to be a dream," she breathes.

"I'll take that as a compliment," I murmur as I close the gap between us. Then I make her dreams a reality with my tongue, gently parting her lips and kissing her the way I wanted to downstairs.

Slowly at first.

Just a sensual introduction between mouths.

One that grows with each passing moment into something more intense. Something more impactful. Something more *us*.

By the time I deepen our embrace, she's practically vibrating on top of me, her thighs squeezing mine as her hands grasp my shoulders. Her nails bite into my skin, leaving marks and claiming me as hers. All while I dominate her mouth.

"I was right," I whisper against her lips. "Chocolate cherries have never been more delicious." I kiss her again before she can reply, my fingers gliding up to fist her hair while I hold her against me.

Fuck, her tits feel perfect against my chest. So full and ripe, those pretty nipples hard and aroused. I'm going to bite them. Suck them. Then bite them again.

Flames, her breasts would look amazing with little droplets of wax painted across them.

I would wipe them away to admire the pink splotches in their wake, then chase away the hurt with my tongue.

That'll be an advanced session, one that will require our little Omega to understand the art of pain and pleasure.

We'll teach her everything.

Show her how best to heighten her ecstasy.

And care for her properly afterward.

Our sweet one. Our Omega. Our *queen*.

I draw her bottom lip between my teeth and bite down a little harder than earlier, then growl as she pants in response.

Already she's showing how she feels about a little stinging sensation while in the throes of passion. "Our king was right," I tell her. "You really are fucking perfect, Miss Marvel."

AILSA

THIS HAS TO BE A DREAM.

Maybe… maybe I'm still asleep and tomorrow is my birthday. Not today. The whole *Drink Me* ceremony hasn't actually happened yet. And I'm just lost in this strange reality where two very sexy men are bathing me in a giant tub.

That makes more sense, right?

Which means… it's okay to kiss them. To touch them. To… to do other unmentionable things with them.

Because that's what dreams are for—fantasizing about what life could be like.

And I very much like this fantasy.

Master Pillar's tongue dances with mine in a sensual caress that has me seeing stars behind my closed eyes. It's so unreal. So intense. So incredibly *hot*.

Every part of me burns, my limbs shaking with some suppressed need that I can't define.

Whatever this is, I like it. I crave more of it. I never want it to end.

I wrap my arms around Master Pillar's neck like I often do in my dreams and press myself closer to him. He responds with a growl that vibrates my chest, causing my nipples to ache with renewed desire.

I want to feel his mouth there. Everywhere. All over

me. Memorizing my skin, tasting my yearning, and fueling the flames building inside me.

It's such a foreign need. One I don't understand, yet fully embrace.

Because this is a dream, I tell myself. *Gods, it has to be a dream.*

It would explain so much.

Or perhaps it's just easier to accept that this is all a dream, to embrace what's making me feel good for just a little while.

It's like I've found a switch in my brain, one I just turn off.

Because I no longer care about anything other than Master Pillar's tongue.

And Krolic's gaze, I think, shivering as I sense him watching me—watching *us*. It makes me feel alive. Desired. *Special.*

I move against Master Pillar, just like I did at the table, and jolt when a sensation zips up my spine.

He's hard, I realize, more than a little aware of what that means thanks to my previous dreams. *Gods, he's so much bigger now.* I'm not sure how that's possible since I've always fantasized about his size before, yet never quite like this.

The water around us does little to temper the heat blossoming between my thighs, his arousal thick and prominent even beneath his boxer shorts.

A devilish part of me wants to strip him of the remaining fabric, to free him and *ride* him. It's so wanton and unlike me. But I'm far more adventurous and confident in my dreams.

I'm not even sure where I come up with these ideas.

I haven't been exposed to much in my twenty-one years. Just a few remarks here and there from Baroness Clarice's daughters. Spending my teen years in their household allowed me to overhear all about their boy-crazy-fueled desires.

I was there when they first fell in love, too.

There when they each lost their virtue.

There when they shared stories of what it felt like.

I… I never wanted to experience it for myself until I heard Master Pillar first speak.

And now… now it's all I can think about as he kisses me. Touches me. *Holds* me.

Gods, I've lost my mind.

But who cares?

Everything is strange here. Out of the ordinary. *Unreal.*

I press myself even more into him, determined to indulge this dream and forget the concept of reality. To feel him beneath me. His heat pressing into my most sensitive part.

But a pair of lips on my shoulder reminds me that it's not just about Master Pillar. Krolic is here, too. My Beast. Only, he's in human form. And what a form that is.

All sensual grace and refined age.

He catches my chin between his fingers and pulls me back to kiss him again while Master Pillar's mouth goes to my throat.

The fire blossoming inside me burns even hotter as Krolic's tongue enters my mouth. He's pulling my head back, forcing me to bend in a way that would normally make me feel unstable. But Master Pillar's arm is around my waist, holding me astride his lap as my breasts push upward toward his face.

I moan as his lips trail down to my chest, his mouth sealing around one of my nipples and sucking it in a way that feels so much more potent than any dream ever has.

"Does that feel good, baby girl?" Krolic asks. "Do you like Catum worshipping your tits?"

A shudder works through me, his words seeming to awaken a part of me I never knew existed. A part that wants more. A part that has me panting, "Yes."

"Mmm," he hums against my mouth. "Such a good fucking girl." He kisses me again, this time with renewed strength, his tongue dominating mine while Master Pillar nibbles on my tender nipple.

I scream when he bites down, shocked by the pain.

Then quiver when his tongue chases away the ache.

"Careful with our Omega," Krolic warns him, a subtle growl underlining his tone.

"Just testing some limits," Master Pillar replies. "It shocked her more than hurt her."

Krolic distracts me with another kiss, his hand moving to my throat as he holds me back against him. I feel owned. Possessed. Utterly captured by these two men.

Which is insane.

I know deep down this is absolutely ludicrous.

Yet I can't stop it.

I want it.

Every part of me is burning with need, stoked alive by endless dreams.

I often woke aroused and wishing it was real. I know tomorrow will be the same. But for now, I follow the fantasy all the way down, allowing myself to just experience what it might be like to be handled by two men.

"Let's move this to the bed," Master Pillar says against my breast.

Krolic rumbles an agreement, his lips leaving mine as he exits the bath.

All too soon, my dream is coming to an end, and I find myself pouting at the thought. I want more of this. More of them. *I don't want to wake up. Please don't let me wake up.*

As though he can hear me, he bends to lift me from the

water, his arms engulfing me in a sea of white fluff. *A towel*, I realize.

"Someone's a little lust drunk," Master Pillar muses as he joins us outside of the bath. "You're beautiful, Miss Marvel."

A quiver traverses my spine. I love it when he calls me that. Love how formal it sounds. How *dominant*.

"So fucking beautiful," he goes on before capturing my mouth with his.

Krolic rumbles against me, his arms holding me in the fluffy cloud while Master Pillar lays claim to my mouth.

It's intoxicating.

Overwhelming.

The best dream I've ever had.

Time seems to suspend itself in that way fantasies often do, and the next thing I know, I'm on the bed with Master Pillar devouring my mouth while Krolic explores my breasts.

"We're going to make you feel good," Master Pillar says against my lips. "So fucking good."

I have no idea what that means, but I believe him. Because I already feel amazing. Treasured. Like I'm actually worth something in this world.

It's a sensation I've never experienced.

One I'm thankful I can find in my dreams.

He kisses me again, demanding that I focus on his tongue while Krolic nips and sucks at my nipples.

Each stroke, each *touch*, makes me burn hotter and hotter.

That inferno builds to an explosive point as Krolic starts a path downward to a space I have only ever investigated in private.

I jolt as his tongue reaches my sex, exploring the intimate layers of my most sacred place.

Oh, Gods…

I… I never knew it could feel like this. His tongue is so much more impactful than my own fingers, so much more *knowing*. Like he's done this to me a thousand times before.

And maybe he has.

At this point, I can no longer discern up from down. Right from wrong. Reality from fiction.

"Fuck, you taste amazing," he says, his voice a low rumble that vibrates my sensitive bud. He gives me another lick that ends in a growl, causing me to jump in response. "Your clit is practically pulsing, baby girl. Do you want me to suck it into my mouth and make you feel good?"

That foreign part of me has me breathing, "*Yes*," in response.

"I love how good you are, Miss Marvel," Master Pillar says against my mouth. "How perfect and needy you are." He captures my lips before I can fathom a reply, then Krolic takes my clit between his teeth and gives it a nibble.

I scream.

Both men chuckle.

And suddenly I'm *flying*.

Or that's how it feels—like my soul has taken flight from my body, soaring headfirst into a burning oblivion of illogical heat.

"Fuck me," Master Pillar breathes, his hand suddenly at my throat. "That's the most glorious sight I've ever experienced."

I have no idea what he's talking about, as I can't see anything. I'm… I'm drowning in a sea of lava, each lap against my skin making me scream.

Only it doesn't hurt.

It feels good.

So good.

"My turn," Master Pillar says, and suddenly it's

Krolic's mouth against mine, kissing me, while Master Pillar licks a searing path downward over my breasts and toward my navel.

I practically melt when I feel his palms on the insides of my thighs, widening my legs to accommodate his size.

Then his mouth is *there*, licking me and nibbling me right where Krolic just did. Except Master Pillar adds his hands, his finger sliding into my slickened channel to explore me in a way no one ever has before. Not even I have stroked myself there. Yet he... he's claiming me. Branding me. *Fucking* me with his touch.

All while Krolic dominates my mouth.

His palm is wrapped around my throat, holding me down as he devours me, forcing me to taste myself on his tongue.

It's sweet. Alluring. Borderline addicting.

I lose myself to him and Master Pillar, reveling in this never-ending dream and loving the sensations these men are evoking from deep within.

So much *warmth*.

So much *electricity*.

So much passion.

I moan, scream, writhe, and *beg*. Because I just want more. I never want it to end.

"That's it, baby girl," Krolic whispers against my mouth. "Come for us again."

His words do something to me. Rip something *from* me. A tidal wave of agony-induced ecstasy.

My vision flees once more, cascading me into a realm of inky rapture where all I feel is the pleasurable quakes assaulting my being.

I am pleasure and pleasure is me.

And I've never felt lighter. More alive. More *aware*.

Yet it's not real, I think dreamily. *Just the ultimate... fantasy*.

Unless it's not.

Unless... unless I really did fall into Monsterland.

Unless I really am an Omega.

I yawn, incapable of analyzing that now. I'm too exhausted. Too replete. *Too pleased.*

"Sleep, Miss Marvel," Master Pillar whispers against my ear. "We'll protect you while you rest."

"We'll protect you for always," Krolic says near my mouth, his lips ghosting over mine. "You're ours now, Ailsa."

"Ours," Master Pillar echoes. "Good night, little one. And sweet dreams..."

CRAZE

It's been a long fucking night.

But seeing Ailsa naked in the bed certainly makes it all worth it.

Krolic and Catum are off searching for a certain cat, their instructions clear—*guard Ailsa*.

I didn't need to be told twice.

A single glance at the sheets—and one sweet inhale— told me they *guarded* her well overnight.

Our replete little Omega still has a pretty flush to her cheeks.

"She's fucking beautiful when she comes" were Catum's parting words. "Enjoy."

Oh, I'll be enjoying a whole hell of a lot.

But first, I want to scrub the stench of death off my skin.

It's an aroma I wear with purpose. One meant to repel. Just like my mask.

It's how I hide here.

I haven't worn my real face in… ages. Centuries. Sometimes I wonder if my varying personalities are here to stay. They come so naturally now, rolling through my mind with a speed I can no longer track.

Ah, well. Such is life, I suppose.

I lock the suite door and set up a card trick that'll ensure no one can come through without meeting a very quick, very *deadly* demise.

Then I arrange a similar trap by the master bedroom door—this one meant to ensnare my gorgeous little minx in case she decides to go wandering before I'm done showering. It won't hurt her, just… capture her.

Which may actually prove to be quite fun. She looked all pretty whilst strung up in that Gum Tree; this would be even more accessible since it would basically tie her up against the door.

Hmm, I hum to myself, then dance off to the shower.

It's as large as the bathtub beside it, making it a silly use of space. Who needs benches in a shower?

I cant my head. *Well, actually*… I can think of a few sensual purposes. Noting those ideas for later, I work on rinsing the paint from my skin. It feels weird to expose myself in this way, but I want Ailsa to know me. The real me. Whoever he may be.

Craze de Hatte.

Mad Hatter.

My lips twist. I'm not… insane. Of course, that's exactly what someone who has lost his mind would think. Which makes it impossible to know.

So I'm about seventy percent sure I still have my sanity. Or maybe closer to sixty percent.

I shake my head. The fact that I'm even considering this is ridiculous enough. There's a naked blonde in the other room, one who may wake at any moment. I would prefer that to happen when I'm stretched out beside her.

I want to see her reaction to my face.

The real me.

Craze. Just Craze.

Will she scream? Try to fight? Run away?

All notions are arousing.

I hum a tune under my breath, the song one I haven't considered in years. It's ancient, like me. Like Catum. Like Krolic.

Ancient compared to our Omega, anyway.

Whistling the hymn, I finish my shower and grab a towel, then saunter back into the bedroom where our sleeping beauty is resting in the large feather-padded bed.

Gorgeous is definitely the nickname I'm keeping for her.

Rabbit may need to go. She's not very skittish. Dainty, yes. But there's a strength to her that I find quite admirable.

It's an impressive feat to fall down the rabbit hole into Monsterland and still retain a sense of wit.

I shake out the droplets from my hair, then head back into the bathroom to continue drying off.

The closet beside it is stocked with everything I could possibly need—pants, shirts, boots, undergarments.

However, I grab a pair of gray sweats and nothing else. I even leave my cards behind, choosing to be simply me for the first time in eons.

This morning—which is technically closer to noon—is all about relaxing.

Running my fingers through my still-damp hair, I waltz back into the bedroom and consider my gorgeous little vixen.

She's going to be hungry when she wakes. Thirsty, too.

Wandering back to the door, I undo the magic trap waiting for her and head into the kitchen to place an order on the lily pad. It's a computerized system highlighted with magic that lets me select all sorts of foods and drinks.

Not knowing what Ailsa will want, I basically order the entire list and send it off.

Catum or Krolic will handle the bill. Typically, they would use their magic to handle the order, too. But I told them I would do it.

They'll probably regret that when they see I ordered, well, everything.

Whistling once more, I return to the bedroom to find Ailsa right where I left her.

She's restless, though, likely from me making noise. Zipping my lips, I crawl into the bed beside her and move as close to her as I can without touching her.

Ailsa releases a soft little noise, one that sounds a lot like satisfaction, and snuggles back into her pillow.

I say nothing and don't move, curious as to if she'll rouse again. But instead, she falls into a deeper sleep.

Hmm. I suppose an hour or two of rest won't hurt anything.

The food and drinks will keep in the dining area, thanks to special Tavern enchantments.

Yawning, I close my eyes.

And startle awake some time later when I hear a gasp from the female in my bed.

Peeking at her through long lashes, I turn and check the time. It's only been thirty minutes. Snorting, I roll back to my side and shut my eyes again. "Go back to sleep, Ailsa."

"*Craze?*"

"Hmm?" I hum, utterly knackered. Which is really her

fault. Had she been awake when I snuggled into the bed, I wouldn't have fallen asleep at all. But now that I've experienced a little bit of rest, I want more.

"Oh my Gods, it was real," she breathes, the cover rustling as she flies upward in the bed. "I… It wasn't… it wasn't a dream at all!"

I peek at her again. "What are you going on about?"

"Master Pillar and Krolic kissed me!" she exclaims. "*Everywhere.*"

Mmm, okay. I appear to be waking up again. Propping myself up on an elbow, I look up at her. "Care to elaborate?" I ask.

She blinks at me. "What happened to your skull face?"

"I washed it off," I tell her before returning to the more important topic at hand. "So where exactly did they kiss you?"

"Why?" she asks.

"Because I would really like to know more about it." I glance down at her exposed tits. "In full detail, please."

"No, I mean, why did you wash it off?"

I slowly return my gaze to her pretty face. "Because I don't have to hide here."

She blinks again. "You normally have to hide?"

"Yes. My face is too easily recognizable without the disguise. And if someone sees me, they'll know Krolic is still alive. Hence, I masquerade as the illustrious Mad Hatter."

It's the name everyone knows me as here, the one I've gone by for centuries.

Craze is reserved for the mate-circle.

And now, Ailsa.

Her brow furrows as she reaches out to touch my cheek, almost as though she doesn't think I'm real. I don't move. I barely even breathe. Because my chosen mate is exploring me.

"Your skin is so soft," she whispers.

I don't bother pointing out that it's because I shave every day. The paint wouldn't pair well with facial hair, making me a little jealous of Catum's and Krolic's trimmed beards. Perhaps when this is all done, I'll grow one, too.

Or maybe not, since Ailsa seems to like my smooth jaw.

"It's nice to see you," she goes on. "The real you, I mean."

I smile. "It's nice to see you, too, Ailsa," I murmur, my gaze dancing down to her breasts again. "*All* of you."

She frowns and follows my gaze, resulting in yet another gasp as she grabs the sheets to cover herself.

My smile disappears. "I was rather enjoying that view, Ailsa."

She closes her eyes and pinches her arm. *Hard*. "Wake up, Ailsa. Wake up. Wake up. *Wake up!*"

I arch a brow when she peeks out at the room. "Still here, darling," I drawl.

She yelps and scoots up to press her back to the headboard, the sheets going with her. "Yesterday really happened. I'm in Monsterland."

"Indeed you are," I murmur, slowly lifting myself up to mimic her position near the pillows. "You were hoping this has all been a dream?"

She doesn't answer me at first, her gaze flitting around the room and going to the wall of windows decorating one side. The curtains are drawn, hiding the view of the clouds. Probably a good thing, given her current reaction.

"No," she says, drawing my attention back to her

mouth. "No, I... I wasn't hoping that at all. I just assumed it wasn't real."

"Definitely real, gorgeous." I reach out to tuck a strand of long hair behind her ear. "Sorry if that disappoints you."

Her gaze finally returns to me, her blue eyes flickering with a myriad of emotions. "Disappointment is the furthest thing from what I'm feeling right now. Shock. Confusion. I'm definitely overwhelmed. More confusion." Her lashes flutter as she starts searching the room again. "I have no idea what I'm doing."

"Well, right now, we're sitting in bed. Next on the agenda is food. Then maybe I'll give you a tour of—"

An explosion at the front door has me leaping off the mattress, my bare feet hitting the ground in an instant. I whistle, calling the remainders of my card deck to my hand, and dash into the living area.

Orange slime covers the floor, the stench of rotting citrus clouding the air. *Fucking orcs.*

Caws echo in the hallway, the sounds crawling along my skin.

Those don't belong to orcs.

Those belong to something far more deadly.

Jabberwaries.

Deadly fucking birdlike creatures with sharp beaks, large wingspans, and venomous spit.

I dart back into the bedroom and slam the door behind me, then cover it with explosive cards. That won't hold for long, but it'll have to do.

"Clothes," I tell Ailsa and gesture wildly toward the bathroom. "In the closet. *Now.*"

She doesn't argue, her naked body practically sprinting across the room as she does what I say. I follow in her wake, grabbing the bathroom door and layering it with more cards.

I meet Ailsa in the closet, where she's putting on a pair of underwear. I find the jeans and sweater that Catum bespelled for her and toss them her way. She catches the items and starts dressing.

I do the same, grabbing a hooded sweatshirt and swapping my gray sweats for a pair of jeans.

Ailsa gasps at some point, probably from seeing my knot. Or, more likely, all my piercings. But there's no time to explain the purpose of a Jacob's ladder right now.

Because the explosion just sounded from the bedroom.

The bathroom is next.

After stuffing my feet into a pair of socks and boots, I grab Ailsa by the waist and run for the glass windows lining the shower.

I don't think; I just turn at the last second to ensure my back hits the panes, and down we go.

AILSA

WE'RE GOING TO DIE.

That thought echoes in my mind as I cling to Craze, my mouth parting on a soundless scream. Soundless because his palm is covering my lips.

Whistling noises whirl around us, the wind seeming to accelerate our fall.

Or that's what I assume until we're suddenly caught in a cloud of mist—one that jolts us right back up into the sky and begins to carry us along some sort of invisible current.

I glance up and then down, goose bumps instantly prickling my nape when I realize just how high up we still are. *Oh, Gods…*

My gaze flies to Craze, but his expression is tight, his lips forming an O.

Because he's the source of the whistling.

I gape at him. However, he doesn't seem to notice me at all, despite the fact that he's hugging me tightly to his chest.

Whatever he's doing is likely the reason we're not falling, so I still and close my mouth.

He must notice that because he removes his hand and resecures his grip around me by lifting me a little higher. I wrap my legs around his waist in response, my arms encircling his neck.

Craze noticeably relaxes but continues to whistle. He has the hood pulled up over his head, hiding his dark hair, but I can still see his makeup-less face.

He's incredibly handsome. Almost in a pretty way. Like his features are too perfect.

I can see why people would recognize him like this; he's stunning.

Krolic has an aged charm to his features, one that commands respect and would easily render me silent.

Catum is all sexy, dominant male, his chiseled jaw and sharp cheekbones marking him as incredibly good-looking.

But Craze... Craze is perhaps the most striking one of the group.

There's just something exceptionally beautiful about his features. He reminds me of the celebrity posters that used to hang on some of the walls back at Baroness Clarice's estate. Her daughters were obsessed with supernatural actors.

Craze definitely fits the description.

Except underneath the clothes is a hard, hot, muscular male.

There were little divots near his hip bones that I didn't know existed until he stripped off his pants.

And his cock...

My cheeks flame.

Oh. My. Gods.

I shouldn't be thinking about it right now, but I can't seem to help myself. I... I've never seen a naked male before. However, I've imagined what they look like. Fantasized about it.

Yet never in my life did I imagine metal. *Down there.*

A row of it. All the way up the underside of his shaft.

I clear my throat and try to erase the image from my

mind. But I can't. I just… it's part of my brain now. Living there forever.

Along with the knowledge of how thick Catum truly is down there.

And Krolic's masterful tongue.

I'm in trouble.

So much trouble.

These males are going to rip the sanity right from my mind.

"Ailsa?" Craze asks softly, making me blink back at him.

Yep. There it goes. No more sanity.

Because at some point we landed on top of a giant—

I frown, glancing down as my feet touch the dotted blue surface below me. "Is this a mushroom?" I ask, my gaze traveling across the top of several rounded heads. In the distance, I can see the stalks, confirming my suspicion.

"Yeah, we're in the Mushroom Jungle." He doesn't sound pleased by that. "I don't know how good the enchantment is on your clothes, so we need to move, and quickly. It's time for plan C."

"And what's plan C?" I ask warily.

"Caverns," he murmurs, making me frown.

"I thought that was plan A?"

"The Black Caves were plan A. The Caverns are another area entirely." I'm still frowning—because *caves* and *caverns* certainly sound the same to me—as he goes down on his stomach to look over the edge of the mushroom. "This is going to be fun."

The sarcastic way he utters that suggests it's going to be the opposite of fun.

"Come here," he says, gesturing to his side. "I'm going to have to hold you on our way down."

The wariness in his tone tells me I'm not going to like this. Not one bit.

I lower to my knees and then to my belly beside him and carefully glance over the edge.

Big mistake.

The ground is *writhing*.

"No," I say, sitting back up. "No, no—"

He grabs me by the waist so quickly I don't have a second to scramble away.

And then we're *falling* again.

I scream, my eyes squinting shut.

But we don't land. We *swing*.

The sensation causes my stomach to drop and my limbs to tighten. I only belatedly realize I'm clinging to Craze again, my legs once more wrapped around his hips, except I'm tucked into his side this time.

He has one arm around me while his other—I peek my eyes open—is grabbing vines. *Plural.*

He keeps releasing them before taking hold of new ones, having us swing with one hand.

I gape at his movements, stunned by his ability to release one vine in midair, just to grasp another to keep us moving forward.

It shouldn't be possible.

The long blue strands are *helping* him.

They're thrashing like live wires, reaching toward us and moving with us as we swing.

I watch in amazement, then yelp when he comes to an abrupt stop as our feet touch the ground. It shifts beneath my shoes—an item I'm really glad I shoved on my feet in the closet earlier—parting to reveal millions of beetle-like creatures.

"Oh, gross," I mutter, suddenly wishing my legs were still wrapped around Craze.

"Shh," he hushes me, his expression hard as he searches the landscape for something I can't see. "There's something strange going on."

No shit, I nearly say back to him as I shake a vibrant blue beetle off my foot.

"Stay here," he says.

"*What?*" I whisper-hiss back at him.

"And be quiet," he adds, his command like a whip to my senses. He's been so jovial and playful that I didn't realize he possessed a serious side. But it's on full display now, his eyes radiating dominance.

I swallow and nod, telling him without words that I understand.

He brushes his knuckles against my cheek before nudging me closer to a mushroom stalk. Once my back touches the cool, hard texture—one that reminds me a bit of a tree trunk—he leans forward to press his lips to my ear. "I promise I'll be back for you. Please don't run. It's dangerous here."

With that soft request—very unlike the snap in his voice from seconds ago—he turns and runs.

I reach out for him instinctively, not wanting to be left behind. His name lingers on my lips, then halts when a growl echoes in the distance.

I swallow.

That… that doesn't sound friendly.

The beetles around my feet scatter, making me jump back into the rough, bark-like stalk behind me. It snags on my sweater, ripping some of the fabric and nearly drawing a gasp from my mouth.

But I swallow it.

And listen as that growling grows louder.

My heart jumps wildly in my chest.

Why do I suddenly feel like bait?

Craze has disappeared. Yet whatever is emitting that grumbling noise is definitely getting closer.

Yeah, I'm definitely bait.

Fucking Craze.

He should have left me on top of—

The mushroom across from me snaps in half as a giant boar-like beast plows right through the stalk.

Oh, I think, watching as the mushroom top crashes into the ground. *Okay. Being on top of the mushroom would have been bad.*

But now that I'm staring down this snarling horned monster, I'm not quite sure being here is much better.

His black eyes immediately lock on me, his tusks creating a tsking echo that stirs the hairs along the back of my neck.

"*Omega,*" he says, his voice raspy. "*Fertile Omega.*" He seems to be tasting the words, his forked tongue licking his lips.

I don't know what this horned beast is, but I'm not interested in being friends with it.

Unfortunately, he seems all too interested.

Because he frolics toward me.

Not charge. Not run. *Frolic.* Like he's dancing on his two hooved feet.

His tongue lolls out of his mouth when he stops five feet from me and bows his head. "My pretty Omega," he purrs.

"Not yours," Craze says from behind him. "*Mine.*"

A whistle sounds through the air as one of the vines appears and wraps around the boar-man, yanking him backward.

The monster snarls, spinning around, only to find himself even more wrapped up in the vine. His hooves claw at the ground as he loses his balance, then the purple ropes tighten and lift him right up in the air.

I gape at the hulking beast and flinch when he snarls his frustration.

That snarl seems to echo, the eerie noise skittering down my spine. It's intense. Loud. And coming from several angles.

Because he's not the only one, I realize as four more come charging into view.

Craze stands in the middle with one of those vines clutched between his hands, holding it like a jump rope.

He's also shirtless.

I have no idea why. And I can't find my voice to even ask.

Because he starts *jumping*.

It's casual at first, the vine seeming to hypnotize the surrounding monsters.

Then he starts to sing, all while jumping rope and twisting his body in a rhythmic manner.

I… I just stare. I'm basically as hypnotized as the boars, if not more so, because wow. *Wow.* His body moves with a grace that shouldn't be possible.

And suddenly the rope flicks out to the side, zapping the nearest boar-man. Then flashes out across the path to another, wrapping around the creature's thick neck and yanking him straight up into the air.

Another rope magically falls into Craze's hands, his dance continuing as he ties up the other two in a series of steps that leaves me breathless. It's all so fast, making it impossible to track his movements.

Which is how I find myself suddenly entangled in a new rope, one cast by his hands as he tugs me into his hard body and tumbles us to the ground.

Except the ground doesn't catch us.

It… it gives out beneath us, sending us spiraling down a hole.

A portal, I belatedly realize as the world spins in darkness.

We land a few seconds later in a room shrouded in obsidian rock.

Craze pins me to the wall, his lips parting on a slight pant, his body vibrating with barely restrained power.

I look up into his black eyes, utterly transfixed by the last few minutes.

He already proved himself to be deadly with those cards.

Now he just demonstrated how lethal he can be with a *vine*.

This Alpha is… *fascinating.*

And beautiful.

And pure, sculpted muscle.

I… I don't even know what to say. I'm too lost to find the words to speak. The ropes tighten around me, holding me captive as his mouth hovers above mine, his hands on my waist.

My heart stops beating.

My lungs cease to work.

All I can do is stare at the man before me.

I don't know if we're safe here. I don't even know where *here* is. I just… give in to the madness. The chaos. The Monsterland mayhem.

And press my lips to his.

CATUM

Where the hell is that damn cat? I wonder, irritated by this futile search.

I received a missive this morning from the enchanted creature, telling me he possessed important information.

But as per usual, that missive came with a riddle, one Krolic and I have spent the last hour trying to decipher.

All I want to do is return to the Tavern and wake Ailsa up with my tongue between her thighs.

Alas, here we are, wandering the Rose Maze just outside of the Royal Palace. If anyone catches us here, we'll be even more delayed.

And potentially ousted.

Both outcomes are undesirable.

"Perhaps the flower on the card isn't a rose," I mutter, pulling it out again to examine. The thorns are rather clear, as is the blood dripping from the tips. But thus far, we haven't found any mutilated flowers.

"How many paw prints were there again?" Krolic asks. "Five?"

I nod, counting the doodling steps around the rose. We

assumed they stood for directions on where to go once inside the maze. Yet everything we've tried so far has failed to reveal the notorious, pink-furred cat. His hair is magenta colored in human form, too. Pretty hard to miss, even in this vibrantly colored maze.

"I have not missed playing this game," Krolic growls as we reach yet another dead end. "I swear the Beta does this on purpose."

"What better purpose than to confuse a king?" comes a soft male voice from right in front of us.

I roll my eyes. "You've been following us around for the last ten minutes, haven't you?" Because that is absolutely something Ches would do.

"Thirty-five," he murmurs as he removes his cloaking spell to reveal himself. "But who's counting?"

"We were right the first time," Krolic says, glaring at the cat shifter.

"No, the third time," he purrs. "Alas, I'll forgive you. You've been out of the game for a while, after all." He saunters toward us, his bright purple pants flowing like a skirt against his long legs.

"We're wasting time by being here," I cut in. "You know it's dangerous."

His lips curl into a smile that is all mischievous feline. "Is it? I had no idea."

"Stop fucking with us, Ches. You said it was urgent."

He presses a palm to his chest, his pale skin blending with his white blouse. "Did I?"

I fold my arms, not saying anything more. He knows what he wrote on that fucking note.

Sexy Caterpillar,

. . .

IHVII4U.

Your Treasure
    Can be
    Found
    Or lost
    Here…

Caterpillar was the pet name he bestowed upon me, similar to how he often referred to himself as *Treasure.*

The jumbled mix of letters and a number was easy enough to decipher—*I have very important information for you.*

And the latter part was decorated with the bloodied roses and paw prints.

"You used to be a lot more fun," he drawls now, his gaze dancing over my torso to my black jeans. "You barely even put on a show last night, *Master Pillar.* I was disappointed."

My jaw clenches at Ches's indication that he was watching me with Ailsa last night. "Things have changed," I inform him.

Because Ailsa won't be shared with the public.

She belongs to me, Krolic, and Craze. No one else. *Never* anyone else.

That was solidified last night when I put my tongue on her cunt. She may not have felt it, but it was a fucking declaration. A vow to make her ours. *A claim.*

Krolic grunts beside me, clearly agreeing with my words.

Watching us share a Beta is a moment of the past. Another lifetime.

Our present and future lie with Ailsa.

And we will not be putting her on display. *Ever*.

At least, not in that manner. As our queen, yes. But how we worship her in private will remain behind closed doors.

"I see," Ches murmurs, his catlike eyes fluttering as he blinks long, pink lashes at us. "Well, I suppose we should get to it, then."

I say nothing. Because that's what I fucking requested several minutes ago.

He sighs and shakes his head. A serious mask overcomes his usual playfulness, his gaze seeming to harden. "The Queen of Hearts is playing the long game," he tells us. "I can't elaborate on what that means, but know that your usual tricks won't work. She sees through your smoky cloaks, Catum. She sees all."

My jaw clenches. "You're saying Ailsa's scent isn't masked."

"I'm saying you need to be very careful when you're above ground." He gives me a meaningful look. "Once a rabbit, always a rabbit." He cants his head, his gaze going to Krolic. "She's always been one step ahead, your sister. Perhaps it takes a woman to beat her at her own game. As they say, the queen is the strongest on the board, yeah?"

With those profound statements, he vanishes, leaving a dusting of purple glitter in his wake.

I scowl. "More riddles." *And a fucking waste of time,* I think, my mind whirring. *Which can only mean—*

"We need to get back to the Tavern," Krolic says, a hint of urgency in his voice.

I'm only half a second behind him in terms of coming to the same conclusion, my hand already waving through the air to create a portal.

Because the only reason Ches would want to distract us and waste our time was if he needed us out of the way.

And he clearly knew where we stayed last night—as evidenced by his *complaint* about the lack of a show.

Fuck.

Krolic and I enter the portal at the same time, both of us drawing our own form of weapons.

Weapons that end up being needed immediately as we step into utter chaos at the Tavern.

There are jabberwaries *everywhere*.

As well as blown walls and shattered glass.

Which meant Craze jumped out the window.

With Ailsa.

And ran.

Krolic must come to the same conclusion as me because he instantly runs back into the portal, and I follow while closing it in our wake before anything can come with us.

We stand in silence for a long moment, lurking between time and space, both of us catching our breath from all the back and forth.

"Plan C," Krolic eventually whispers.

"Plan C," I echo, knowing exactly where to go.

But I'm not sure it'll matter.

Because it seems Ches was right about one thing—my cloaking isn't working.

Which means Ailsa is a damn beacon for chaos.

Although... he did say we needed to be careful *above* ground.

Was that a hint? Or another game?

Ches's allegiance has always been to himself first and foremost. But I considered him an ally, once upon a time.

Perhaps he really did mean to warn us.

Or, like everything else in Monsterland, it's a trick.

I run a palm over my face, exhausted from this morning's mindfuck.

There's really only one way to find out if Ches's words were truly a warning or just one of his ploys.

The Caverns are underground.

Let's see if my cloak holds down there…

CRAZE

AILSA'S LIPS provide the sweetest relief. She's all sugar and innocence, making me want to corrupt her. Taint her with my darkness. *Fuck. Her.*

I should pull back.

I shouldn't take advantage of a vulnerable moment.

But there are lots of "shoulds" and "should nots" in life. Yet I never do what is expected or right.

Because I'm not a white knight. Or a good man.

I'm fucking Craze.

And I show her what that means with my tongue.

I take her with abandon. Fucking her mouth. Grabbing her hips. Devouring my sweet little rabbit until she's panting against my bare chest.

I lost my sweatshirt earlier, the loose fabric not conducive to my weapon of choice. The vines would have caught on it, derailing my movements.

But I'm pleased with that decision now. Pleased that I'm shirtless. Pleased that I can feel her nails clawing at my back.

My Omega is hungry. *Starved*. And ready to play.

Fuck waiting.

Fuck patience.

Fuck whatever the fuck I'm supposed to think.

I'm panting. Hard. And so pent up that I might burst in my damn pants.

The ropes writhe around her, their magic listening to my command as I tell them to massage her breasts while they move. Her arms are free, but her midsection is wrapped up in enchanted vines. It's fucking hot. Fucking perfect. Fucking *beautiful*.

She gasps, her long lashes fluttering as she holds my gaze.

I'm fucking feral for this female. I have been since the moment I caught her scent. Fuck, maybe even from the day I found out she existed.

Or before that.

When I dreamt of having a mate.

A queen.

An Omega.

Now my Omega has a face—a very beautiful, fucking *stunning* face. One that's blossoming with shades of red as she kisses me again, her need an aroma I can taste on my tongue.

Graves, I want her.

And I show her that by pressing my thick cock against her, fully aware that our jeans won't mask my desire.

She stills, her nostrils flaring as her eyes widen. "I want to see all of you," she tells me, the bold request seeming to take her by surprise because her cheeks turn even redder.

I smile. "You can see whatever you want of me. And *do* whatever you want to me."

Because I'm hers.

Her Alpha.

Her Enforcer.

Her everything.

Krolic and Catum played last night. Now it's my turn.

But I want to do this on her terms. Let her lead.

At least… a little.

Dominance comes naturally to me. Just as I suspect submitting comes naturally to her.

However, in this, I want to meet her needs. Do whatever pleases her. *Anything* that pleases her.

"I… I want to understand… your…" She trails off, her porcelain features a crimson shade now. "You're pierced." The words come out as a whisper, one that curls around me in a tantalizing caress.

"Yes, I am," I say, leaning even more into her trapped form.

Oh, she could move if she desired it.

But something tells me she's more than happy to stay right here.

If she expresses otherwise, I'll release her.

And if she doesn't… I tell the vines to slither over her again, causing her to gasp. "Gods, what are you doing to me?"

"Indulging," I murmur, running my nose along her cheek to her ear. "Exploring." The ropelike vines glide lower, slipping between her legs to add a subtle friction. "Teaching."

She jolts as a rope tightens right over her clit. "*Oh, Gods…*"

"Craze," I tell her. "Just Craze." I nip her thundering pulse and tell the vines to writhe again.

Her body vibrates in response, the scent of her slick a beacon to my senses. Thank the *blades* that this cavern is shrouded in Catum's magic. Because these cloaked clothes were not doing the trick.

Granted, the Tavern seems to have failed, too.

Maybe her Omega fragrance is just too powerful to disguise.

It's like a fucking drug. It makes me want to do wicked things to her. Teach her all about my preferences. Force her to experience the highest of highs.

I tell the vines to loosen their hold, then replace the friction between her legs with my hand. She arches into me, her full lips parting on a pant I can taste with my tongue.

My mouth reclaims hers, our kiss turning bruising in an instant. I'm not soft or tender. I'm unhinged. Psychotic. And one hundred percent hers.

She can tame me if she wants to. I'll allow it.

But until then, I'll show her exactly who I am.

The ropes fall to the ground as I pull one of my cards from my pocket. The sharp edge teases my thumb, drawing blood. "Do you trust me, gorgeous?" I ask Ailsa.

She shivers. "I shouldn't."

"You shouldn't," I agree.

"But I…" Her forehead crinkles. "I do."

I arch a brow. "You don't sound very sure about that."

"Because I shouldn't trust you."

"True," I agree again. "Except you should trust me." I bump my nose against hers, my lips whispering across hers. "Because I'll never hurt you, Ailsa. Unless it's for pleasure. Then all bets are off."

She swallows. "What does that even mean?"

"Want me to show you?" I ask softly, my voice as smooth as silk. There are a dozen ways I could demonstrate my words. All of them would be introductions. My version of *slow*.

"Okay," she says. "Show me."

I smile against her mouth. "You're so fucking good for me, gorgeous." I bring the card up to her throat and let her feel the razor edge along her tender skin.

She freezes.

Which makes me grin even more. "Try not to move." Because I don't want to cut her yet. Just… tease.

Ailsa seems to stop breathing as I draw the blade lower, snagging on her sweater.

She's not wearing a bra, something I know because she never grabbed one in the closet.

Ripping the card downward, I slice through the fabric like butter, exposing her tits.

She gasps, her breath an alluring pant against my mouth.

I don't give her a chance to vocalize a response, my tongue eager to dance with hers. She's still frozen, yet her lips move with mine.

Because she's fucking phenomenal.

A natural to my unnatural.

I nip her bottom lip, my card going to her jeans. She stops breathing again as she feels the blade touch her hip.

Then I jerk it downward, easily slicing through the side of her pants down to the middle of her thigh.

"I… I could just remove them," she whispers.

"No, Ailsa," I reply, my forehead meeting hers. "Because your job is to take off my pants while I finish freeing you from yours." I utter that last line while switching the card to my opposite side and creating another gash down her jeans.

She shudders, her gaze hooded as she stares up at me. "You're insane."

"Yes."

A hint of boldness enters her features, one that has my knot throbbing with eagerness.

Because yes fucking please.

I like that glimmer in her eyes.

"I want to be insane, too," she tells me. "I want to be insane with you."

My lips curl. "It's a date, gorgeous." I kiss her again, loving that she's giving in to the madness. The impulses. Her instincts.

Is it fast? Maybe for someone wanting to indulge in the ordinary.

But there's nothing *ordinary* about Ailsa Marvel.

She's an Omega.

A queen.

A fucking goddess deserving of worship.

I lick her bottom lip and pocket my card. Then I yank on her jeans, tearing them off her in a harsh pull that nearly has her knees buckling.

She stands before me in her panties and shoes, looking fucking edible.

"You have fantastic tits, Ailsa," I murmur, admiring her full breasts. "I want to make them bleed."

She trembles, her eyes widening.

I catch her throat before she can run, my palm squeezing her delicate neck to cut off the air. "You told me to show you what I mean about hurting you for pleasure." I squeeze her a little more, causing her hands to fly up and claw at my wrists. "Unbutton my pants, and I'll let you breathe again."

She swallows against my palm, her eyes huge. My name forms on her mouth, her voice nonexistent.

"Now, Ailsa," I say, giving her a dose of my dominance.

The way her nipples bead against my chest tells me she likes it, even if her mind hasn't caught up to her body's reactions.

A little growl vibrates her chest, making me growl right back at her.

Her legs tremble in response, a hint of shock entering her expression.

Then she grabs my jeans and unfastens them in an angry jerk.

I press my lips to hers as I let up on her throat and blow oxygen into her mouth as she gasps, forcing her to breathe me in, to accept my crazy, to *enjoy*.

"*You're insane,*" she snarls.

"You've said that already," I remind her, kissing her again.

She bites my tongue. *Hard*.

Which makes me chuckle. "You're learning," I praise, loving the sting she's created in my mouth.

I draw my thumb along her raging pulse, my hand still grasping her throat.

She tries to shove me back, but I don't move, instead kissing her again and allowing her to taste my blood.

She bites me a second time.

Which only makes me kiss her harder.

And suddenly she's moaning as she sucks my tongue deeper into her mouth.

I'm an Alpha. Her aphrodisiac. Her *craving*.

And blood play is just the beginning.

She practically claws at me as she tries to climb up my body, eager for more. Eager for me. Eager for *this*.

I cut off her airflow again, my nose bumping hers. "Now unzip me."

This time, she doesn't hesitate or try to fight, just yanks the zipper down.

I shudder as my head parts the fabric, my rock-hard cock more than ready to play with this delectable little Omega.

"Push the pants down," I say without letting her breathe.

Her hands do my bidding as she stares me down with lust-blown pupils.

She likes this.

My dominance. Her fear. The newness of *us*.

I wait until panic enters her gaze, then I release her like I did before—with my mouth against hers, forcing her to breathe me in again.

She inhales harshly.

Then we're kissing.

Biting.

Exploring.

I kick off my jeans and shoes, then pin her to the wall again, my hands going to her panties and ripping them off her.

"I have no idea what we're doing," she pants as I lift her in the air, my cock instantly settling against her blistering heat.

"Learning," I tell her as I begin carrying her through the cavern. "And soon, we'll be *fucking*."

Perhaps not in the traditional sense.

But I will absolutely be penetrating her in some way.

Her mouth.

Her pussy.

Her ass.

I don't fucking care.

But my Omega wants a lesson, and I fully intend on delivering one she'll never forget.

I drop her onto the bed I slept in just last week, this lair the one I've hidden within for centuries.

Her light hair gives her an angelic glow against my black sheets. "Oh, sweet Ailsa," I say as I crawl over her. "I can't fucking wait to corrupt you." I nip at her chin. "Every fucking inch of you is about to become mine."

"*Ours*," a deep voice interjects.

Catum.

Grinning, I glance over my shoulder at him and Krolic, their expressions thunderous. "Welcome home," I tell them. "I was just about to teach our Ailsa a lesson in pleasure and pain. Feel free to pull up a chair and enjoy the show."

AILSA

CRAZE PARTS my thighs beneath him, his hard flesh pressing against me once more. I shudder at the sensation of skin and metal, utterly transfixed by the madman on top of me.

I should be screaming.

Running.

Doing anything other than allowing his lunacy to overwhelm me.

But I... I can't. I'm lost to this man's touch.

Knowing Krolic and Master Pillar are here, too, just escalates the forbidden desires growing inside me.

I don't even know who I am here. What I do know is that I need these men. I *want* them.

When I woke up and realized my experience wasn't a dream at all, but reality, I felt relieved. Because a part of me would have been devastated to learn what happened between the three of us was just a fantasy.

It's real.

All of this is real.

I'm... I'm an Omega.

And these Alphas believe I'm theirs.

I could fight it. I *should* fight it. Especially after the *lesson* Craze just gave me with his hand around my neck.

But I enjoyed the feel of his dominance.

Just as I like how it feels to have him on top of me now.

Gods, it's all sorts of messed up. However, this world is crazy. So why can't I just indulge in it and be free? Why do I need to be concerned with anything else?

This is my life now, right?

As an Omega in Monsterland.

With three very sexy men who seem to think I'm their mate.

One of whom is tenderly kissing my neck, like he's apologizing for choking me. It feels good. Warm. *Safe*.

But before I can get too comfortable, he palms my breast and pinches my nipple. I gasp, conflicted by the varying sensations.

"Craze," Krolic says, a hint of authority in his tone. "She doesn't know what a knot is yet."

The male on top of me pauses, his fingers releasing my bruised flesh as he lifts his head to look down at me. "Is that true, gorgeous? Those two didn't properly knot you last night?"

I shiver, uncertain of what he's talking about. Master Pillar and Krolic pleasured me with their mouths. However, knots…? I clear my throat. I have no idea what *knot* truly means.

"Is that the metal?" I ask him, referring to the glimpse I caught of him naked. I can feel some of it now, too. Right against my sex. "The, um, piercings?" I try again, unsure of what else to call it.

I'm familiar with the concept of piercings—Baroness Clarice's daughters had their ears pierced. But the kind Craze has, well, that's not one I've ever seen or heard of before.

He chuckles. "You really are innocent, Ailsa." He presses a kiss to my lips before I can respond to that. "Corrupting you is going to be the highlight of my life."

I shiver. He used that word right before Krolic and Master Pillar arrived, saying how he couldn't wait to corrupt every inch of me.

I want that, I think. *I really want that.*

Except he rolls off of me now to his side, leaving me sprawled out on his bed as he props himself up on his elbow. "Explore me, gorgeous. Consider it your reward for being such a good girl for me."

Gods, why do those words make me blush?

All three men have said similar things to me, praising me for being *good* or following an order. It should be condescending. But something about the way they say it, like they consider my acquiescence to be a gift, makes me feel revered.

I was never worth anything in my world.

Everything changed with a single drink.

Because these men—these *Alphas*—treat me as though I'm important.

They talk to me. Answer questions. *Protect* me.

And now… now Craze is offering to let me *explore*.

I lick my lips and slowly face him, my gaze running over his completely nude state. At some point, he lost his socks. I did, too. I don't know when. I don't care. We're both… *naked*.

The lighting isn't harsh, just subtle, reminding me of candlelight. And it glints off the metal bars lining the underside of his shaft.

"You can touch me," he murmurs. "You can touch them, too." He gestures toward Krolic and Master Pillar, both of whom are still dressed and standing near the foot of the bed. "Or we can make them watch."

My throat works as I take in the two Alphas—Krolic with his jeans and white T-shirt and Master Pillar in another all-black suit.

Both of them are staring at me hungrily, just like last night.

"You all have… metal knots?" I guess, my gaze darting to their groins and the impressive bulges behind their zippers.

Craze chuckles beside me. "Look at my cock, Ailsa."

I blink, his words sounding like an invitation more than a command. Yet my eyes travel to his piercings like they're under a spell, being pulled by his words alone.

My throat works as I take in his thickness and the ladderlike pattern starting at the head and traveling all the way down to his bulging base.

He's… large.

Very large.

And, um, well decorated.

I kind of want to lick him.

No. I *really* want to lick him. Just to see what he tastes like. Especially the head.

It's a foreign craving, one I'm certain I've never experienced before—my fantasies with Master Pillar never included anything like this—but the urge hits me right in the lower belly.

Maybe it's a result of last night, of knowing how good it felt to be licked between my thighs.

I indulge in the desire, leaning down to trace his metallic knots with my tongue.

"*Fuck*," he breathes, his hand suddenly in my hair. "I didn't expect you to be so eager."

A response lingers in my mouth. However, I fail to voice it. A groan escapes me instead as I reach his tip, causing a forbidden flavor to erupt on my tongue.

I don't know what that was, but I need more of it.

I lick him again, then take his head into my mouth, my instinct to suck overwhelming me.

I want more of his flavor, his spicy essence.

His cock rewards me with another taste, making me moan with delight. He curses, his grip tightening in my hair as he rolls to his back and pulls me with him.

"Graves, you're a fucking natural, and you don't even realize it." His voice sounds huskier than before, his abdomen flexing with the effort to speak.

Or maybe it's from something else.

His grasp is secure, yet I feel him shaking, like he's holding himself back.

The bed dips beside us as Master Pillar sits on the edge, his brown eyes capturing and holding mine while my tongue dances around Craze's bulbous head.

"Give me your hand," Master Pillar murmurs.

I'm about to sit up, but he shakes his head firmly.

"No, Miss Marvel. Keep sucking his cock, and give me your hand."

The mattress moves on my opposite side, a palm drifting up my spine to my nape. "Do what he says, baby girl," Krolic murmurs.

I tremble, their surrounding presence lighting my blood on fire.

Three men.

Three Alphas.

All focused on me.

Oh, Gods…

Swallowing around Craze's head, I slowly lift my hand toward Master Pillar.

He takes it gently, aligning our fingers together, and brings our joint touch to the swollen base of Craze's arousal. He's hot here and so large I can't quite wrap my hand around him.

"This is a knot," Master Pillar says as he presses my

fingers and thumb against the thick part of Craze. "We all have this."

Krolic kisses my shoulder, his hand squeezing around my nape. "It's how we secure our bodies to yours, Ailsa. How we fuck. And how we *breed*."

Another quiver traverses my spine. That last word does something to me. Something I shouldn't like. But it feels… right.

Which is strange because I didn't feel that way when I knew the Silver King wanted to breed me.

But Krolic… if he's the real Silver King like he says he is… I may not mind that as much.

"It extends out of our shafts and connects us to you— our Omega—and unleashes pleasure unlike any of us have ever felt," he adds. "It'll very likely render you unconscious. But you'll wake up wanting to experience it all over again."

Craze's dick leaks again, making me moan around his head and eagerly swallow his essence.

"Fuck, this might make me come," he says, sounding almost pained.

Master Pillar presses down on my fingers again. "Massage his knot while you suck on his head," he instructs me. "Then try taking more of him into your mouth."

Craze curses with the words, his grasp twisting in my hair like he's trying to stop himself from guiding my actions.

But I don't need him to.

Everything Master Pillar just said is something I *want* to do.

"Graves, that feels so fucking good, Ailsa," Craze says as I slide my mouth down.

"Make sure to relax your throat," Master Pillar

murmurs. "If you feel like you're about to choke, pull up a little, breathe, and try again."

Krolic's thumb massages my neck while I do what Master Pillar says—suck Craze down while fondling his throbbing base.

More of that delicious flavor touches my tongue, making me groan around him.

"Fuck, hearing you enjoy this only heightens the experience," Craze grits out. "Your little moans are so fucking hot, Ailsa."

"Keep going," Master Pillar encourages me. "Let's see how deep you can take him."

Krolic applies pressure to my nape, guiding me down. I gag a little as Craze hits the back of my throat, and the pressure lessens, allowing me to retreat and breathe like Master Pillar instructed.

Then I try again and look up to see Craze practically panting in response.

Is this what I looked like last night? I wonder. *Blissed out and constantly on edge?*

Because it's a very alluring sight, one I want to strengthen by making him feel good. By making him lose control.

It's such an intrinsic desire, one that burns through my veins and drives me to swallow more of him. All while applying pressure to his knot. And reveling in the metallic piercings running along the underside of his shaft.

I've never experienced anything like this.

Never tasted something so exquisite.

Or felt this sort of texture against my tongue. It's smooth, yet punctuated with steel. Hot, yet cool. Soft, yet so incredibly *hard*.

"You look amazing with my cock in your mouth, gorgeous," Craze says, his voice holding a growl to it.

"He's right," Master Pillar murmurs, his hand still covering mine. "You're exquisite, Miss Marvel. Like a sexed-up goddess."

Krolic rumbles his agreement, his body shifting on the mattress as he releases my nape. I feel a sudden loss at the withdrawal of his touch. But then I sense him moving behind me, and soon his palms are touching me again. Only lower. Between my thighs. Parting my legs. And… and…

Oh, Gods…

I feel his shoulders touching my legs as he positions himself *under* me.

"Focus on Craze, Miss Marvel," Master Pillar says, demand underscoring his words. "Suck his cock while our king eats your pussy."

Eats my… Ohhh…

I moan as Krolic's tongue parts my sex and goes straight for my throbbing clit.

I shudder, barely believing what's happening.

Because I'm straddling his face.

His hands are on my hips, holding me to him, all while I play with Craze's knot.

Master Pillar grounds me by guiding my hand, Craze urges me on with his grip in my hair, and Krolic… Krolic is *devouring* me. I barely notice when he slips a finger inside my slick channel, the wetness acting as a lubricant for his penetration.

He adds a second and begins scissoring them, the sensation unlike anything I've ever experienced. I can practically feel my eyes rolling into the back of my head.

But a tug on my hair brings me back to Craze, his arousal seeping into my mouth.

Gods, I want more.

And I tell him that by hollowing my cheeks around him.

He curses and Master Pillar praises me, telling me how good I'm doing, how I'm teasing Craze in the best way.

"Look at him, Miss Marvel. You're doing that. Your skilled mouth and beautiful tongue are driving him mad."

"Can you feel how close he is to coming? How his knot is pulsing for you?"

"Are you ready for your reward, sweet one? Because Craze is about to explode down your throat. Can you swallow for him?"

Master Pillar's ongoing commentary is driving me closer to the precipice of no return. Between his sensual words and Krolic's tongue against my clit, I'm barely able to see straight. Pair all that with Craze's addictive flavor and I'm… I'm…

"*Fuck*," he groans, his fingers harsh as he fists my hair and pushes his cock impossibly deeper into my throat.

I startle, unable to breathe.

"Relax," Master Pillar says, his lips right by my ear. "Use your throat, Miss Marvel. *Swallow*."

My eyes widen, but I do what he says, my insides seeming to burn as I take Craze's ecstasy into my body.

It's intense.

And he tastes so amazing.

I… I… I *scream* as I follow him into oblivion, my world dissolving into a series of orgasmic waves.

My instincts take over, my throat working around Craze while Krolic pleasures me below.

Breathing no longer matters.

Just this. The pleasure. The darkness. Craze's exquisite essence. Krolic's tongue. Master Pillar's deep voice.

"Fucking beautiful," he tells me. "So fucking beautiful."

"Graves, I've never come so hard before in my life," Craze adds, sounding wrecked. "And I'm still fucking hard."

Krolic growls against my clit, his fingers still moving in and out of me. "She's ready."

"Ready for what?" I ask as I release Craze from my mouth.

"Ready to take our knots," Master Pillar tells me, a sinful twinkle in his brown gaze. "We're going to fuck you, Miss Marvel. And show you what it means to be well and truly knotted."

KROLIC

AILSA DOESN'T IMMEDIATELY REACT to Catum's words, instead going still as she digests what he's just said.

"You're not in heat yet," I tell her. "So this isn't about breeding, Ailsa. This is about showing you who we are together. Teaching you about Alpha and Omega dynamics."

If she says no, we won't push her.

But this does feel like the best way to demonstrate our future together.

Oh, it'll be about a lot more than fucking. However, we're sexual beings. It's important for her to understand what that means. To understand who she really is in this world.

Omegas are sensual beings, and they love being taken care of by their Alpha mates. That very much includes sexual needs, in addition to a myriad of others.

Though, this is the basis of our connection, how our bodies interlock and thrive together in moments of pleasure.

"Knotting you also doesn't make this permanent," I add. "This isn't the mating ceremony." That... is a rather primal event. One I hope to experience soon. But that's not today's purpose. "We value your consent, Ailsa. And while we'll absolutely enjoy knotting you, this isn't about taking your choices away."

Craze snorts. "I don't need the primal ceremony to devote my life to her. After that blow job, I'm forever worshipping at her altar. Consider me yours for eternity, gorgeous." He almost sounds drunk. Not that I can blame him. I feel the same way after feasting on her cunt.

She's fucking delicious and still dripping down my chin.

I move my fingers inside her again, my lips brushing her swollen clit.

She moans in response, the first sound she's made since Catum informed her of our intentions to knot her.

"Will you let us show you what it means to be knotted, Ailsa?" I ask against her damp flesh. "It'll be a first for all of us."

Because we've never been with an Omega.

"Betas and other Alphas can't take a knot," Catum elaborates. "Only Omegas can, which makes you even more precious to us."

He must punctuate the word *knot* by squeezing Ailsa's hand because Craze mutters, "Fuck you, Catum. *Fuck you.*"

"You already had some fun," Catum retorts. "Now it's your turn to watch." He pulls Ailsa's touch away from Craze and lays her palm on the bed before standing— something I feel more than see as the mattress shifts.

But I suspect he's disrobing when I hear Ailsa gasp.

Or perhaps that's a result of my tongue tracing lazy circles against her sensitive nub.

"Do you want to feel our knots inside you, Miss Marvel?" Catum asks, a subtle growl underscoring her last name. "See what it means to be properly taken by your Alphas?"

She quivers on top of me, her upper half seeming to

fall to the bed. But Craze catches her and pushes her up to fully sit astride my face while going up onto his knees beside her.

Ailsa looks down, allowing me to see her flushed cheeks. Moons, she's stunning like this. A purr rumbles to life in my chest, my need to express my adoration hitting me square in the gut.

Because *fuck*, this female is everything.

I've waited two years to indulge in her, to love her, to *cherish* her. And we're finally here, just days before her heat.

I lick her deep, loving the way it makes her squirm on top of me.

"It'll just be an introduction," Catum goes on, the sound of a zipper following. "A sexual courting, if you will."

Craze chuckles, his fingers weaving through her hair as he pulls her in for a long, sensual kiss that leaves her trembling over me.

I tongue her cunt, causing her lower half to move in response.

She likes this.

Wants it.

Craves it.

But she still hasn't spoken the words we need to hear before we fuck her.

I take my fingers out of her and grab her hips.

Craze must sense what I'm about to do because he moves, allowing me to pick her up and flatten her on the bed. She yelps as I come down over her, still fully clothed, and pin her arms over her head. "We need your words, baby girl. Your *consent*. Or we won't be giving you our knots."

Her blue eyes widen, her pupils flaring with desire.

"As I said, this is an introduction," I tell her. "Not a vow. Nothing permanent. Just a way for you to experience what we're offering. We'll never force you, Ailsa. That's not the point of any of this."

"It's also why I diluted the elixir," Catum adds as he settles on the bed beside us, completely naked now.

Ailsa swallows and glances at him, her gaze running over the long length of his exposed form and zeroing in on his colorful dick.

Her brow furrows, obvious confusion highlighting her features. "He's tattooed," I explain to her. "Craze is into piercings, hence the Jacob's ladder. And Catum is into ink."

Catum grabs his cock and gives it a stroke, the blue-and-green design twisting with his movements.

"His nickname is Caterpillar," Craze muses. "A play on his name, but also his dick."

Ailsa's mouth forms a little O in response.

"My shadow-monster form is all black," Catum adds with a shrug. "I wanted a little color in my life."

"Shadow monster?" Ailsa echoes.

He smiles. "Want to see my inner monster, Miss Marvel?" His hand begins to transform, his skin shifting into an obsidian shade that's contrary to the vibrant colors decorating his shaft.

Her eyes widen even more as the ebony shades crawl up his arms to his neck, painting him in dark waves of midnight. His body doesn't change size, but every part of him becomes black before turning translucent—just like a shadow.

However, he doesn't take it that far.

He merely shows her his shadowy arm. "All of me becomes this, including my cock." He returns to stroking it as his skin reverts to his tan coloring. "I can fuck you in that form, if you prefer. But it'll feel better for both of us if I stay like this."

"You won't be able to feel anything if he's in his shadow form," I clarify when I see she's still confused. "He's literally a shadow." I gather her wrists in one hand, my opposite going to her chin to return her focus to me. "And I will not be fucking you in wolf form."

If she could shift, we might have another conversation.

But fucking as my wolf just… doesn't appeal to me.

"That's not to say my inner beast won't be driving some of my more feral desires, though," I admit, my lips curling at the thought. "His savage needs are my savage needs. But we'll work up to that, baby girl. All you need to do right now is agree to let us knot you. The rest is up for negotiation."

She stares up at me, her lust-blown expression telling me her decision before she's even voiced it. But I'm not going to accept that as a response.

I need her words.

"This is crazy," she whispers. "But I want it."

I smile. "It's not crazy, Ailsa. It's who we are. And we've spent the last two years subtly preparing you for it. Through my companionship and protection, Catum's dominance and dream walking, and Craze's preparation in Monsterland. Everything has brought us to this moment."

"Except I didn't know any of that was happening."

"True, but you know now," I murmur, my nose skimming hers as I lower my lips a hairsbreadth away from her mouth. "And your soul has always known." Something she'll understand once we mate her. Once we *claim* her. "Tell me you want us to knot you, baby girl. Tell us to fuck you and we will."

She swallows, her body practically vibrating beneath me. "I… I want you to knot me."

"Just me?" I ask. "Or all three of us?"

Her pupils dilate even more, her breath fanning across my lips. "Oh, Gods…"

"Alphas," Catum murmurs. "The only godlike being in this room is you, Miss Marvel."

"Our goddess," I agree, my nose trailing along her cheek to her ear. "Now tell us you want all three of our knots inside you. Not together at once—not yet—but I need you to tell us to fuck you, Ailsa."

She shudders, her nipples hard even through the fabric of my shirt. "I want all of you to… to knot me," she finally says. I'm about to make her say it with a little more confidence when she adds, "I want all of you to fuck me."

My dick throbs in response, drawing a curse from my lips.

Because *moons*, that's hot.

I love it when a woman says what she wants, when she voices her consent.

And I know Craze and Catum like it, too, because both of them groan in response.

"Such a good girl," I whisper against her ear. "Now stay right here for me, baby. Legs spread. Pussy wet and needy. Because I'm going to be the first one inside you."

She's the picture of sensuous debauchery as I crawl off of her.

Catum doesn't move, just lounges beside her as he strokes his dick, his gaze on her tits.

Craze lies on her opposite side, preparing himself for another round by massaging his knot.

Yet her eyes are on me as I disrobe, no doubt wondering what my cock looks like.

"Sorry to disappoint you, Ailsa, but all I have is a

knot," I tell her as I remove my jeans, socks, and shoes. My shirt is left, the fabric disappearing with a tug over my head. "However, don't let the lack of ornaments fool you. I absolutely know how to fuck."

Her legs tremble as I get back on the bed and kneel between her splayed limbs.

"You didn't move an inch," I murmur, pleased. "You know what that means, sweetheart?" I lean down to kiss her clit. "You deserve a reward." I lick her as both Craze and Catum lean in to take her nipples into their mouths.

They know me as well as I know them. When it comes to fucking, we're in sync in the best way, and Ailsa learns that now as we drive her to the brink of no return with our mouths.

My fingers slide right into her slick heat once more, easily resuming my earlier preparations.

She's so fucking ready for our cocks.

Our knots.

Our brand of pleasure.

But I want her to come again before I fuck her, make her so delirious with pleasure that she doesn't even realize I'm inside her until she feels the pinch of her innocence rupturing around my thick cock.

She's panting, moaning, clutching at the pillow above her head.

Because she still hasn't moved.

"Such a good fucking girl for us," I say against her weeping pussy. "We're going to make you come so fucking hard, baby."

Over and over again, I add with my mind.

But I'll let that part be a surprise.

Catum moves up to capture her mouth while Craze grabs her abandoned tit and tweaks her nipple, causing her to scream against Catum's lips. Only it's not a scream of pain, but one of pleasure as she erupts on an orgasmic wave that squeezes the shit out of my fingers.

Moons Almighty, I need to feel her do that around my cock.

Right. Fucking. *Now*.

Catum and Craze move as I crawl up her, my fingers still lodged deep in her pussy while my thumb applies pressure to her clit.

I want to stroke her pleasure, keep her coming.

But I also can't wait any longer.

I need her.

Removing my hand, I bring it up to her mouth and part her lips with my damp fingers. "Suck," I tell her, sliding them over her tongue and forcing her to taste herself on my skin.

It has the desired effect of distracting her and prolonging her rapturous state as I position myself at her entrance.

Then I thrust inside her without warning, making her take me all the way to the hilt.

Her eyes fly open, a garbled sound escaping her.

"Shh," I hush her, not moving an inch as I allow her body to acclimate to my size. She squirms, clearly uncomfortable, so I grab her hip with my free hand and hold her in place. "You can take it," I promise her. "Just give yourself a moment."

She's shaking her head, tears glistening in her eyes.

I remove my fingers from her mouth and kiss her before she can speak, my tongue whispering a sweet apology against hers, all while my thumb draws circles of encouragement against her hip.

"It hurts right now," Catum whispers against her ear, his palm holding one of her hands back against the pillow.

"But I promise it's going to feel so fucking good, sweet one. Trust us."

She's still crying, her agony hurting my soul.

I don't mind mingling pain and pleasure, but this is hard for her. We're Alphas. We're not just larger; we're stronger, and a hell of a lot for a small Omega to take.

However, Catum is right.

She's going to love this soon.

She just needs to get past this first step; then it'll be pure bliss.

Craze leans forward, his nearness causing me to pull my lips from hers and let him take over. Only, he laps up one of her stray tears first, then feeds it to her with his tongue.

My palm goes to her throat, my opposite one still against her hip, as I wait for her to calm down.

Whatever magic Craze uses on her seems to calm her, his mouth clearly speaking to hers. By the time he finishes kissing her, she's no longer crying. But she's not all that enthused either.

At least, not until I subtly move.

Just half an inch to readjust myself inside her.

However, it's enough to make her nostrils flare. And not in a bad way.

Her eyes meet mine, shock radiating from her blue irises. There's still a watery sheen to them that makes her look incredibly pretty, if a little innocent. However, that glimmer soon turns sensual as she shifts her hips. A new kind of sound leaves her, one that's part moan, part breathy purr.

I smile. "There's our pretty Omega." I press a kiss to her jaw. "Ready, baby?" I skim my nose along her cheek as Craze rolls back to his side. "Tell me to move."

She shudders, her lashes still damp with her tears. But

nothing in her expression is sad now. It's all heat. Desire. *Intrigue*. "Fuck me," she says instead, her command going straight to my balls.

"You're such a good student, Miss Marvel," Catum murmurs on a groan, clearly having enjoyed her demand as much as I did. "Flames, you'd better fuck her, K. Or I'm going to be the first knot she feels in that pretty cunt."

CATUM

CHALLENGING the Silver King isn't a wise decision.

But *fuck*, I need to be inside this woman. *Right fucking now.*

So if he doesn't start moving, I'm going to throw him off of her and take over.

We've engaged in the ultimate game of delayed gratification. It was fun for a while. But now... now I need our Omega.

"Hmm," Krolic hums, the sound one that can be good or bad.

I decide it's the latter when he pulls out of her pussy, his cock head stained with her innocence. I half expect him to make her lick it off of him, but instead he says, "I want you on your knees, Ailsa."

She blinks up at him, partially dazed from his abrupt withdrawal. "What?"

"Hands and knees, baby girl. Catum needs you to suck his cock while I fuck you," he tells her.

Ah, the hum was good, then, I realize, pleased with this development.

When Ailsa doesn't immediately move, he grabs her hips and rolls her to her stomach. Then I help by fisting her hair and pulling her head up as I move to kneel in front of her.

She scrambles, her palms finding the mattress with Craze's assistance as Krolic guides her to her knees.

Her eyes are huge as she looks up at me, the surprise in her features rather alluring. "Part your lips, Miss Marvel," I tell her.

Like a good girl, she does, then screams around the head of my dick as Krolic enters her from behind. I don't let her pull back, instead holding her in place while tears gather in her eyes once more.

Only these tears are not born of pain.

They're from pleasure.

A pleasure that mounts as Krolic truly begins to fuck her, just like she requested.

The aged lines of his face are taut with agonized pleasure, his enjoyment palpable as his hips move against her.

There's nothing in this world like an Omega's pussy. Or that's what we've all been told, anyway. And it seems that rumor is very, *very* true.

But I want to feel this Omega's mouth.

"Take me deeper," I tell her, my fingers still woven through her hair, my other hand clamping down on her nape.

Her nails bite into the sheets as I arch her head back a little more to find a better angle.

Then I push myself into her widening mouth, loving the way her eyes flare in alarm.

Because yeah, I'm longer than Craze. Wider, too.

And my knot is bigger than Krolic's as well.

She's in for a world of unique pleasure where my dick

is concerned, something she already seems to be learning as my tattoos hum to life inside her mouth.

They're *writhing*, something that's going to feel fucking magnificent for her when I knot her.

"Remember to relax your throat, Miss Marvel," I tell her as she begins to choke. Krolic is evoking too many sensations below, driving her to the brink of madness with every thrust.

He wasn't lying when he said he didn't need any fancy enhancements to properly fuck her.

He's a king.

And he's showing her what that means right now.

"Suck her clit for me," he tells Craze.

The infamous Mad Hatter grins. "Only if I can nibble, too." The sadist loves to evoke pain.

Krolic nods while Ailsa's eyes go huge.

But she can't exactly protest with my cock stuffed in her mouth.

"If any of this becomes too much for you, fist your hand and lift it in the air," I instruct her, realizing she needs a safeword, as well as a motion to make when she can't otherwise speak.

She swallows around me, her eyes rolling into the back of her head as Craze makes his way beneath her.

"Demonstrate for me, Miss Marvel," I demand, squeezing her nape. "Show me you can make a fist and lift it in the air."

Her gaze darts back up to me, a hint of clarity in her features, perhaps because Craze hasn't quite started playing with her yet, and Krolic has slowed his pace. Both of them realize how important this is.

"Make a fist, Ailsa." Krolic's words are underlined with dominance, his kingly state coming out to wrap an invisible hand around our Omega and force her compliance.

Her lashes flutter as she lifts her hand in a fist-like motion.

I relinquish my grip on her nape and draw my hand around to brush my knuckles down her cheek. "Good girl, Miss Marvel. Repeat that action now if you need us to stop."

She lowers her hand instead, her gaze defiant and making me grin.

"If you change your mind, you know what to do." I graze her cheek once more, then grab her face and push myself deep into her mouth.

She gags and splutters, then groans as Krolic resumes thrusting.

All while Craze tortures her clit.

She screams every time he bites down, and moans whenever he soothes the pain.

It's a glorious fucking sight, one that has me so close to coming that I nearly give in to the impulse.

But I want to knot her.

To tie us together. To feel the bliss of her hot channel clamping down around me as we come together in unison.

She's about to experience the beginning of that now with Krolic. I can tell he's close, see it in the way his pace has turned savage. He's letting go. Falling into the climax he knows is going to knock him off-kilter.

It's a rare moment of peace for him. One where he's trusting Craze and me to protect both him and our chosen mate.

And something about that just makes all of this more powerful.

We're a circle for a reason.

A shared unit of Alpha power.

As Second, I'll be the temporary king as Krolic gives in to his pleasure.

Then he'll reassume his throne while I fuck our Omega into oblivion.

"*Fuck*," he groans, his head falling back as his orgasm rips out of him, his knot shooting into our Omega and making her scream around my cock.

I nearly come with them, the sensation of her choked gasps almost enough to drag me over the edge. But I pull out before she destroys me with those clever lips and yank her up onto her knees so Krolic can grab her chin and guide her back into a kiss.

She's utterly spent, her goddess-like form pink from exertion as she climaxes with our king.

It's a fucking erotic display, seeing him pulse inside her like this, his cock deep in her pussy as he holds her like an offering for us to worship.

Craze is half mad with lust, gazing up at them from the bed, while I remain on my knees, loving this feral display of pleasure.

Krolic has her head twisted to the side so he can better devour her mouth. His other arm is around her middle, supporting her weight as he unleashes his ecstasy inside her.

It goes on for minutes, their embrace one that has Craze and me panting with *want*.

But we give them their moment.

Allow her to feel her first knotting.

All while knowing we're next.

"Fuck, baby," Krolic whispers against her mouth, his forehead touching hers. "*Fuck*." He kisses her again, his rapture ongoing.

She's quivering in his arms, her body overwhelmed by the unending orgasm.

It's a sensation I can't wait to experience with her.

I give my dick a stroke, fully anticipating what's to come next.

Because it's my turn to be inside her.

My turn to experience the bliss of an Omega's—

My hand stills, the hairs along the back of my neck standing on end as a sizzling sensation hums through my veins. Not a pleasant one, but one of warning.

Craze and I share a look, his dark eyes glittering with understanding because he senses it, too.

I lunge for Ailsa and Krolic, my arms encircling them both as I engage a portal on the ground, one meant to take us to the Ice Planes.

So much for it being safe underground, I think, furious for allowing this distraction. This cavern has been a safe haven for hundreds of years. The fact that anyone has discovered it proves Ailsa isn't masked at all. They can scent her right through all my magic.

Which is a huge fucking problem.

Because we still have five days before her heat.

Krolic's arms are around me as we cradle Ailsa between us, the three of us rolling through the portal and onto the snowy fields. The chill burns my bare skin, this plane aptly named. It's high up in the Garnet Mountains and shrouded in clouds, making it difficult to see through the fog.

But I feel Craze rolling onto the ground behind us, his presence a scent that's ingrained in my memory. I quickly shut the portal, then scan the icy tundra for any incoming threats.

Plan D is one of our last resorts.

"Shit," Craze mutters, taking the word right out of my mouth as he leaps to his feet. "Bringing her here was a mistake. We should never have let anyone know she exists."

Krolic is already shaking his head. "Monsterland deserves to know their queen."

"Sure, *after* she's carrying your heir," Craze growls, one of his more antagonistic personalities on display. I can't say I blame him, given the situation.

But Krolic is right. "Our queen also deserves a choice," I add.

"What choice are we giving her exactly?" Craze demands. "We've already claimed her. Fuck, we've been taking out everyone and anyone who comes within a few feet of her. How is that a choice?"

I untangle myself from Krolic and Ailsa so I can sit back on my heels. I'm not having this conversation whilst strewn about on the ground.

Running my fingers through my hair, I attempt to regain control of my mental faculties.

Krolic, however, is faster. "Her choice is whether or not she wants to accept her role in Monsterland."

"And if she doesn't?" Craze retorts. "We just take her back to her realm? Or we let another Alpha-circle claim her?"

Krolic releases a low rumble at that and sits up with Ailsa in his lap. Thankfully, he doesn't appear to be inside her anymore, his knot likely having subsided the moment we hit the Ice Planes.

"We all agreed to this plan, Craze. Complaining—"

"I didn't," Ailsa interjects. "I don't even understand what's happening, or what *plans* you've made or why I'm here or… or *how* w-we ended up h-here." Her teeth begin to chatter over that last part, the frigid air not at all kind against her exposed skin.

"Let's move this discussion into the cabin," I tell them, gesturing to the sheet of ice about ten yards in front of us.

Ailsa frowns at it.

Considering how it looks from the outside, I'm not surprised.

Krolic stands with her in his arms, and I leap up to my feet to get ahead of him.

Craze just stomps off after us, clearly pissed.

Talk about a mood shift, I think warily.

When I approach the wall, I press my hand to the center and a door appears, one that only manifests when one of the three of us touches this specific sheet of ice.

Pushing through the threshold, I hold the door open for Krolic to bring in Ailsa. Craze follows right behind them and heads to the bedroom without a word.

I assume he's getting dressed until he returns with a T-shirt for Ailsa.

Krolic takes it from him and puts it over Ailsa's head, fashioning a temporary dress of sorts as Craze marches off again.

"I'll be back," Krolic mutters, following Craze and leaving me alone with Ailsa.

She hasn't said anything at all, not since mentioning her own frustrations outside.

"I'm sorry, Ailsa," I murmur, meaning it. "You're right. We should have focused on our plans, not…" I nearly say *our knots* but clear my throat instead. "How about you sit down over there while I make you a hot chocolate?"

"Will I even be able to enjoy it?" she asks, sounding exhausted.

"The only monsters up here are snow creatures, and most of them are loyal to Krolic," I tell her. "And they don't take kindly to intruders."

She glances at me. "If you're saying this is safer, then why didn't we start here?"

"Because I thought my cloak would be enough to mask

your presence while we worked on a few other details," I tell her.

"What details?" she asks.

"Details regarding the royal court." I turn toward the kitchen, determined to make her something to eat and drink. I'm guessing she needs it after… everything.

"Tell me what that means," she demands, standing only a few feet behind me. "What details did you need?"

"Final plans for attempting to reclaim the throne," I tell her. "But it's all been a moot point. We haven't been able to sit in the same place long enough to finalize anything. And, honestly, it really doesn't matter. Our allies will either stand with us or they won't."

"What allies?" she asks. "Because everyone I've met so far seems to want to kill me."

I shake my head and look back at her. "They don't want to kill you, Ailsa. They either want to fuck you or take you to the Imposter King."

She rubs her temples. "Master Pillar, I—"

"Catum," I interject, turning to fully face her. "Formalities can be fun, but right now, we need to be Catum and Ailsa. All right?"

She swallows, her exhaustion palpable. "Catum," she whispers, making my lips tilt up just a little.

"Good girl," I praise, leaning in to brush my mouth against hers. "Now, why don't you take a seat at the counter since you didn't want to relax in the living room. I'll make you a hot chocolate, then we'll talk more."

She takes a step toward the stools, like she's going to obey, then pauses and frowns. "No."

"No?" I echo.

"I can't sit right now."

My brow furrows. "Why not?"

"Because… because…" She gestures at her thighs and

then her hidden mound, the oversized shirt more like a dress on her. "I'm *leaking*."

I bite my lip to keep from chuckling.

She notices, though, because she scowls. "It's not funny."

"You're right," I agree. *It's hilarious*. But it's also not the time to be laughing, so I don't add that clarification out loud.

Instead, I step toward her and lift her into my arms, causing her to yelp in response. "What are you doing?" she shrieks.

"Taking you to the shower," I tell her. "Where I'm going to clean you up while someone else makes something to eat."

That last part is for Krolic and Craze—both of whom just joined us in the kitchen.

"She wants some hot chocolate," I tell them, aware that Ailsa never actually said that, but I think she'll like it. "Prepare food to go with it. We'll be back in thirty minutes."

AILSA

Master Pillar—*Catum*—pulls the shirt over my head and drops it, his heated gaze roaming over me in a sweeping caress while the shower runs beside us. There wasn't a knob or a handle to turn it on. Instead, all he did was wave his hand beneath the head, and water began to pour down over the blue marble floor.

I have no idea where we are or why we're here. Or how these men have so many homes. I realize Krolic is royalty, but I've gathered that they've been hiding. "Are all of these places yours?"

For whatever reason, that's the first question I ask.

Maybe because I'm just so lost and confused that I have no sense of organization when it comes to how to proceed with any sort of conversation.

"We have homes all over Monsterland," he murmurs before pulling me beneath the warm water.

All I hear is the shower raining down on me for a long moment, the repetitive noise almost comforting.

"They're like safe houses," he adds after guiding me back toward him. "We've enchanted them to hide our presence, which has worked for hundreds of years. But your scent is apparently too powerful to mask."

"Yet you wanted everyone to know about me...?" I

hedge, recalling some of what they've said to me about needing Monsterland to know I'm an Omega.

He nods. "It's part of the mating ritual." He pulls a bottle of shampoo off a shelf and squirts some into his hand, then starts massaging it into my hair. "But it's also a way to ensure the kingdom knows you're real, making your choice incredibly important."

"My choice," I echo.

"On whom you mate," he replies before gently pushing me beneath the water again. His fingers comb through my hair, washing the soapy suds from my long strands while continuing to massage my scalp.

It feels good.

Relaxing, even.

Yet his words play through my mind, everything these men have told me looping through random strings of logical and illogical twists.

They brought me here to spread my scent. To ensure all of Monsterland kind knew I existed.

However, we continue to run every time someone finds me, because the Alphas either want to fuck me… or take me to the Imposter King.

I shiver. *What am I missing? What are they not telling me?*

"What's the mating ritual?" I blurt out, stepping back from the shower and away from Catum.

He stares down at me, a hint of darkness lurking in his brown eyes. "It's a hunt."

"A hunt?" I echo.

He nods. "Where the Omega in heat runs and the Alphas… hunt."

I swallow. "And how…? How is that *my* choice?"

"Because an Omega only submits to the strongest Alpha-circle, and the strongest Alpha-circle is typically the one the Omega chooses."

I slowly shake my head. "That doesn't make any sense."

He drags his fingers through his thick hair and blows out a breath. "The elixir awakens an energy inside the Omega that drives her heat. But with that comes a magical element. Omegas are quite literally the diamond of the Monsterland world. Inside you rests a power unlike any other."

"Except I'm human," I remind him.

"A human can't take a knot, Ailsa," he returns, grabbing my chin and forcing me to hold his intense stare. "I saw Krolic's knot shoot into that pretty pussy between your thighs, confirming who and what you are. Embrace it, Ailsa. You're not human. You're an Omega. Which makes you utterly remarkable."

He grabs me between the legs in the next breath, his fingers sliding into my slick channel and stroking me deep inside.

I groan in response, his movements unexpected and harsh, yet arousing at the same time.

But all too soon, his touch is gone and his fingers are at my lips. "Open," he demands, pressing inside without waiting, and forcing me to taste myself.

No, not just myself.

Krolic.

Because his essence is still inside me, the warm substance exactly why I didn't want to sit down earlier.

"You taste that, Ailsa?" he asks, his fingers in my mouth preventing me from responding. "*That* is our king's seed dripping from between your thighs. Seed that is only released when an Alpha *knots* a potential *Omega* mate. You're not human, sweet one. You're something else entirely. Now *suck.*"

Oh, Gods… Why does this man's dominance make me so weak in the knees? And why am I so eager to obey him?

"Good girl," he murmurs as I do exactly what he says.

That, I think in the next breath. That *is why I obey him.*

His praise makes me feel warm.

Cherished.

Important.

"Now tell me you're an Omega," he says as he removes his fingers from my mouth.

I swallow, loving the taste he's left behind. It's me and Krolic, with a little bit of Catum mixed in. *Decadent*, I decide, my throat working once more.

"Miss Marvel." The authority in his voice makes me shiver.

"Craze told me Omegas can be any type of being, including humans," I whisper, remembering what he said. "So I'm still human, and also… an Omega."

Master Pillar narrows his gaze, considering me for a moment. "Craze is right—Omegas can be any type of being. But what he apparently didn't elaborate on is when the elixir is imbibed, it awakens the Omega soul inside that being. And that soul takes over, Ailsa. Whatever weaknesses you may perceive you have no longer apply."

He walks me back under the water to continue rinsing out my hair, then pulls me close again to work on the conditioner.

I shiver, my nipples beading as they brush his hard chest.

He's naked.

And colorful, I think, sneaking a glance down at his impressive manhood. He's bigger than the other men, his knot even more impactful.

I'm a little afraid to take him, especially after how much Krolic's initial thrust hurt.

But oh, the pleasure afterward... the way his knot attached to me and held me in a downward spiral of oblivion... I liked that. I liked that *a lot.*

"The ritual requires you to be presented in front of the kingdom," Catum tells me. "That's the purpose of having you take the elixir, and for bringing you here. Monsterland needs to know an Omega has been found. The oldest of our kind will demand that the ritual be honored."

"The ritual that requires me to run," I translate before he dips me back beneath the water.

His fingers massage my scalp again, his touch hypnotic and nearly making me forget what I asked. But he remembers and responds the moment he tugs me free of the showerhead.

"Yes, the ritual that requires you to run and Alphas to hunt. We don't trust the Crimson King to follow protocol. We believe he'll lock you in a cage and breed you, thus claiming you as his because of the heir inside you."

I swallow. "That's what the voice said after the ceremony—that I would be bred."

Catum grunts. "That voice was Craze being a lunatic and trying to scare you."

My lips curl down. "That was Craze?"

Catum nods. "Yeah, he likes to perform. But he also wasn't wrong. The Crimson King won't play by the rules. Impregnating you will solidify his rule."

"Why?" I ask, not understanding that part. Unless... "Is that the outcome of the ritual? Me... being pregnant?"

He grabs a bar of soap and begins lathering it between his hands. Then very quietly, he says, "Yes. That's how the claim is solidified."

My eyes widen. "By impregnating me." I can't help the shrill quality of my voice. "What if I don't want to be pregnant?"

"Then it's your choice to refuse all suitors," he murmurs, his eyes meeting mine. "If that's your decision, we will respect it. And the rest of Monsterland kind should, too."

"Given what I've experienced so far, I have a hard time believing that," I tell him.

"Because Monsterland is not what it used to be." He sounds almost sad as he says it, his gaze drifting to my upper body as he begins spreading the soap along my shoulder and arm. "We want to restore it, but to do that, we need an Omega. Everything is upside down here, and it's been that way since Heart started fucking with the hierarchy."

Heart. Krolic's sister. "But it's the Crimson King you keep insinuating that I should fear."

He focuses on switching arms before replying, "Both of them are equally villainous. But Crimson is the only one who can impregnate you. Heart has a lock, not a knot."

"A… lock?" My brow furrows, confusion swirling through my mind.

"You know how Krolic's knot secured you together, making it impossible for you to move away from him?"

His words evoke a pleasant memory, one that has my thighs tingling—a sensation that increases as he begins soaping my breasts. "Y-yes," I manage to stammer out.

"A lock is the opposite. It's when an Alpha female traps a male's cock inside her," he tells me matter-of-factly. "But more than that, an Alpha female has no seed. And you, my sweet Omega, need Alpha seed to create a baby." His palm moves to my belly while he speaks, a wistful glimmer entering his gaze.

"And you want that," I whisper, my throat going dry.

"Yes," he admits without missing a beat. "We all do, Ailsa."

"But we just met."

"Did we, though?" he asks, his gaze returning to mine. "Perhaps you and Craze, yes, but can you truly deny how things feel between us?"

I... I can't.

However...

"How much of what I feel is... real? Is the elixir...?" I trail off, unable to finish asking that question. Because somewhere deep down, it feels wrong to even think this way.

These men have been courting me for two years. Perhaps strangely, but this is where our definitions of *normal* differ.

They approached me the way they felt was right.

Can I punish them for that? Can I deny how I feel because of that?

"The elixir inspires your heat, which, yes, can alter your frame of mind," he replies. "In a few days, you will be begging for our knots. But that instinct hasn't arisen yet."

I say nothing, simply thinking through what he's said.

I have felt a little out of sorts, making irrational decisions—like playing with their knots—but I... I feel alive as a result of those choices.

While I've absolutely embraced the insanity of this realm, that doesn't mean I've lost my mind, does it?

"I diluted the elixir, Ailsa," he goes on. "Well, kind of."

I frown. "What do you mean, 'kind of'?"

"The ritual elixir is meant to take three days to kick in. That's part of the hunt timeline." His lips twist. "But Crimson altered the formula centuries ago to make it more potent, because he's desperate to send an Omega into heat immediately. The only part of the ritual he's kept the same is the twenty-first birthday requirement, and I think he only did that to ensure the elixir worked properly."

I can't help but notice he's no longer referring to him as the *Crimson King* but *Crimson*, suggesting that's the mysterious imposter's real name.

But I table that thought and focus on what he's saying regarding the elixir. "So you… reverted the elixir?"

"Yes." He resumes soaping my torso before adding, "But I made it even less potent to give you time. We also wanted to ensure that others in our world discovered your existence. If Crimson takes you now, there will be a riot. He has to play by the rules and let the Alphas hunt. Or it's possible his claim will be contested."

"Except he's already not the rightful king…" I let that sentence hang as he gently rotates me to start soaping up my back.

"Correct. He's pretending to be the Silver King."

"Yet you call him the Crimson King because Crimson is his real name…?" I phrase it as a question.

"Crimson is his last name," he murmurs. "Like Silver is Krolic's last name. They're rival wolf packs."

"My mother chose the Silver mate-circle," a deep voice adds as Krolic enters the bathroom with a tray. "And the Crimson mate-circle never forgave her for it."

Catum kneels before me as he begins lathering suds along my legs. I shudder when his touch moves inward over my inner thighs and up to my sensitive flesh. "Are you sore, Miss Marvel?" he asks softly.

I swallow and shake my head. "No." That was evident when he shoved his fingers inside me a bit ago. I wasn't sore at all.

"Another sign of your changing genetics," he murmurs, leaning forward to kiss me right on the clit. "You're no longer an ordinary human, sweet one."

I nearly fall backward when he kisses me again.

Only, he doesn't continue, just simply leans back on his heels and resumes soaping up every inch of me.

"Is she questioning her Omega status?" Krolic asks, one eyebrow arching high. "Because I am more than happy to prove her wrong again."

"She's conflicted on what it means to be human and an Omega," Catum tells him before reaching around to my backside. "She's learning, though. Right, Miss Marvel?"

"Yes, Master Pillar," I reply on an exhale.

He smiles up at me and winks. Then stands and helps me rinse.

"Next time we shower, I'm going to help you shave," he says against my ear. "While I appreciate your groomed pussy, I really want to see you bare."

My cheeks flame in response to his unexpected words, then heat even more as he presses a kiss to my pulse.

He's behind me with his chest to my back, allowing me to feel his hardness against my ass. His heat is reminiscent of a brand, his touch filled with promise.

Yet he merely walks around me to wash himself off, giving me a glorious display of all his muscles while he cleans himself off and washes his hair.

Part of me wants to offer to help, but he's a good foot taller than me, and there doesn't appear to be a bench or a stepping stool in the shower.

By the time he turns off the water, I'm panting. But all he does is wrap me up in a towel and pass me over to Krolic, who is waiting with the food.

He brings something red to my mouth that I accept without studying it. Flavor bursts on my tongue, the savory bite reminding me of tomato soup. Except it's chilled.

Catum finishes drying himself off, his white towel low across his hips as he saunters toward me to feed me the next bite.

Grilled cheese, I think, moaning in delight. It's one of my favorite meals from back home, a meal I rarely made because the kitchen wasn't mine to use. But sometimes I snuck in to fry up a cheese sandwich and steal leftover soup.

Krolic would know this since I often brought it with me outside to eat in private.

It's a simple thing, but an important one. Because it drives home what Catum has been saying—these men know me.

Not in the conventional sense.

But that's okay.

I like unconventional.

I like *them*—Catum, Krolic, and Craze.

"So what's the plan?" I ask Catum and Krolic. "What's next?"

Because I want to understand everything. Understand them. Understand my choices. Understand the future, the present... *the ritual.*

"We're safe here for the time being," Krolic says. "But it won't last long. Which means we need to discuss plan Z."

"And what's plan Z?" I wonder aloud.

"We take you back to your realm," he replies, sounding unhappy with that idea. "It's not ideal, but if Monsterland isn't going to respect your choice—which I'm starting to question, given all these recent attacks—then we need to remove you from the situation."

My lips curl down. "But what about your throne?"

He lifts a shoulder. "We'll win it back in a different way."

"A different way," I echo.

His green eyes flash as he looks down at me, his expression exuding a sadness that hurts my heart. "Yes. By turning Monsterland on its head."

KRⵔLIC

I FEED Ailsa another tomato bomb.

While I didn't hear most of her conversation with Catum, I understood the gist of what they discussed—the elixir, the mating ritual, and my family feud with the Crimson pack.

My blood boils like it usually does when I think about the Imposter King and Heart. They've destroyed everything, including this kingdom.

I meant what I said to Ailsa—if we can't fix this with the mating ritual, then we'll be forced down a much more violent path.

Thus far, we haven't permanently killed anyone, just severely injured those who have posed a threat. Primarily because we're still not entirely sure if the attacking beings are of sound mind or not.

They don't want to hurt Ailsa. Yet they seem inclined to take her by force.

Craze told me about what happened in the Mushroom Jungle with the snout men.

"They were overrun with lust," he muttered back in the kitchen. "They've all been overrun with it, K. And it's clear they're not interested in her consent. Just that she's a fertile Omega."

"Is that what they called her?" I asked, frowning at the term *fertile*.

Her heat hasn't started yet. So while she will soon be in estrus, she's not yet. And therefore, by definition, not *fertile*. Hence the reason I could knot her without impregnating her.

Craze went on to confirm that was the phrase one of the snout men used before trying to stake his claim.

Traditionally, interested Alphas and their mate-circles hunt a desired Omega during the ritual period. And the Omega chooses whom to submit to by succumbing to the eventual rut.

However, Omegas can refuse all suitors.

It rarely happened in the day when rituals were more common. But it did occasionally occur, and that Omega chose to live without mates.

Ailsa could take a similar path.

Unless Monsterland doesn't allow it.

In which case…

"War," Catum says, answering a question Ailsa just asked about what I mean by turning Monsterland on its head. "He's talking about war."

Yes, I think, hating the word. Alas, he's right.

"We've avoided a fight for what feels like eons," I add while bringing another fried cheese ball to her lips. "Our hope has always been to find an Omega to complete our circle, and to remind Monsterland of our rituals. Because somewhere along the way, the Alphas lost their sense of purpose."

"That happens when their leader is absent," Craze interjects as he joins us in the bathroom. "Or, in this case, hiding his true identity."

"I can't tell if you're insulting me or the Imposter King," I mutter, not at all amused by his commentary.

"A bit of both, I imagine," he drawls before stealing one of the tomato bombs.

Except he doesn't eat it.

He puts it between his teeth and feeds it to Ailsa via his mouth. She moans in response, not too dissimilar to how she was moaning earlier in our bed.

Craze grabs her hips and holds her against him, his shoulders seeming to loosen in the process as his personalities visibly switch to someone softer, gentler, more nurturing.

By the time they're done sharing the tomato bomb, he seems much less aggravated, which is good because his irritable side was starting to grate on my nerves.

If anyone has a right to be upset about not knotting Ailsa, it's Catum. Yet other than the obvious erection beneath his towel, he seems fine.

"You said Crimson is hiding his identity," Ailsa murmurs. "Pretending to be the Silver King."

"Yes. His wolf is white, so he only ever shows himself in wolf form while Heart translates his edicts for the masses," I elaborate. "Everyone assumes it's a sister supporting her brother."

"And there's speculation that the king never shifts into his human form because he lost his mate-circle," Catum adds. "The kingdom thinks Craze and I are dead."

"Hence, I'm the Mad Hatter," Craze muses, his eyebrows dancing as he plucks another tomato bomb from the tray and eats it.

I take a cheese ball to give to Ailsa, but she doesn't immediately accept it. "So what changes if he takes a mate?" she asks. "Why would that make him reveal himself? And won't that just piss everyone off?"

"The kingdom fell to me as the strongest Alpha," I say, trying to explain how hierarchy works in our world.

"However, that role isn't official until a king takes a mate. Continuing bloodlines is very important in this world, but with the lack of Omegas..." I trail off, swallowing.

The disappearance of Omegas started with my mother's death. Then no new Omegas were born, making it impossible for me to officially claim my title.

Thus, we began hunting the way a mate-circle should.

And it took centuries for us to find Ailsa.

If she refuses us...

I can't even finish the thought. It'll always be her choice. But our circle won't move on from her. She's it for us. And not just because Omegas appear to be on the verge of extinction. It's *her*. She's been our choice since the moment I first scented her.

Our strong-willed, adventurous Omega. The female who never shied away from my beast, even when she thought I meant to eat her.

She's always been strong. Forward. Confident in her own right.

Perhaps shy externally with Catum, but bold inside her mind and in her dreams.

The perfect mate.

"Omegas have always been rare," Catum continues for me as he leans against the counter, his arms folded across his chest. "And Omegas only mate strong Alphas."

I nod. "If the Imposter King takes a mate under these current conditions, he'll be visibly seen as the strongest Alpha among us. And no one will care how it was done. Unless, of course, they are made to realize that he's ignoring the rituals."

"Right. Otherwise, he can spin it that the Omega came directly to him and declined the ritual, as proven by the heir in her belly." Craze utters the words with a hint of malice, his dislike palpable. "That was the reason we presented you to Monsterland—to provide proof that you are not denying the ritual."

"To give you a choice," I rephrase. Because that was the point of all this—we want her to willingly choose her mates.

And, of course, we hope that choice will be us.

We are the strongest Alphas in Monsterland. Deep down, her Omega soul knows that.

It's the human part of her that needs to understand all this, to accept it.

"So with the ritual, I… I run. And you chase?" She voices it in a breathy tone that goes straight to my knot.

And I'm not the only one who feels it. Because Craze groans, "Graves, now I'm hard again."

Catum just smirks, but I'm certain he's not unaffected by our Omega's words. "You run and Alphas chase, yes," he confirms. "And you choose which circle to submit to."

"For a rut," she says slowly, like she's tasting the term. "Which means…?"

"Fucking," Craze growls before grabbing her and pulling her into a kiss. "Lots and lots of knotting. And coming. And pleasure."

She melts into his touch, her lips rounding on a moaned "Ohhh."

Craze smiles against her mouth. "You like that, don't you, gorgeous?"

She swallows. "I… I might."

"You will," he promises, kissing her again. "You'll fucking love it."

"Assuming we proceed with the ritual," I interject, hating that I have to be the voice of reason. But it's my job. My role. My burden. "If the Alphas won't respect Ailsa's choice, then it's too dangerous to continue with our plans."

"Thus taking us to plan Z," Craze says with a sigh as he steps back from Ailsa.

"Taking me… home," she summarizes, her lips curling down. "And then what?"

"Then we handle the issues here and come back for you later," I tell her. I hate this plan, but it's our last resort. "We hoped your presence here would reignite some of our old ways. However, thus far… it seems to have proven just how lost Monsterland has become."

I look at Craze, his words from a few minutes ago swirling in my head.

"That happens when their leader is absent."

It's my darkest fear come to life.

It took us so long to find a potential mate, thus allowing Monsterland to deteriorate beneath the Imposter King's rule.

We searched for an Omega out of necessity. But I would be lying if I didn't admit to myself that our reasons went deeper than just saving the kingdom.

We wanted a purpose.

A future.

A queen.

Perhaps that makes us selfish in a way.

Only, I thought bringing Ailsa here would unite the kingdom, not divide it more.

We anticipated the Imposter King's minions trying to drag her back to his lair, but thus far, the only Alphas who have come after her are ones who want to knot her themselves.

Except for maybe the Tweedle brothers and Brandt. Although, we never actually waited to hear their reasonings. We just assumed they were there at the behest of the Imposter King.

Have we been looking at this wrong from the beginning? I wonder. *Has the betrayer on my throne sent anyone after her at all?*

"We need to move forward with plan Z," I say slowly out loud, my mind trying to solve all the puzzles of the last few days.

Hell, if I'm honest, these puzzles date back *centuries*. And now they're made even more complicated by the Imposter King not doing what we anticipated.

Which makes everything here an unknown.

I do not like unknowns.

"Ailsa will be safer outside of Monsterland at this point," I continue, still thinking aloud. "I know we have allies here, but I currently don't trust anyone. We need to regroup and determine who we can actually rely on in Monsterland. And we can't do that with her essentially serving as bait for chaos."

Our Omega frowns at the term *bait*.

But it's an accurate one.

She's a fucking beacon for mayhem.

"Someone has to stay behind to protect her," Craze tells me. "Her realm is too connected to ours for us to just leave her there."

He's right. There's a reason the Imposter King's edict is so strongly obeyed across all the realms. We're the heart of all magic, our monster influence having spread far and wide.

The Imposter King has informants everywhere.

Which is why we won't be taking Ailsa back to her district or anywhere she'll be noticed and discovered. Thanks to technology and media reporting, everyone in her realm will know she's an Omega, as the results of her ceremony would have been broadcast worldwide.

She'll be recognized everywhere she goes.

And that's why the Imposter King would never expect us to take her back there.

However, like in Monsterland, we have homes in her world. Places we can tuck her away while we work through the issues here.

"You'll go with her," I tell Craze.

Not because he won't be useful here, but because he's a master of disguise. If anyone can protect Ailsa while simultaneously moving around the realm, it's him.

That's why he was chosen to be her initial escort here.

And why he needs to be the one to go with her now.

He dips his chin. "All right."

"Do I get a say in this?" Ailsa asks.

"You do," Catum says before I can respond. "It's always been your choice, Ailsa. It will always *be* your choice. But that's precisely what we're trying to accomplish now. And since we can't guarantee your ability to choose here, it makes sense to move on to plan Z, just like Krolic has said."

"Or we could devise a whole new plan," she offers. "One that involves me choosing you now and giving you the heir you need. Then you could just reclaim the throne, right? Do exactly what Crimson planned to do and say I chose not to indulge in the hunt?"

My heart pangs at the idea, my soul immediately declining the option.

Because it's not who we are.

We don't take by force.

And we're not going to mate our Omega under false pretenses.

We will do this the right way.

Or we won't do it at all.

"I'm not Crimson," I tell her, my voice gruff. "I can't… *won't*… hide behind a technicality. If—*when*—we retake the throne, it will be the right way. Because I'm a king who respects Monsterland kind. Not a coward who hides behind mirages and outright lies."

She stares at me for a long moment. Then she steps around Craze to reach me and goes up onto her toes to press a kiss against my lips.

"I understand." She cups my jaw, only then making me realize I've clenched my teeth together at some point during my speech. "But my forgoing the hunt and choosing you would never be a mirage or a lie. Because I think I chose you and your wolf the first time we met."

I lean into her touch, my eyes drifting closed. "As much as I wish I could do it this way, I can't. For the sake of the kingdom, we must perform the ritual," I tell her. "They need to be reminded of our ways."

But it needs to be safe enough here for us to perform the hunt the way it is intended to be performed.

"Okay," she whispers, going up onto her toes to kiss me again.

I clasp her nape and pull her even closer to return the kiss, this time allowing my tongue to part her plump lips and deepen our embrace.

She shivers in response, then presses herself more firmly against me.

My free arm slides around her waist, holding her to me as I claim her. Worship her. *Devour* her.

Moons, she's addicting.

Perfect.

Beautiful.

Mine.

My wolf purrs inside, pleased with her acquiescence. Thrilled by her presence. Loving her affection.

We've hunted for a mate for so long, finally finding the

perfect one in a forest just outside a small, unsuspecting manor.

She lived in a mountainside district, her life not one of prestige but of work. And something about that made her even more perfect.

Because she's never been put on a pedestal. Never been one to direct others or put anyone else down.

She's youthful. Vibrant. *Alive.*

Hardworking. Dedicated. And full of dreams.

Dreams I want to make come true.

She deserves everything and more.

"We're going to prepare Monsterland for you," I promise. "And we'll come back for you, Ailsa. I vow it."

She swallows and nods. "If you don't, I'll find another portal to fall into."

I smile. "You didn't fall, baby girl. You jumped."

Her brow furrows. "I definitely fell."

I lift a shoulder. "If that's how you choose to remember it, that's fine. I'll simply recall my own version." Where she bent over to touch the portal and basically dove right in. "You are destined to rule this kingdom, Ailsa Marvel."

"You'll be the Monsterland Queen," Catum says, coming up behind her to kiss her nape. "And we'll be your knights."

"Your personal court," Craze adds, stepping forward to complete the circle around her. "We'll all bow to you as our mate."

"And worship you as our goddess," I conclude, my lips against hers. "I'm sorry, baby girl." Because I hate that she can't stay. Hate that Monsterland needs our intervention now. Hate that I have to say *goodbye.*

Craze meets my gaze as I glance at him, my chin dipping in a nod.

He needs to take her now.

Before I change my mind.

Before I decide to take her up on her offer.

Not that I can. She has to be in heat, and I refuse to give her another dose of that elixir just to speed up the process.

That's how the Imposter King chooses to play.

But as I told her, I'm not him.

I'm the Silver King. The true heir to the throne. The motherfucking Monsterland King.

And my mate-circle is the strongest in the land.

It's finally time we remind our kingdom of our place at the top of the hierarchy.

It's time for the Imposter King and my dear sister to pay.

Just as it's time to temporarily say goodbye, I think, looking down at our chosen mate. I kiss her one last time, then let Catum turn her in his arms to do the same.

She's still dressed in just a towel, but Craze will find her something to wear in her home realm. He'll hide her. Protect her. And ensure no one can find her.

His gaze tells me as much as he pulls her into his arms.

"We're going now?" Ailsa asks, sounding breathless.

"It's as good a time as any," he tells her. "Hold on, Ailsa. The ascension isn't as easy as the fall."

Her lips curl down. "What?"

Craze doesn't elaborate, just calls a portal and pulls her into it.

The swirl closes half a beat later, leaving me and Catum staring at one another.

"Who's first on the kill list?" he asks me casually, like we're not about to go annihilate half the fucking kingdom.

"I want to talk to Brandt first," I tell him. "Find out if he's of sound mind." And if he is, then he'll be the first Alpha we make an example of.

Catum nods. "All right. I'll—"

The ground cracks beneath us, sending me backward into the counter and Catum into the shower he recently vacated.

Both of us frown, the rumbling intensifying as a portal swirls open where Craze left seconds ago.

He comes flying out of it, a towel in his hand—the towel that was just around Ailsa when he left with her—and crashes into the ground.

Unconscious.

Alone.

And covered in blood.

AILSA

I blink.

Then frown.

"Craze?" I whisper, my mouth incredibly dry. "Why…?" I swallow, my voice a mere rasp of sound. *What happened?* I marvel, blinking again.

One minute, we were in the bathroom.

And the next…

I don't remember.

I just… I'm here.

My brow furrows more. *I'm in my bed.* I can feel the familiar lumps beneath me, see the cracked wallpaper decorating the drab wall. There's minimal light, the slender window above barely allowing any sunlight to stream into my basement quarters.

Musk taunts my nostrils.

But beneath it is the subtle lingering scent of cinnamon spice.

And smoke.

And the forest.

Craze. Catum. Krolic.

Where are they?

And why am I here?

Rolling to my side, I instantly regret the decision and curl my knees into my stomach. Because *ugh*. I feel sick.

Like I haven't eaten in days and still have no interest in eating.

What's wrong with me? I wonder, my head spinning as I close my eyes. Dizziness assaults my senses, worsening the rolling sensation in my abdomen.

Gods, Craze wasn't kidding when he said the ascension would be worse than the fall.

But where is he?

I peek again, searching for his dark hair and sinful eyes. Even his masked face would do right now. But he's not within my field of view, and I'm not sure I can sit up to survey the rest of the room right now.

Didn't they say I wasn't going back to my district, though? I think, frowning once more. *Something isn't right.*

"Ailsa?" a feminine voice murmurs, startling me.

Baroness Clarice.

"Are you finally awake, girl?" she asks, the subtle impatience in her voice making my stomach churn.

She only ever calls me *girl* when she's displeased.

I swallow, my still-dry throat barely working. It takes all the energy I possess to roll onto my back and then rotate my head toward the basement door. "I... I don't feel well, Baroness Clarice." My scratchy voice barely travels the space between us.

Yet I can tell she heard me by the way she folds her arms. "Well, no, I imagine not. You missed your birthday ceremony, and you've been out cold for days."

What? I blink at her. "I..."

"I told you that wandering around in the woods was unhealthy," she goes on like I didn't try to speak and starts sauntering down the stairs, her stiletto heels clacking against the wood. "Maybe now you'll listen to me, hmm?"

She flips on the lights, causing me to wince and cover my eyes. The fluorescent tubes are far too bright for the area down here, but she says it helps her confirm that I'm keeping my quarters *clean*.

Not that I have much space to make dirty.

One twin bed cot.

A single dresser, plus a wardrobe for my uniforms.

And a bathroom with a mediocre shower.

That's all.

What did she mean about me missing my ceremony? I wonder, trying to focus. *I… I definitely went to my ceremony. Drank the elixir. And… and met the most amazing men.*

"Doctor Tav will be by soon to evaluate you. I want to make sure that you can properly recover." She comes to stand by the bed, her lips pursed as she stares down at me. "You're three days behind in your chores, Ailsa. This is very inconvenient for all of us."

"I'm sorry," I manage to say, my mouth thick.

Was it all a dream?

"Hmm," she hums, tapping her foot. "Well, I'll have Tabitha bring you something to eat while you wait for Doctor Tav. Just do exactly as he says. We can't have you dying down here."

With that lovely sentiment, she flips her long white-blonde hair over her shoulder and leaves the way she came.

I don't breathe until the sound of her heels is nothing but a memory.

I'm home. In my district. And I missed my birthday ceremony.

That… that can't be right.

I was in that bathroom in a towel, telling the three Alphas that I didn't need to be hunted, that I would say I chose them.

Craze brought me here.

I was still in the towel. And I…

Frowning, I glance down to find myself clothed in my

usual servant uniform—dusky brown pants and a plain white T-shirt.

Pushing myself upright, I look to my partially open wardrobe and spy the blue-and-white ceremonial dress hanging from the mirrored door.

My stomach clenches. *No. No, that can't be right.*

Craze, Krolic, and Catum are real.

Everything we experienced… it was too much to be a dream.

Except even the shoes are sitting on the ground, waiting to be worn.

My hands begin to shake, the tremble working its way up my arms as Tabitha appears on the stairs. Her head is bowed as she descends, her timid demeanor reminding me of my own when I first started in Baroness Clarice's manor.

Only, Tabitha seems a bit more on edge now. Maybe because she's had to work overtime the last few days to cover for my absence.

She creeps toward me with the tray, not once looking up.

We don't know each other well; she just started working here thirteen months ago, and she's eight years younger than me. Still, I don't like her posture. It's a little too broken down, as though something happened recently to completely break her spirit.

"Are you okay?" I ask her under my breath, aware that there are listening devices everywhere in this manor.

Baroness Clarice takes her security seriously, and that includes monitoring her staff. But she hasn't taken much interest in me these last few years, likely because I've been with her home long enough to know my place and how to properly do my job.

Although, her security is how she learned about my frequent trips to the forest.

She didn't like my "little adventures," as she called them, but she never told me to stop them. Just said it wasn't safe and that I'd better not catch a chill.

It seems I failed that requirement.

Assuming I've truly been ill, I think, frowning again. *It couldn't have been a dream. My Alphas are real. I can still smell them. Can still* feel *their touch.*

Krolic marked me between my thighs.

I can sense it.

The way his knot pulsed inside me.

His seed.

That wasn't a dream.

Tabitha sets the tray down, reminding me of her presence and the question she has yet to answer. I glance up into her violet gaze, noting the thin cluster of pink lashes framing her catlike eyes. She's human, but there's always been an otherworldly quality about her. One that seems highlighted by her facial features. The hints of pink in her hair also seem unnatural.

But only humans are servants in this world.

And she's a servant.

Ergo, human.

"Don't drink the tea," she whispers, her words barely audible.

Then she turns and leaves without another word, leaving me in stunned silence.

I glance down at the tray, noting the small tuna salad sandwich and the teacup beside it.

Something isn't right.

My brow furrows even more as another part of me snaps, *No shit.*

Craze, Catum, and Krolic are real. I'm certain of it. They're my… my mate-circle. Sort of. Not really. Not *yet*.

I shake my head and instantly regret it, the sense of delirium hitting me all over again.

I was in Monsterland. I'm an Omega. I… I shouldn't be here.

Not a dream. Not a dream. Not. A. Dream.

But how is the dress in perfectly good condition? And the shoes?

I destroyed those in Monsterland.

Blowing out a breath, I scrub my hand down my face. None of this makes any sense.

And while my stomach is killing me, I don't want to eat.

Don't drink the tea, Tabitha said.

Biting my cheek, I study the contents. It looks normal.

Bending down, I take a sniff. Smells normal, too.

But that doesn't mean I want to taste it. Especially not after Tabitha's warning.

Shaking my head, I push the tray aside and force my legs to move toward the ground. They feel heavy, confirming that perhaps I have been asleep for a while.

Or drugged, I think.

I'm not quite sure what that would feel like, but I've heard about drugs from Baroness Clarice's daughters. Well, not directly from them. Just in the movies they used to watch.

Move, Ailsa, I tell myself.

But I can barely feel the cement floor beneath my bare feet. It's like I'm numb.

"Where is she?" a deep voice booms, sending a chill down my spine.

"In her room, resting," Baroness Clarice replies in a

light purr. It's a voice I've not really heard her use before. She's usually exasperated or stern, not... flirtatious.

"Take me to her," the male growls.

There's something in his voice that has all my instincts flaring to life. A feeling of wrongness that I can't explain. A sense of *warning*, one that makes me want to run.

Except my legs are lead weights, and my head is pounding.

Gods, this isn't good. This—

Footsteps on the stairs have me glancing toward the entry to my basement bedroom just as a man with black pants and a white button-down shirt begins to descend.

He's tall. Wide. Similar in size to Krolic, Catum, and Craze.

An Alpha, I realize, then frown at my knowledge. *How do I know that?*

How do I even know this is happening?

Maybe... maybe I passed out in the portal and this is just a nightmare.

Or... or none of it ever happened and it was just the most fantastic dream. Until I woke up in reality.

"Miss Marvel?" the deep voice asks, a note of softness underscoring his tone.

I clear my throat and focus on the approaching male, noting the deep lines near his eyes—eyes that are a vibrant blue that contrast with his black hair and pale skin.

He's handsome.

Undoubtedly so.

But he doesn't smell right.

Which is strange. My nose isn't usually this sensitive, but there's something in his cologne that's a bit off. *Sandalwood*, I think. *Not the right kind of tree oil.*

Krolic smells like cedar and pine.

This Alpha... his scent is too soft. Too *other*.

I need the forest.

I need *Krolic*.

"Hello, Miss Marvel," the Alpha murmurs, his eyes lighting up as he runs his gaze over me.

I swallow, uncomfortable with his nearness. His *wrongness*. I… I don't know how I sense any of this, but I'm not going to ignore my instincts. Not when everything else feels so unreliable.

"I'm Tav," he tells me as he sits beside me on the cot.

"Doctor Tav," Baroness Clarice interjects, earning a cold look from the Alpha before me. I'm not even sure how I know he's an Alpha. His size, perhaps. But I'm certain of it now.

And come to think of it, Baroness Clarice… she's an Alpha, too.

How have I never noticed that before?

She's tall. Slender. And exceptionally dominant.

Only, I've never realized her status. She's always just been Baroness Clarice, a being of unknown supernatural origin who happened to own the manor I worked within. I never asked questions. Never wondered about her heritage. Just obeyed.

However, I'm innately certain of her classification in this moment, like I suddenly have an awareness for identifying those with Monsterland traits.

Is this a result of the elixir? I wonder. *Or have I lost my mind entirely?*

"She needs to respect and obey her betters," Baroness Clarice hisses in response to something Doctor Tav just said. I missed it, too lost in my head to hear. "She's fully aware of her position. And she will address you as *Doctor*."

The male Alpha releases a sound of displeasure before clearing his throat and looking at me again. "I hear you've been unwell."

Understatement, I want to say.

But I don't want to antagonize him or Baroness Clarice.

Their Alpha presence is... suppressing. Intense. Demanding submission.

Very unlike Krolic, Catum, and Craze. While I could sense their domineering personas, they never made me feel like I needed to supplicate or beg for their favor. I obeyed them to please them.

With Baroness Clarice and Doctor Tav... my obedience would be derived from fear.

Except, I don't quite fear them.

It's a strange feeling, one I don't fully understand.

And I'm not ready to embrace it.

Not until I understand what is happening.

So, instead, I clear my throat and say, "I'm not sure what happened, but I've been asleep for a while." That feels truthful—I've definitely been asleep for some time. Which explains the grogginess, headache, and general feeling of dead weight.

But I'm hoping they also assume I'm buying Baroness Clarice's story about me missing my ceremony.

I didn't miss it. My mate-circle is real.

The dress must be a replica. That's the only explanation I'll accept.

Because life without Catum, Krolic, and Craze... just no. I won't even entertain that. Not after spending time with them and receiving a taste of what we could be together. I need more. I need them. I need the potential for our future.

Doctor Tav doesn't immediately say anything, instead reaching around me to pick up the tea. He gives it a sniff, and his nose visibly crinkles. "What is this?" he demands, his gaze going to Baroness Clarice.

She simply looks at him. "Tea."

His expression hardens. "Remake it."

"Excuse me?"

"You heard me, Heart. *Remake it.*"

I flinch, the name *Heart* serving as a bolt to my heart, one that causes my pulse to race. *Krolic's sister.*

Is that… is that even possible?

Why would she be here?

Maybe I misunderstood.

"Sorry, little one," Doctor Tav says, his hand grabbing mine and sending a cold blast through my veins. I nearly shiver in response, his touch so wrong that I can barely think straight. "I didn't mean to growl."

Growl? I repeat to myself. *Oh.*

He thinks my pulse is racing from his snarl, not from hearing *Heart.*

Did I even hear that correctly?

"Remake the tea," he says again without looking at me.

"I don't *make* tea," Baroness Clarice—*Heart?*—snaps before taking the tray and stalking off toward the stairs. "And I don't submit to you, either."

Doctor Tav grunts. "Don't I know it."

The baroness flips her long blonde hair over her shoulder like she usually does and sashays up the stairs, then slams the door behind her.

Doctor Tav sighs, his thumb tracing unwelcome circles against my wrist. "We're not a match, are we?" he says in a low voice.

I blink. "What?"

He cants his head to the side, his blue eyes almost kind. "You heard me, Miss Marvel. We're not a scent match."

This time, I can't stop the shiver from vibrating through me.

And he releases my hand, his fingers going to his dark

hair as he shakes his head. "Nothing is what it seems here. Nothing at all."

"What do you mean?"

"I hoped we would be a match, to at least make this palatable. But I should have known fate would never reward me with such a gift." He glances up the stairs, his mouth grimacing. "She won't care, though. She never does."

"I… I don't understand."

"No, I suppose you don't," he murmurs. "And for that, I'm sorry. Fuck, I'm sorry for a great many things. Alas, apologies are a concept of the past."

He stands.

"I'm going to go make sure your food and tea are safe to eat and drink," he says, finally looking at me again. "You're going to need your strength, Omega. The next few days are going to be taxing on both of us."

With that, he leaves.

All I can do is gape at the stairs.

He called me an Omega.

It's real. Everything… is real.

And I'm pretty sure I just met the Crimson King.

CRAZE

WHAT THE FUCK JUST HAPPENED? I wonder, my head pounding as my eyes slowly open.

There's water everywhere.

Soaked in blood.

What in the hell? I sit up, splashing the warm liquid all over the marble siding.

"Oh, good, you're awake," Krolic says. "About fucking time, too."

"What?" I blink. "Why the fuck am I in a bathtub?"

"Because you were covered in blood and bleeding out," Catum mutters. "I had to do something to heal you quickly. But it still took two fucking days."

"*Two days?*" I try to jump out of the tub, but my usual agility fails me, my head forcing me to fall right back down in the bath.

"You're making a mess," Krolic chastises.

"Oh, I'm sorry," I snap at him. "I'll just drown instead."

He grunts.

And Catum sighs. "We'll clean it up later. What matters is bringing you up to speed."

"Up to speed on what?" I ask, laying my head back against the marble siding and closing my eyes. "Did I get attacked by an ogre again?" Those things are always trying to beat me to a pulp, and I definitely feel like one of them snuck up on me. Probably hit me in the head with a stone bat or some shit.

"The Imposter King has Ailsa," Catum tells me, causing my brow to furrow.

Ailsa Marvel.

Potential mate.

No, not a potential *mate.* Definite *mate.*

My eyes fly open as I force myself up and out of the water again. This time, Krolic simply throws me a towel rather than giving me a hard time about making a mess. I catch it but don't use it, instead gaping at Catum as my memories begin to resurface.

We were in this very bathroom, talking to Ailsa about the mating rituals. A little about Crimson. Then we decided... on plan Z.

I made the portal.

And we...

I frown. "I don't remember what happened after stepping into the portal." It's all a blur, like a big black hole.

"My sister happened," Krolic growls as he bends to begin emptying the massive tub. It won't take long, magic whirling through the air to speed it along and clean up the mess left behind. Krolic's worries are for naught.

At least about the bath.

His concerns regarding his sister, however, are definitely proving valid.

"What did she do?" I demand, needing to understand, to fill in the gaps of my missing memory.

"She set a trap. *Above ground*," Catum mutters, the words seeming to irritate him. "The fucking cat warned us not to take Ailsa above ground. I thought he meant in Monsterland. But no, he meant to her realm."

"Which is sometimes referred to as going above ground," I translate, realizing what he means. "Fuck."

"Yeah, *fuck*. She's been hiding in plain sight the entire fucking time." Catum sounds furious. "I even *met* her as Baroness Clarice but didn't pick up on her presence at all. She's been playing us for two fucking years."

"Longer than that," Krolic says, sounding just as furious.

But I... I'm a little lost on a key part of this conversation. "Baroness Clarice?"

"My sister is Baroness Clarice," Krolic says through his teeth. "Or rather, she's turned the woman into a puppet of sorts. A *shadow self* would be the appropriate term, I suppose."

"She's basically possessed her, and she's existing inside her as though she is her," Catum explains. "It's fucked up."

"Clearly," I mutter. "Heart can't even shift into a wolf. That's why she was never strong enough to rule."

"She still can't shift," Krolic says. "But it seems she's tapping into other magic—old, dark magic—to solidify her rule in varying ways." He sounds irritated by that, probably because it's the first we're hearing of it.

But it could explain how she managed to kill their parents and brothers.

And also how she escaped prison all those centuries ago.

Catum folds his arms. "The cat's cryptic riddle included a part about how she's always been one step ahead of us. We assume this is why."

"Just as we hope the part about Ailsa being the key to bringing Heart down—a queen against a queen—is also accurate," Krolic adds.

"Exactly." Catum moves to turn on the shower. "You need to rinse, Craze."

I nearly tell him to fuck off, but the bloodied towel in my hands suggests he's right. I toss the soiled linen into the still-draining bath, where it disappears along with the water.

"What's the plan?" I ask as I step under the cold spray. It'll warm up soon. But I don't fucking care about the temperature. I care about our lost time and how we're going to get our Omega back.

"Storm the palace," Catum says.

I snort. "Sure. I would love that. But we need an army. What's the real plan?"

"Storm the palace," Krolic echoes.

I gape at both of them. "You've had one too many cups of my tea, mates. That's a suicide mission."

"Not exactly," Krolic murmurs. "We've been busy while you've been napping."

I arch a brow. "I wouldn't say I was *napping*."

"Regardless, we've met with some old friends of yours," Krolic goes on.

"Friends?" I repeat. "I have no friends." Except for the two assholes watching me shower right now.

And Ailsa.

I would like to call her a friend, too.

As well as a cock-sucking goddess.

But I'll discuss that nickname with her later. When we

find her. Because we will find her. *And I'll kill anyone who has touched her,* I decide as I begin shampooing my hair.

"Brandt," Krolic tells me. "And the Tweedle brothers."

My hand stills. "*What?*"

"I had a little conversation with them about why they tried to attack Ailsa. It was very… enlightening."

"Did they call her fertile like the snout men did?" I wonder aloud.

"They did," Krolic confirms. "Only, they don't remember why they felt that way, and they were rather horrified by their own actions."

I stare at him. "So they felt… possessed?"

"So it would seem," Catum drawls. "Just like Baroness Clarice."

"Just like Baroness Clarice," Krolic echoes. "To say Brandt and the Tweedle brothers were livid by this revelation… would be an understatement."

"But are they free of her hold?" I ask.

Catum and Krolic grin. "They are now," Krolic tells me.

"How?" I wonder aloud.

"By pledging their fealty," Krolic says, making me blink.

I blink at him. "What?"

"We realized the snow creatures up here have never been impacted by her magic—because they swore fealty to me ages ago. Apparently, it's as simple as a vow." Krolic shrugs. "So as we said, our plan is to storm the palace. And while you were getting your beauty rest, we gathered some friends to help."

I ignore the jibe about my *beauty rest* and focus on what matters most. "You really have been busy."

"Yes," both men say.

"This is still going to be a suicide mission," I tell them. Because the fealty thing feels too easy. "But fuck it. I'm in."

I earned my Mad Hatter title for a reason. *This* reason. If my best friends want to storm a fucking fortress to rescue our Omega, then I'm the right Enforcer for the job.

I finish rinsing my hair and skin, then turn off the water and grab a fresh towel.

There's really only one thing left to say.

"I'm going to need my cards."

Because the Queen of Hearts is going to pay. That bitch is going down, even if it means sacrificing myself in the process.

Time to play.

AILSA

I DON'T TOUCH the food or drink on the new tray. Tabitha brought it down shortly after *Doctor Tav* left. But I refuse to eat it. I don't trust the contents.

Hell, I don't trust *anything* here.

The door to my room is locked. I know this because I tried to open it about thirty minutes ago.

Normally, that would be fine—I've slipped out of the basement window dozens of times.

Only now, that window doesn't budge.

Because it's not the same window.

I made that discovery shortly after finding the door locked, and I've been trying to figure out what it means. Obviously, I'm not really home. But why go through all the charades of pretending I'm here? Why tell me the ceremony never happened, only for the Imposter King—or who I'm about ninety-five percent sure is the Imposter King—to call me an Omega?

None of this makes any sense.

Is Baroness Clarice actually Heart? Or is Heart just masquerading as Baroness Clarice?

I pace the room, my mind racing.

Where are Catum, Krolic, and Craze? Was Craze hurt somehow? Did he lose me in the portal?

I stalk over to the wardrobe to finger the blue-and-white ceremonial dress. It feels like the one I wore the other day. And the shoes are that same too-small size.

My teeth grind together.

Is this all an elaborate ruse to make me feel insane? Because it's working. I—

The lock clicks upstairs, causing the hairs along my nape to stand on end.

But the sense of anticipation dies when I see that it's just Tabitha.

She quietly slips into the room, closing the door behind her, and creeps down the stairs like she's a silent little cat. "You didn't touch your food."

I look at her and arch a brow. "Are you here to force me to eat?" It comes out a little harsh, which isn't my intention. But I'm really over all of this nonsense.

At least the rasp in my voice has disappeared.

Strange, because I didn't drink anything at all. Yet I actually feel somewhat normal again. Even my stomach has stopped rolling.

Tabitha stares at me. "I think you should at least try the tea."

I blink at her. "Earlier you—"

"It's really good tea," she stresses, cutting me off. "Trust me."

My brow furrows. An hour ago, she told me not to drink the tea. Now she wants me to try it?

I walk over there, determined to grab the teacup and either chuck it at the wall or dump the contents down the drain in the bathroom. But when I lift the medium-sized ceramic cup, I spy a piece of paper folded neatly beneath it.

Or I assume it's a paper, anyway. It's small, the missive having been folded several times to more or less hide beneath the tea.

I set the drink to the side and grab the note.

When I look up at Tabitha, she has a finger in front of her lips.

Frowning, I unfold the letter and arch a brow at the four words. *There are ears everywhere.*

I snort. *No shit*, I want to say back. But since I can't, I let my eyes convey that message for me.

Tabitha grabs the tray. "Well, since you don't want to eat anything, I'll just take this back upstairs." She takes a step, then trips over her own two feet, sending the contents all over the floor. With a loud gasp, she says, "You *pushed* me."

Both of my eyebrows fly up. "I did not."

"Yes, you did!" she accuses, sounding furious. "Now I have to go get cleaning supplies to fix your mess. What the hell is wrong with you, Ailsa? Why are you so fucking ungrateful?"

With that glorious speech, she stomps off and up the stairs, leaving me gaping at her departing form. "Everyone is insane here." That's... that's all I've got.

I take the note she left me, shred it, and throw it into the bathroom bin.

"How utterly helpful," I mutter.

"You have no idea," a silky voice says, making me yelp and turn around just as the bathroom door closes.

The shower starts a second later as a male forms just beside the tub. I run for the door, but he's faster, grabbing me by the wrist and yanking me back to him.

"I'm not going to hurt you, Ailsa Marvel." His bruising grip on my wrist says otherwise. "But I need to deliver a message."

I take in his vibrant pink hair and matching eyelashes and immediately frown. "You look like Tabitha."

"Well, relatives often look alike," he drawls. "But I'm

not here to discuss familial resemblances, darling pet. I need to know how much you've learned about the ritual."

I stare at him. "The mating ritual?"

"No, the graduation one."

My frown deepens. "What?"

"Of course I mean the mating ritual, darling girl," he snaps, his mercurial mood swing making me want to step back. But his hand is still clamped down on my wrist. "Tell me what you know."

"That it's a hunt—"

"No, tell me what you know about how it begins," he interjects, his lack of patience starting to piss me off.

"Look, I don't know who you—"

"Darling," he interrupts, a subtle purr underlining that word. "I'm destined to love you and worship you as the future Monsterland Queen, but right now, I need you to focus. You're the new player on the board, the unknown queen. You have the power to fix all of this, but you need to listen to me."

"Says the man who keeps asking questions," I retort.

He makes a noise in the back of his throat that almost sounds like a strangled laugh. Yet his catlike eyes radiate annoyance. "You have no idea how the ritual begins."

I arch a brow, choosing silence over confirmation. He's the one who said I need to *listen*, after all.

"Of course you don't know how it begins." He sounds annoyed. "I warned them, Ailsa. I warned them not to take you above ground, yet did they listen? No. Fucking Alphas."

He finally releases me and takes a step toward the door to press his ear to the wood. After a second, he nods and returns to the tub.

This small bathroom suddenly feels even tinier with the two of us sequestered inside it.

"Right, we don't have much time." He glances at the door, then back at me. "The palace has eyes and ears all over the grounds. Remember that, my queen. *Use* it. If you declare your desire for a hunt, the ritual must be offered. But you have to truly want it. Shout for it. *Beg.* And find the Story of Alice. It's written in the walls. Her words… *are everywhere.*"

Those last two words are a whisper on the wind as the male disappears before my eyes.

The door flies open a second later, causing me to yelp and jump back toward the running shower.

Baroness Clarice stands there, eyes narrowed as she scans the room. "I heard voices."

I swallow. "I… I was talking to myself. A-about the tray." It's an asinine thing to say, but if I've learned anything from my time in Monsterland, it's that insanity is currency. "I didn't push Tabitha."

The baroness rolls her eyes. "I couldn't give two shits about your food and beverage, Ailsa. Now clean yourself up. We have a ceremony to attend."

"A ceremony?" I repeat.

"Yes," she hisses. "The one you missed on your birthday. Remember? So take a shower and get dressed. I'll be waiting for you upstairs."

The door slams before I can say anything else.

Why is she pretending like I haven't gone through the ceremony yet?

Does she want me to take the elixir again? I wonder. *The more potent one? To force my heat?*

But if that's the case, why would the Imposter King call me an Omega? Why tip me off that he already knows who and what I am?

I run my fingers through my hair and turn to stare in

the mirror. "What the hell am I supposed to do?" I demand, the steam from the shower fogging the glass.

I'm about to reach forward to wipe it clean when a single word appears. *Run.*

My gaze widens. "I…" I swallow, my voice dropping to a whisper. "I should run?"

Run disappears, only for *Yes* to take its place.

I jump back into the wall, my hand to my chest.

"This can't be happening." I've officially lost my fucking mind.

Another word appears.

Go.

I shiver, my head beginning to sway back and forth as the glass fogs once more.

To the, follows, causing me to gape at the mirror.

Courtyard is the final word.

"And do what?" I ask the strange figment.

Beg for, the invisible being writes. *The ritual.*

"Are you the pink-haired man?" I ask warily. "You're still here?"

No.

"Then who are you?" I demand, still whispering.

Alice.

I stare. "That's the name the pink-haired guy gave." Which makes me instantly suspicious.

I'm.

An.

Omega.

The sequence of letters leaves me breathless.

"You're an invisible Omega?" I whisper. "How…?"

Free us is all the figment writes back. Then two lines appear under those words, punctuating them.

"By demanding the ritual," I say.

Yes.

"You want me to be hunted by the Alphas."

Yes.

"What if…?" I can't finish the question. There are too many unknowns. *What if the wrong Alpha takes me? What if they force me to breed? What if my mate-circle doesn't reach me in time?*

The figment is already drawing again.

Don't.

Submit.

Until.

The.

Right.

Circle.

Finds.

You.

That sounds ominous.

Yet I understand, thanks to my Alphas explaining some of the process.

Only, I'm not sure how to demand the ritual. "Do I just… beg to be mated?" I ask, swallowing thickly.

Yes.

In the.

Courtyard.

"And that's how the hunt begins?"

No, the figment returns. *Growls.*

"Growls?" I repeat. "Alpha… growls?"

Yes.

I'm not sure what that means exactly, but I suspect I'm going to find out. Assuming any of this works. And that I haven't completely lost my mind.

But it's Monsterland.

Embrace the madness, I think. *Experience the mayhem.*

I huff a laugh. "I've gone absolutely mad."

Good, the figment replies. *You're ready.*

I gape at the mirror. "Okay…"

I shake my head and step into the shower.

I'll clean up, don the dress, and pretend to be the obedient little Omega that Baroness Clarice expects me to be.

Then I'll run the moment I find the courtyard. If I see it, anyway.

After that… *I'll beg.*

AILSA

The moment I step out of the basement, it becomes clear to me that we're in some sort of illusion. One I don't quite understand. *How is Heart doing this?* I wonder, glancing at the woman I know as Baroness Clarice.

She arches a brow, likely expecting me to bow as I normally would.

I nearly defy her, my urge to stare straight at her hitting me square in the gut.

But I grit my teeth and curtsy the way she anticipates, pretending to play this game.

Find the courtyard, I tell myself. *How am I going to do that if I can't see through this illusion?*

"Stop stalling," she snaps, her heels already clacking.

Bitch, I think, standing.

Her demeanor isn't different. She's always been this way. But I… I feel different. Maybe it's the ability to notice her Alpha traits, or my instincts that tell me she's not who she seems. Perhaps it's related to the elixir awakening my inner Omega, or being exposed to my intended mate-circle.

Regardless, I can feel the change, sense that nothing here is right.

Because it's not real.

At least, not in the way it should be.

The hallways all resemble the manor I spent the last nine years of my life in, but the scents are not right. The general feel is all wrong, too.

This isn't Baroness Clarice's home.

It's not my home either.

But it could be, I think, glancing around once more. *This is Monsterland.*

I recognize some of the aromas from my brief time here, just as I can smell my mate-circle.

Fire.

Spice.

Cedar.

I inhale, allowing their presence to ground me. *Are they nearby? Or just somewhere within the realm?*

"What are you doing, Ailsa?" Baroness Clarice—*Heart*—demands. "Hurry up."

I apparently paused in the hall, lost to my surroundings. "Sorry," I say, feigning an apologetic grimace.

She snaps her fingers and I quickly obey, skipping forward, and resume following her. All while trying to discern the source of the illusion, how to see through it.

Because I won't be able to find this elusive courtyard if I can't break through this mirage.

Assuming the courtyard is real, I think.

I give myself a mental shake. *It's real.*

Everything in Monsterland is insane. I just have to embrace the mayhem. Accept that the unordinary is the new ordinary. Believe that I'm meant to be here, chaos and all.

I'm an Omega. And I want to engage in the ritual.

It's how we'll win back Monsterland. Break through whatever spell this female Alpha has woven over the kingdom. And demolish her illusions.

Expose the Imposter King.

Although, I'm questioning how much he's behind all of this now.

Heart seems to be the mastermind.

How long has she been Baroness Clarice? Did she know I was an Omega the whole time?

The answer to the latter question is likely yes. Which means she knew Krolic and Catum were in my district. She let them take me away.

Why? I wonder.

Or perhaps… perhaps they thwarted her original plans by reacting quickly. Maybe she didn't mean for them to take me at all.

Which would suggest she never accounted for how much they would tell me, how much I now know.

From what I've gathered of her, she thinks little of Omegas. She wants me to supplicate. She doesn't see me as a queen. Or respect me as her equal.

"She's fully aware of her position," she said to Tav earlier. There was a hint of pride in that statement, almost as though she was pleased that she'd taught me to be inferior.

She no doubt assumes it worked since I'm acquiescing and trailing after her like a good little pet. That I clearly bought her story and believe none of my "dream" was real.

Oh, it was very real, I think at her. *But this place is not.*

We're outside now, and I can taste the difference in the air. There's something sweet nearby. Floral. *Like roses*, I think, inhaling. I've only caught that aroma once— when Master Pillar brought a vase of them to sit on the altar.

I remember sneaking up to inhale the pretty flower, curious as to what they smelled like. It was my first time seeing roses in person, and these were particularly unique, as they were purple.

Why am I smelling roses now? I wonder, scanning the drab countryside of the mountain. *There are no flowers nearby.*

The closest sunflower field is almost a mile away.

I glance toward the forest edge where I would normally run, and frown when I find it missing. Narrowing my gaze, I realize there are a lot of details that don't exist here. Just like the lock on the window in the basement.

It's an imperfect mirage.

So what happens if I run toward something I know to be inaccurate?

I bite my lip, considering if I should make my move. It will blow my obedient cover, but what else am I going to do? Follow her all the way to whatever ceremony she has in mind?

No.

No, I will *not* be doing that.

Because I know what it'll do. Catum purposely diluted my dose. I won't be countering his work, not until I'm certain the ritual will be honored.

It's my due as an Omega. My fate. And I accept that path.

Swallowing, I glance at the baroness, note that she's walking with purpose toward the chapel. The details of it are perfect.

But the forest edge still isn't.

Particularly the place I ran through during my escape after the ceremony.

She didn't see it, I realize. *Which means she didn't anticipate it.*

Something Catum, Krolic, and Craze did threw off her game.

Or maybe… it was simply *me.*

She's aware of their skills, has engaged in a careful strategy against them. But I'm an unknown.

What was it that pink-haired man said?

"You're the new player on the board, the unknown queen. You have the power to fix all of this."

By declaring I want a ritual, I add.

But I have to be heard.

I have to be seen.

And I can't accomplish that in this illusion.

Time to run…

I don't second-guess my instinct; I merely bolt toward the forest.

Baroness Clarice never spent time in there. She won't know the details like I do. It should be enough for me to burst through her mirage and finally see what's all around me. To finally embrace Monsterland and all its mayhem.

The Alpha in disguise roars behind me.

But I don't obey her. I don't listen. *I don't submit.*

Kicking off the stupid, ill-fitting flats, I run faster. Harder. And burst through the tree line into a land of roses.

I knew it!

Only it's an endless sea of colors and hedges, the maze sprawling before me in chaotic twists and turns.

It's not a courtyard, but it's also no longer hidden from my view.

I take off alongside it, eager to find more, to locate a central place, to take advantage of what the pink-haired man said about there being eyes and ears everywhere.

I have a declaration I need to make.

A request that can't be denied.

Ritual. Ritual. Ritual. The word repeats in my head with each step, reaching a crescendo as I find a set of ornate stairs that seem to lead to a break in the maze.

The rose garden–like hedges part around the bottom, forming an oval wall of sorts with several arched openings. But the area before it is a massive fountain, one that can be reached if I descend the grand staircase.

It's not a courtyard. At least, not in the traditional sense. However, there's nothing traditional about this place.

And it looks official with the stone statues decorating the fountain area.

This has to be it.

I take a step, only for a blur of white to catch my attention out of the corner of my eye. I spin toward it, my lips parting at the sight maybe ten yards from where I stand.

"Beast," I breathe, instantly running in his direction.

But when I'm just a few feet away, he darts away from me, leading me to another staircase, one that goes up.

My stomach twists, the direction not feeling right.

But it's Krolic as his wolf. He's clearly trying to show me something.

I ascend a few stairs, his name on the tip of my tongue when his scent curls around me.

My steps slow and I inhale deeply, expecting to be overwhelmed by his woodsy cologne. Only... I smell ash instead. Like a burning tree.

I frown.

The scent is all wrong.

Beast pauses at the stop of the stairs, his green eyes holding an expectant look to them.

Krolic's commentary about how Crimson masquerades as the Silver King whispers through my mind.

Except this scent doesn't belong to Tav, either. He reminded me of sandalwood oil, and this fragrance is reminiscent of what happens when a tree burns.

Was I wrong about Tav being Crimson? Is this the Crimson King?

I shiver and take a step back down.

The wolf growls in response.

Not Beast.

I turn and run back down, then sprint for the other staircase.

I should have followed my instincts. But I let this wolf distract me.

I can feel him bounding after me, his scent all wrong.

"I want the ritual!" I start yelling, terrified that he's going to catch me first. "I want to be——"

Something hard hits me from behind, knocking me forward.

I don't think; I roll with it, letting the momentum take me down the hill alongside the grand stairs.

Sharp thorns catch on my dress, tearing the too-tight fabric. But I don't care. I let it rip as I spin all the way down and land on a gravel path that frames the rose maze.

Snarls erupt near my head.

I ignore them, pushing through the agony to shove to my feet and run barefoot across the rocks toward the fountain statues.

"I'm Ailsa Marvel!" I shout, my heart hammering in my chest and in my years. "I'm an Omega! And I want the ritual! Hunt me!"

I have no idea if what I'm saying is even correct. But I keep shouting it as I reach the fountain, only to be tackled to the cobblestone-covered ground by a raging wolf.

He snarls in my face as Baroness Clarice snarls, "Foolish girl." She's walking down the stairs, her clacking heels echoing throughout the fountain. "You have no idea what you've done."

She's seething. I can feel her fury like a hot wave to my

senses, the weight of it almost more intense than that of the wolf on top of me.

The animal growls, his snout lowering to my neck to open his jaws along my throat.

I freeze, the dominant gesture intimidating in the worst way. If this were Krolic, I would tilt my head to the side in submission. But this Alpha isn't Krolic. He's an unknown. A foreign rival. *And not my mate.*

Someone tsks in the distance, the sound an echo around us that has the wolf snarling against my neck.

"Ah, ah, ah. You know the rules, Spaten," a voice singsongs.

The pink-haired man, I recognize, swallowing.

"The Omega has requested the ritual. So all of Monsterland kind has been invited out to play, and I don't think they'll be very pleased by you demanding her submission before the games even begin."

"*You*," the baroness hisses. "You've been meddling. I told you what would happen if—"

"Your threats are unnecessary, Queen of Hearts," he inserts coolly. "A new round has begun. You and I will continue our dance should you win."

She growls, the sound of it vibrating the stone beneath me as the wolf echoes the snarl against my throat.

Then a louder, more intense growl rumbles the earth as the familiar scent of cedar washes over me.

Beast.

My *Beast.*

Krolic… is here.

KR⊖LIC

Spaten.

I can barely believe my eyes, but I would recognize my eldest brother anywhere.

He's supposed to be dead.

Killed by our dear sister.

But he's currently standing on top of *my* Omega.

I growl again, making his ears twitch as his green eyes —the same shade as my own—lock on me.

All this time, I thought Heart was behind the deaths of our parents.

But I see it clearly now.

It was Spaten. It's always been Spaten.

That's why his wolf looks identical to mine. How his presence lingered here as king. Why some of the kingdom chose to follow him.

He's an heir.

Not *the* heir, but an acceptable one nonetheless.

And his aura is riddled with darkness.

Magic? I wonder. *Is he the one weaving spells over those in the kingdom?*

I thought it was Heart. Now I don't know what to think.

Especially since my sister appears to still be possessing Baroness Clarice.

Or maybe she is the baroness.

I can't smell Heart's tangy scent anywhere. Which means either she's not nearby, or she's donned a clever disguise.

As though hearing my confusion, her skin begins to melt away to reveal the sister I know beneath the mask.

A shape-shifter, I realize, my heart stilling in my chest. *Heart's become a shape-shifter.*

How? I want to demand. She's never had a wolf. Never been able to shift. And yet, she's transforming into her true self now as though she's done this thousands of times before.

"That's a new trick," Craze drawls from behind me. "Can you grow a knot, too?"

My sister snarls at him.

"Well, I see your manners have taken a step in the right direction," he muses dryly. "Better than your supposedly dead brother, anyway." His gaze narrows at Spaten. "Growl at our mate one more time and see what happens."

"She's not your mate," my sister hisses at him.

"She's not yours either," he bites right back. "She wants a mating ritual. So let's give her one and see whose knot she chooses." His gaze drops to Heart's lower half. "Oh, wait… I guess you'll have to sit this one out."

Ches chuckles somewhere in the distance, the cat having vanished when he sensed our arrival. He's probably playing in the hedges again, observing every moment.

He's not the only one.

There are several monsters lurking in the maze. That's where the ritual will begin. I don't know how Ailsa knew to demand her rights here in the ceremonial courtyard, but I'm glad she did it. Her voice carried across Monsterland, inviting all the Alphas out to play.

And thus far, the only one who seems hell-bent on taking her by force is my brother.

He has yet to release her neck, despite her refusal to submit.

Oh, she's gone still. But she's not tilted her head.

She won't give him what he wants.

Yet she's given it to me before. The first night we met, I pinned her in a similar manner, my mouth instantly going to her neck.

She tilted to the side, just as an Omega should when her Alpha demands her submission.

But he's not her Alpha.

We are her Alphas.

Poor Spaten is about to learn that lesson the hard way.

Catum appears behind him, his shadow form hiding him from view. But I feel him there. Know what he's about to do. And give him a subtle go-ahead by tilting my chin.

This is my fight, which makes it *our* fight. As a unit. A circle. A proper fucking royal court.

That's what my sister and brother have failed to realize.

It's a lesson that is about to cost them dearly.

I made the mistake of imprisoning my sister, once upon a time. I realize now how she escaped—with Spaten's help.

Then she must have faked his death before actually killing our other brother.

Their betrayals have tainted Monsterland, creating a darkness that's reminiscent of a disease.

It's a disease I fully intend to cure now.

By ridding this realm of their presence. *For good*.

I have no idea where Crimson is, but I imagine he'll be appearing at any moment. We'll handle him, too.

Then... we'll claim our daring little mate.

She's still refusing to submit on the ground despite

having my brother's teeth pressed against her throat. I can feel her determination. Her *anger*.

Such a good fucking Omega, I think. She knows her wolf, and that animal on top of her isn't him.

I growl, low and with warning. *Release her*, I'm saying. *Release her or face the consequences.*

Said consequences are standing right behind Spaten.

My brother rumbles back at me, then does exactly what I wanted him to do—lifts his head to stare me down in challenge.

I nearly smile inside.

But the instinct disappears behind my beast's howl as Catum bodychecks Spaten, sending my brother flying across the courtyard into a nearby sculpture. The hit is so intense that the stone cracks. But my eldest sibling is instantly on his paws and charging—not toward Catum, but toward me.

I brace myself for impact, ready to spar.

It's been a long fucking time.

And I have no idea what powers my brother has seemingly inherited.

But I'm ready. My mate-circle is ready. *And our Omega is watching.*

Craze goes for my sister while Catum runs toward me and my brother.

Then everything is a blur of white fur as Spaten and I tumble across the earth.

He's big. Slightly bigger than me. And he's fighting like his life hangs in the balance.

Which it very much does.

I snap at his neck, his scruff, his throat, all while trying to gain purchase.

But he's fast—faster than I remember.

And fucking insane.

He tumbles both of us into the nearby fountain, causing my ears to fill with water, thus drowning out all the sounds around me.

So much so that I almost miss the thundering echo of approaching Alphas.

However, as I surface, I see them coming.

A hungry mob.

All of them with their sights set on Ailsa.

Possessed, I recognize.

Catum must see it, too, because he shifts focus, running for our intended to protect her.

But there are too many of them. Too many salivating beasts.

My wolf grumbles as my brother tackles us once more, our momentary distraction giving him the upper hand.

I take a mouthful of water, my lungs screaming for the need to inhale. I went down before I took a proper breath.

Shit!

I claw at the ground, only to find my paws waterlogged.

This is bad.

I spin, using my back legs to kick Spaten off of me. But that sends me deeper.

My back hits the floor, probably ten feet beneath the surface now.

I whirl again, determined to push off the ground to reach the air I desperately need.

Except just as I shove off the bottom, Spaten checks me again, driving me right back down.

My wolf releases a sound I can't hear over the bubbles in my ear, my insides demanding that I inhale.

No, I fight back. *No!*

But the dots… the darkness… it's starting to seep in.

And with that comes doubt.

Fear.

Terrible. Unadulterated. *Fear.*

I can sense Catum fighting for his life. Sense Craze doing the same.

We didn't underestimate our opponents. We underestimated Monsterland. Their ability to be manipulated. To be *controlled* by the dark villain in their midst.

My siblings never respected my rule.

It's clear now.

And they didn't respect our parents' rule either.

What is this world without respect? I think, furious. *What happened to Monsterland? The kingdom I love? The kingdom I once revered?*

With a roar, I give it one last push, refusing to go down like this. Refusing to let go of my throne. My purpose. *My destiny*.

Spaten tries to keep me down, but something from below shoves me higher, the force of it allowing me to break the surface on a much-needed gasp.

Which is when I see the bedlam occurring in the courtyard.

Catum has yanked out the hearts of almost a dozen Alphas, but he's wounded and bloody and panting.

And Ailsa is standing behind him with a vial in her hand.

One that says *Drink me*.

My eyes widen inside, my beast instantly trying to swim toward her. *No!* I want to shout. *Ailsa, don't!*

"You want me?" she asks the crowd, a note of steel underlying her tone.

I watch with horror as she tips the contents into the back of her throat. Swallows. And shouts five words that ignite the chase.

"Then come and get me!"

AILSA

A Few Minutes Earlier

"Ailsa," a voice whispers in the wind, causing my head to whip around as I try to find the owner of that sound.

A pair of lips appears in the space before me, making me yelp.

"Shh," he hushes, the rest of his face appearing, followed by a head of pink hair. "You need to take the elixir."

"What?"

His hand appears as he holds it out to me. "Take it. Then tell them to chase you."

I shake my head. "I don't—"

"Look around you," he demands. "Look at the statues. Really look at them. Then check the water."

I blink at him as vicious chaos breaks out around me.

Craze stabbed Heart a few minutes ago, but she instantly recovered, making him growl about dark magic spells as she tossed his card right back at him.

The pair of them are fighting a few yards away while Catum whirls in a blur of black and blood, fighting off snarling Alphas.

Alphas I *really* don't want to play a game of chase with right now.

"*Look*," the pink-haired male says again. "Please, Ailsa. Just... *look*."

Swallowing, I glance at the statues—noting the feminine angles and angelic features. Their lips are all rounded as though they're lost in song.

I glance at the fountain, momentarily distracted by Krolic and the other wolf fighting near the deeper end of the pool. Or what I assume is deep, anyway, since they keep going under.

But as they disappear behind the center fixture, I start to see the reflections that the pink-haired man mentioned.

I frown.

The gentle innocence of the statues disappears the longer I look. Their expressions are grotesque and agonized instead, as though they're *screaming*, not singing.

I shiver. It's a horrifying juxtaposition. "I don't understand."

"Drink and declare the chase," he whispers, shoving the vial into my hands. "But make sure you touch the water before you flee."

I shake my head, his words telling me what to do without providing any context as to how that relates to the statues and their strange reflections.

But when I glance back at him, he's gone.

And all I have is the vial.

Drink me, the label says.

I close my eyes.

If I take this, I'll go into heat. Perhaps immediately since I already have some of this elixir in my system.

Maybe that's what he means by initiating the chase.

But... but how does that solve any of this?

The Alphas stalking toward me are half crazed, their auras radiating pain as they come for me.

Catum is the only one stopping them from ripping me apart.

I don't want to make that worse.

Unless something about the ritual will snap them out of it? I wonder. The pink-haired man hasn't led me astray yet.

And Alice told me to start the ritual in the courtyard.

Maybe this is the final step.

My eyes open once more, my spine steeling as I stand. "All right," I mutter to myself. The craziest solutions are what have worked so far in this world. Why not try this one, too?

Clearing my throat, I fix my focus on the Alphas coming at me from the side. They're walking over the remains of the others who came before them without even glancing down, their eyes fixated on me.

"You want me?" I ask them, my voice exuding a calm I don't quite feel.

A calm that fizzles out of me as I force myself to knock the contents into the back of my throat and swallow.

"Then come and get me!" I shout, bolting toward the water and Krolic's watching form.

His eyes meet mine, a note of panic lingering in his gaze that I can't quite ignore.

Maybe I made the wrong choice.

Who the hell even knows?

But I run through the shallow area of the water, the liquid a blessing against my bare feet. A tingling sensation crawls up my skin, nearly making me stumble.

It feels like magic.

Healing, I realize as the aches on my soles begin to subside. *How... fascinating.*

So fascinating that I can't help but stop and look down.

It's a stupid thing to do, especially when I have a horde

of Alphas bellowing in my wake. However, the water feels so inviting, like it's calling me home.

Almost like the portal in the cave, I think, recalling how the dark hole intrigued me enough to touch it. Almost as though it was beckoning me to fall in.

My knees bend of their own accord, my fingers reaching for the water again now, curious as to why I feel so compelled to touch it.

Someone shouts my name.

I ignore them, too consumed by the need to run my fingers across the chilly water.

The liquid seems to hum in response, utterly entrancing me.

At least until a hand grabs mine and tries to pull me in.

I yank back, a scream billowing up from my throat.

Then a pair of bright green eyes meet mine from beneath the water, the ash-blonde-haired woman petite like me. Except she's older. Similar to Krolic's age.

Her nails bite into my wrist as she tugs on me again.

I jerk my hand out of the water.

And bring her with me.

She gasps, the sound seeming to echo throughout the entire courtyard.

Then she releases me to drop back down.

Only, she doesn't go under; she hauls another woman out.

Followed by two more.

I blink, my own hand joining hers as a male clasps my fingers.

Rather than think about how impossible this is, I just help him to the surface.

Everyone continues the process until half the fountain seems to be filled with people.

Omegas, I realize. *They're all... Omegas.*

Krolic is no longer in beast form, but standing as a human a few feet from me, his eyes filled with awe. "How?" he breathes.

I… I just shake my head.

Because I have no idea *how* any of this is happening.

"Thank you," the original blonde says to me, her voice a rasp. "*Thank you.*"

"Mom?" Krolic breathes, blinking at the female. "H-how?"

She smiles fondly at Krolic, her hand reaching up to cup his jaw. "Your Omega chooses you."

His brow furrows. "We haven't completed the ritual yet."

"I know," she whispers. "But her soul has already chosen, and it was enough."

"Enough for what?" he asks, staring at her like he can't believe she's here.

I understand the emotion because I feel similarly.

None of this feels real or possible.

Which, of course, means that it's all entirely plausible.

Because nothing is ever what it seems.

"To break the curse," she says before shifting her focus to the other Alpha in the water—one who is also no longer in wolf form. He's standing there, gaping at Krolic and his mother, a note of horror in his features.

Features that remind me of Krolic's.

"You and your sister have a great deal to atone for, Spaten," the woman announces, her voice carrying as it loses the raspy quality. "First, you killed my mate-circle. *Your own father.* Then you banished me to the depths of the ritual fountain. But you had no idea the Fates would send all of Omega kind with me, did you?"

She looks for Heart—who is kneeling on the cobblestone with Craze behind her, one of his cards against her throat. His opposite hand is locked in her blonde hair—the same color as Krolic's mom's. As well as Baroness Clarice's, but I already gathered that Heart can shape-shift. That was pretty obvious when she transitioned into another woman right before my eyes.

Just like Krolic being able to turn into a wolf at will.

An eerie quiet falls over the courtyard as the fountain —which I now realize is more of a small pond due to the depth in the center—shuts off.

Krolic's mother has lifted her hand into the sky, creating a dark hue that overtakes the sun and cascades the courtyard into darkness.

A blinding light soon follows as a bolt comes sailing through the air to strike Heart in the chest.

Craze releases her just in time, jumping several feet back a second before it hits. He curses. "A little warning next time, Alice," he mutters, his words carrying due to the astounding silence.

A soft churning noise echoes next, the sound of it seeming to be radiating from Heart's skin as it literally turns to stone.

I realize with a start that all the other statues no longer exist.

Because they were the Omegas, I suddenly comprehend.

That's why the pink-haired man told me to look at the reflections. I do it again now and see Heart's face frozen in horror.

Another bolt jolts through the night-like sky, this one striking the Alpha in the water.

His body vanishes, only to reappear alongside Heart's, his reflection showing a snarl rather than one of terror.

"Crimson," the woman calls out.

The maze parts to reveal a new arc, allowing the male I met just hours ago to step into the courtyard. "Your

Majesty," he replies, bowing low. "It's good to see you in the flesh, Alice."

She smiles. "Likewise, Tav."

Krolic frowns. "He's aligned with Heart."

"He's not," she murmurs. "He's aligned with me. And he has been for a very, very long time."

Tav goes to one knee on the edge of the pond, his head bowed. "My fealty rests with the Silver Queen."

"As does mine," the pink-haired man says as he appears beside Tav, both men on their knees.

"I should have fucking known," Catum grounds out, making the pink-haired man grin.

"Queen Alice will always be my first and only love," he says.

Queen Alice's lips curl. "I won't be queen for much longer." She looks at me. "That honor falls to you, Ailsa Marvel. So have your chase. Run free." She shifts her attention to Krolic. "And enjoy your hunt."

The night clears, revealing the sun once more as amusement meets her proclamation.

"Happy hiding," she whispers to me as she walks past me to reach Tav and the other man.

Both of them stand in sequence, heads still bowed in reverence.

"You'll always be queen to me," the pink-haired one purrs.

"Stop flirting with me, Ches," she replies.

"Never," he says back to her.

Tav simply shakes his head. "You see what you left me to deal with these last few hundred years?"

"Are you saying my presence is more irritating than Heart's?" the pink-haired one asks, sounding offended. "Because that hurts, Tav. It really hurts."

Queen Alice laughs. "I've missed you both."

"Not as much as we've missed you," Tav replies, pulling her into a hug.

Ches joins from the other side, the three of them embracing for a long moment.

"Thank you for hearing my call," she says to them.

"Thank you for entrusting us with the honor of helping to save Omega kind," Tav returns.

"He's disappointed that his efforts didn't result in the Fates sending him his own Omega," Ches interjects, earning a snort from Tav. "He chose the Silver Pack over his own. That has to earn him some favor, right?"

"Fuck off, Beta."

Ches grins. "Tell me I'm wrong. Tell me you don't want a reward for picking the right side of the battle?"

"There is no battle," he grumbles. "Not anymore."

Ches shrugs. "For now, anyway."

"The Crimson Pack isn't what it used to be," Tav grits out. "Leave it alone, cat."

There's clearly a story here. One I'm intrigued to learn more about. Krolic's expression tells me he feels similarly.

All this time, he assumed Crimson was the Imposter King.

I doubt any of them ever guessed he was actually on their side. But I see a hint of respect in Krolic's gaze now as he looks at Tav. That same glimmer is echoed in Tav's eyes as he glances back at Krolic.

"The Fates will honor you both in different ways," Queen Alice interjects, her voice soothing. "Now let's stop distracting our future queen." She gives me a knowing look. "That elixir is already doing its job. You need to run."

With that profound statement, she waves her hand, creating a portal in thin air, one that she walks through with Ches and Tav at her back.

And then they're just… *gone*.

I frown. Her connection with the two men didn't seem all that romantic. I'm not sure how I recognize that. Maybe because of the way they spoke to each other, or because of how they looked at one another. There was fondness there, but not the same kind of fondness I sense in Krolic's eyes now as he stares at me.

I meet his gaze, then glance around to find that we're the only ones in the pond-like fountain.

Catum and Craze stand just out of reach, their expressions expectant.

Everyone else is just… *gone*.

"Where…?" I trail off, confused by our sudden aloneness.

"Home," Krolic tells me, making me frown.

"What?"

"You were going to ask where everyone is, and I'm answering simply—*home*. Which is where we're going to take you once we catch you."

"Catch me?" I repeat, a strange warmth seeming to hum to life inside me.

He dips his chin in a single nod. "You need to run, little bunny."

I gape at him, not just because of the abrupt change in atmosphere, but because the nickname is new. "*Bunny?*"

He grins. "I'm a predator. And you, my sweet girl, are officially *prey*."

Catum and Craze growl in agreement, both of them studying me with intense stares.

"We… we just… All of this… I." I shake my head. "Don't you think we need some time to digest everything that has happened?"

Craze grins. "It's chaos, gorgeous. Our lives wouldn't be the same without it. So we don't need time to think about anything. In fact, I believe I speak for the mate-circle when I say that none of us want to think at all right now. We just want to *chase*."

"So *run*," Catum growls. "Now."

My nipples bead in response, my body instantly primed.

"This is madness," I breathe.

"This is Monsterland," Craze counters. "Welcome to the mayhem, little rabbit."

"You called for a hunt, baby girl," Krolic drawls. "You initiated the ritual."

"Yes, because… because…" *Because the pink-haired man told me to* rests on the tip of my tongue, but it feels wrong. Like a lie even though it's technically true.

However, deep down… I… I wanted this.

I can sense it now, that intrinsic desire to be chased. Caught. *And claimed*.

Krolic smiles, his mouth radiating sin. "We'll be nice and give you a head start."

"Thirty seconds," Catum clarifies. "Beginning… *now*."

"You can't—"

"Twenty-nine," Catum says, interrupting me. "Twenty-eight."

Oh, Gods…

They're serious.

"Twenty-seven."

Shit!

I don't know when I went to my knees in the water, but I stand now.

And then I do the only thing I can think to do—*I run*.

CATUM

I'M SO FUCKING hard I can hardly think straight.

Between the fight and hearing Ailsa declare her need for a hunt, I... I'm enslaved to my instincts. Lost to the drive to *claim*.

Because our Omega has started the most primal of games.

And she's running through the hedge maze.

Krolic joins me by one of the many entrances, his eyes narrowed. "Split up or hunt as a team?" he asks.

"Team," I tell him.

"Always as a team," Craze echoes.

If either male is stunned by what was revealed today— that Queen Alice was stuck in a fountain with over a dozen other Omegas—neither of them shows it.

Perhaps because we've all seen extraordinary events in our very long lives.

Or, more likely, because none of us can get Ailsa Marvel out of our heads.

The ritual has begun.

The elixir has been drunk—*again*.

And our delicious Omega is about to go into heat.

Fuck, I can't wait to knot her. I'm going to claim every part of her, just as I'm sure Craze and Krolic will do the same.

Her scent grows stronger with every step, her cunt already slick with need. I can practically taste her on my tongue.

"Oh, we're going to rip you apart, Miss Marvel," I purr, aware that my voice will carry directly to her on the wind. "And you're going to love every fucking second of it."

Craze and Krolic growl in agreement, the echo of their hunger no doubt sending a chill down our Omega's spine.

This is part of the fun.

Part of the draw.

Part of the *foreplay*.

I pause as I feel her move, her presence close yet too far away.

She's running.

Searching.

Desiring a place to hide.

I smile.

There is nowhere she can hide in this maze. We will find her. And we will fuck her.

For days.

"Graves, she smells amazing," Craze says under his breath. "I can't wait to rip that fucking dress off of her."

"I can't wait to be inside her," I growl, my knot practically throbbing with need. Delayed gratification is not my thing, and yet I've staved off my orgasm for *days*.

Hell, years, really.

My hand did the job just fine, but fucking our mate will be a lot more than fine. It'll be *exquisite*.

Craze starts skipping through the maze, a whistle weaving into the air around him as he taunts our intended.

Krolic adds to the tune, his inner beast rumbling in a low snarl of sound.

A purr vibrates my chest, creating a baritone that rivals Krolic's.

I can practically hear our sweet Omega moaning in response. Her thighs are probably drenched with need, the elixir having heightened every sensation, every reaction, every *craving*.

"We're coming for you," I whisper, my magic carrying the words to our panting Omega. "Run faster, Miss Marvel."

I can hear her heart beating. Or maybe it's my own.

But I take off toward the sound, determined to find her.

Craze and Krolic are right behind me, their excitement as palpable as my own.

We hit a dead end, one that has me grinning because Ailsa's scent is all over this area. She was here.

Which means we just missed her.

I turn and keep prowling, my nose leading the way as I track her sweet fragrance all through the maze.

Krolic grabs my arm, his finger brushing his lips as he cants his head to the side.

Frowning, I follow his movement, my nose instantly rejoicing at the perfume lingering in the air in that direction.

I nod for him to lead, acknowledging that he's the king.

Or the future one, anyway.

With Alice actually being alive, she's the current monarch.

But once we claim Ailsa, Krolic will officially take the throne as the Monsterland King. I'll be his Second. And Craze will be the Enforcer.

Just as it used to be.

Just as it should be.

Just as it will be.

Krolic pauses at the edge of a colorful rose-decorated hedge, then holds his hand up in a waiting signal.

I understand why an instant later when I hear the soft patter of feet coming our way. Ailsa's fragrance grows with each passing second, then suddenly she appears, her damp dress sticking to her like a second skin.

She yelps upon seeing us waiting for her and turns to run in the opposite direction, but Krolic grabs her by the waist and yanks her back, spinning her into our waiting circle.

We close in on all sides, our Omega shrieking in response as she whirls around, searching for an escape.

But there is none.

"You're ours now, Miss Marvel," I growl, catching her by the nape and yanking her in for a devastating kiss. She pushes against me, trying to free herself, which only makes me kiss her harder. She gasps when I draw blood, her eyes wild with an intoxicating mixture of fear and arousal.

"Catum," she breathes.

I nearly correct her, desiring the formality of *Master Pillar* on her lips. But there's a vulnerability to her that has me wanting to allow her use of my first name. At least for now.

"Ailsa," I return softly, then kiss her again, this time with all the reverence I feel blossoming deep inside me.

She practically melts into me, no longer trying to fight.

I love it.

Love this.

Love *her*.

She's our intended.

And we're about to thoroughly worship every fucking inch of her.

Craze rips her from my arms, not to kiss her but to tear the dress off of her, his movements bordering on feral. Ailsa shivers, her hands going to cover her breasts on instinct. But I catch her wrists and yank them back down. "No more hiding," I say against her ear, my chest to her back. "You're ours to fuck now, sweet one."

"Ours to knot," Krolic agrees, grabbing her next and kissing her while Craze shreds her panties with one of his cards.

He doesn't wait for her consent or for her to say anything, just goes to his knees from behind, spreads her legs, and starts eating her cunt while Krolic kisses her.

"*Ohh,*" she says against our king's mouth.

"Let him tongue-fuck you," Krolic tells her, his hand around her nape as his opposite arm clasps her waist. "He's going to make you come. Then you're going to straddle Catum while Craze takes your ass." His grip shifts to clasp her chin. "And I'm going to take your mouth."

She shudders.

"Do you hear that, Miss Marvel?" I ask, leaning over Craze to press my lips to her ear again. "We're going to take all three of your holes. All at once. Claim you in the basest way. Make you *ours*. And drown you in our seed."

I can't tell if her trembling is from my words or Craze's actions below. Probably both.

I step back to loosen my tie, my jacket and cuff links long gone, thanks to the bloody battle in the courtyard. Some of those Alphas will never recover.

Others will eventually regenerate.

I'm, thankfully, already healed.

It was a dark day.

But it will culminate in light.

In beauty.

In a future bond.

My tie falls to the ground as I undo the first two buttons of my dress shirt. The sleeves are already rolled to my elbows, so I leave those alone.

All while Krolic whispers sensual promises against our Omega's mouth, telling her how good she's going to look stuffed full of our cocks.

She's nervous. But she's also extremely turned on, as evidenced by Craze below. He's practically drenched in her slick, the elixir more than doing its job.

Fortunately, she's still of sound mind.

Soon, that will change.

But we'll guard her through the process. Protect during her moments of mental weakness. And knot her into oblivion, just the way she needs.

I unbuckle my belt, then unfasten my pants, but I don't take them off.

I want Ailsa to soak my clothes with her arousal.

To claim me in her own way. Mark me as hers. Saturate me with her essence. And tell the world that this Alpha… no, *these Alphas* are hers.

She jolts as Craze begins to prod her backside, preparing her for his cock. It's that or we share her pussy, which I don't think she's ready to do.

That'll be a more advanced session for later in her heat.

Just like wax play.

Knife play.

Blood play.

All play.

We're going to fucking debauch our little Omega. Introduce her to pleasures beyond her imagination. Show her what her future will be with us.

Unbridled rapture.

Intense orgasms.

Delirious states of being.

Subspace.

Flames, I can't fucking wait.

"Do you remember the safe motion that Master Pillar taught you?" Krolic asks her, using my formal title because he knows I like it.

Ailsa blinks groggy eyes at him but nods.

"Show us, Miss Marvel," I demand. "What's your nonverbal safe motion?" Because she's absolutely going to have her mouth full over the next few days. Whether it be sucking our dicks, keeping our cocks warm, or kissing us, there won't be much talking.

Because we're going to be inside her constantly.

Her nipples are tight little points that I long to suck and nip. *Or cover in hot wax.*

Fuck, her tits will look so good with pink marks on them.

I can't fucking wait to play.

But we need to finish this first, claim our prey. Accept her submission. Make her take all three of us as one.

"Oh, Gods," she says as Craze attacks her clit with his mouth. He has three fingers in her ass now, his vigor making her knees shake.

"The motion, Miss Marvel," I remind her. "What is it?"

She fists her hand and lifts it over her head, then grabs on to Krolic as she falls apart.

Fresh slick scents the air, her pussy convulsing in her dire need to be *fucked*. The elixir will have made this orgasm even more intense for her, which explains the soft cries leaving her now as tears trail down her cheeks.

Krolic licks one up with his tongue, then kisses the hell out of her while Craze works her through the passion, his touch no doubt restoking the flames even as she continues to come.

She's panting by the time it's done, her body visibly quivering.

"You're doing so good, baby girl," Krolic says, his fingers in her hair now as he tilts her head back for a better angle against her mouth.

Her breasts are pushed up against his bare chest, making me slightly envious.

Because I want to feel her. To touch her. To take her.

"She's ready," Craze growls, causing her to yelp in surprise. Because he said it right against her clit. She screams then, suggesting he just bit her there, too.

"Shh," Krolic hushes her. "Your body is ours to care for over the next few days. Let us play."

She jumps as Craze repeats the motion, her hand flying down to yank him away. But he doesn't let up, instead grabbing her ass and pressing his face even more into her heat.

"*Craze*," she says on a snarl that quickly morphs into a moan. "What are you doing to me?"

"Owning you," I say as I come up behind her again. "Now get over here and straddle me, Miss Marvel."

She swallows, her eyes finding mine and watching as I go to sit on the ground. I've left my pants undone for her. It'll be her job to pull out my cock and take me into her cunt.

"Go to him," Krolic tells her. "Show him with your hands and your mouth how much you want him."

Her pupils dilate as she considers Krolic's and my words.

Craze slides out from between her thighs, his face saturated in her pleasure and a little bit of blood.

I don't know whether he cut her with one of his blades

or bit her too hard, but the sight of it has my knot throbbing. Because I love the savage way he plays. Love even more that she allows it.

When she turns around, I don't see any evidence of him having truly hurt her. But her thighs are soaked with arousal.

I rest back on my palms.

"Stand near my face first," I tell her. "I want to see what Craze did to your little clit."

She visibly swallows, then walks forward and grabs my shoulders. She's too short to stand directly over my head, but she goes up onto her tiptoes to let me see her pretty pussy.

I don't reach for her.

I simply inhale her.

Then I slowly lean forward to give her a long, sensuous lick. *There*, I think, finding the small cut near her clit, but not on her clit. *Sadistic bastard.*

Yet I can't say I hate it.

The taste of her blood is an aphrodisiac. One that has my cock exploding from my boxers. I lave the wound, loving the way she moans in response.

Our little Omega likes the bite of pain.

That's good.

Very good.

"You want my cock, Miss Marvel?" I ask against her weeping sex. "You want us to fuck you?"

"Yes," she whispers.

"Prove it," I demand. "Show me with your mouth."

CATUM

Ailsa trembles, her legs shaking with the effort of having remained on her toes. But she gracefully moves back, then kneels between my legs. Her eyes hold mine as she parts my pants. However, I stop her when she tries to take them off. "No, Miss Marvel. My clothes are staying on until we're back in the nest. So get creative."

Her brow furrows, like she's not sure what I mean.

Craze must take pity on her because he makes a show of taking his own cock out and giving it a stroke without removing his jeans.

Her nostrils flare, her focus on his decorated shaft.

Then she looks down at my groin and reaches for my boxer shorts.

She finds the opening inside them and guides my dick out, the head already beading with precum.

"Your mouth, Miss Marvel," I remind her, the challenge in my tone unmistakable.

Just as her acceptance of the challenge is noticeable as she leans down to suck the droplet from my head, all while holding my gaze.

"Fuck, that's good," I tell her, pleased. "How deep do you want me in your pussy? Just the tip?"

She narrows her eyes, catching the hint, and takes more of me into her mouth.

"So halfway in, then?" I say, taunting her.

Our sweet little Omega growls, her lips moving downward as she grips my knot and gives it a violent squeeze.

"*Fuck...*" I've been beaten at my own game. Because *that* was exactly what I needed from her. Exactly what I desired. A little fire. A way to know our Omega is still with us and not at all afraid to voice her own needs. "Again, Miss Marvel. Do it *again.*"

Craze goes to his knees behind her, his pants having disappeared along with his shirt. He meets my gaze over her back, and I give him a nod, aware of what he wants to do.

He grabs her hips, causing her to yelp around my cock.

"Focus on my dick, Miss Marvel," I command. "And let Craze play."

He lifts her rump into the air, then positions his cock at her slick entrance.

She screams as he slams inside her, his head falling back in a display of beautiful agony.

"He needs to lubricate his cock," Krolic says softly. "It'll help him take your ass, sweet girl."

Ailsa's eyes water, making her exceptionally pretty with my shaft sliding in and out of her plump lips. I tell her so and smile when she moans.

Because she likes our praise.

Our compliments.

To know what she does to us.

"If you keep clamping down on Craze like that, you're going to make him come," I tell her. "And I'll be very upset. Because I want to knot your pussy next. So stop taunting him."

She whines and Craze fucks her harder, torturing her with his pierced dick.

Because those metal beads are texturized for her pleasure, and I know the head of his cock is hitting that spot deep inside, the one that makes her want to come.

"Don't you dare orgasm," I tell her. "If you clamp down any harder on Craze, he'll knot you. Hold it back, Ailsa. Wait until I'm inside your pussy."

She looks ready to fall into oblivion, her expression blissed out and almost unaware.

So I reach down and tug on her tit, purposely twisting her nipple along the way.

It's enough to drag her back to us, to stave off her orgasm and keep her on the edge.

Which is exactly where we need her.

Craze and I lock gazes again, another wordless exchange happening between us as he eases out of her cunt. "Crawl up there and put Catum inside you, gorgeous," he says against her ear.

She's barely coherent, her body primed and ready to explode.

I tug her off my dick, my fingers fisting in her hair as I continue to hold myself up with one hand on the ground behind me.

"Come fuck me, Miss Marvel."

Her eyes nearly roll into the back of her head. But a smack on her ass from Craze has her moving, her slick thighs instantly parting over my hips as she rubs herself wantonly against my colorful shaft.

I can't wait to show her what these tattoos do.

I'm about to remind her of what she's supposed to be

doing when she goes up onto her knees and brings my cock to her entrance.

My fingers clench in her hair as she starts to lower herself onto me, her quavering body reminding me of a sexed-up goddess.

"Fuck, you feel amazing, Miss Marvel."

"Likewise, Master Pillar," she purrs, her words nearly shocking me out of my oblivion.

She's learning.

And I fucking love how quickly she's picking up on what makes each of us tick.

I pull her into me, kissing her soundly as she takes me all the way into her slick channel, her tight little body pulsing around mine.

Amazing is no longer the right adjective.

Unbelievable.

Unreal.

Fantastic.

None of those words are good enough.

And I stop trying to find the right one the moment our tongues touch.

She moans, kissing me with a passion I feel to my very soul as her hips begin to move.

But Craze stops her, his heat joining ours as he kneels behind her once more. "Reach back and spread your cheeks for me," he says against her ear, making her jolt.

"Do what he says, Ailsa," Krolic murmurs. "Because the sooner he's in your ass, the sooner I can fuck your mouth. And I'm feeling particularly left out over here."

He's standing right beside us, his hand massaging his knot as he prepares himself for her throat.

She's probably going to choke on his seed.

But that's all right. We'll help her through it.

Her limbs are still trembling as she reaches behind to

expose herself for Craze. He curses, clearly pleased with the invitation, and wastes no time pressing himself at her back entrance.

"This is going to be intense," I warn her. "Just try to breathe through the burn, Miss Marvel. Once he's seated, we'll make you see stars."

Hell, she'll probably pass out.

Ailsa goes rigid as Craze starts to push forward.

"Relax," I whisper against her mouth. "I promise this will feel so fucking good once we start fucking you. But you need to let him in."

She bites her lip, and I lean forward to suck that poor bottom lip into my mouth. Then I lave it with my tongue before kissing her deeply.

Her arms are tense as she continues to expose herself to Craze, her body frozen at an extremely sensual angle.

I'm sure it's driving Krolic mad seeing her like this. But he's as patient as I am, if not more so.

"So fucking tight," Craze groans, his head falling back as he shoves his hips forward, forcing her to take the rest of him in a single thrust.

She screams against my mouth. I tighten my grip on her hair, commanding her to stay right where she is as I devour her. But she starts to move her hips like she's trying to get away from us, like it's too much to take.

Which feels so fucking good that I can't help but growl. "Keep doing that, Miss Marvel, and you'll be getting my knot sooner than expected."

Craze grunts, his hands suddenly on her hips. "Where do you think you're going to go, gorgeous? You're impaled on both our cocks. Fucking accept that, or you'll end up hurting yourself."

Ailsa releases a soft cry, one I swallow before gently kissing her.

She's no longer holding herself open for Craze, but shoving against my chest.

Yet not once does she lift her hand into a fist.

This is just her body fighting the inevitable.

And once we get moving, she'll understand the purpose of the pain.

"Do you feel full, baby girl?" Krolic asks softly. "Stretched in an unimaginable way, perhaps?"

She nods, tears trailing down her cheeks. "It's too much."

"It's not," he promises her as he brushes his thumb along her jaw. "Soon, you'll beg us to double knot your pussy."

Her eyes widen. "Double knot…?"

"We'll work up to it," I whisper, tilting her head toward Krolic. "Now part those pretty lips for our king, Miss Marvel. Let him fuck that delectable mouth while Craze and I make you feel good."

Her throat works, her pupils blown wide with lust.

A lust that only grows hotter as Krolic takes control of her chin and angles his cock toward her mouth. "Ready, baby girl?"

She seems torn on nodding and shaking her head but leans forward to lick him like the good little Omega that she is. Then she parts her lips around him and takes him as deep as she can without gagging.

"Good girl," he praises. "Don't overexert yourself. We have a long few days ahead of us."

She practically vibrates in response to his words, the sensation making my balls tighten in anticipation.

I once again meet Krolic's gaze and give him a look I know he understands because his lips curl.

Craze slowly drags himself out to the tip, then rams

himself back in, causing our Omega to jolt and scream. Except it's a garbled sound since her mouth is full of cock.

"Careful with your teeth, baby girl," Krolic tells her, a hint of dominance in his tone. "I like pain, but not that kind of pain."

She swallows around him, then braces as Craze does it again.

"Relax," I remind her. "We're going to take care of you, Ailsa. Just trust your body to accept this. I promise you'll love it."

Her eyes close, and I allow it for the moment. She needs a few seconds to mentally regroup.

Craze slides in and out of her a third time, then a fourth time, and by the fifth, her cheeks are flushed.

On the sixth, she groans.

And on the seventh, I reach between us to thumb her clit.

Her eyes fly open once more, revealing lust-drunk irises. "There's our pretty Omega," I murmur. "Look how much you love this." I apply a little more pressure against her sensitive nub. "You're submitting so beautifully, Miss Marvel."

"So fucking perfectly," Krolic echoes, his grip shifting to her nape as he starts to fuck her mouth. "Keep that throat relaxed for me." He still has his other hand on his knot, likely to stop it from exploding down her throat. He'll hold it back while his seed slides over her tongue.

Craze probably won't hold his back in her ass. He'll want her to feel the undercurrent of pain while she experiences the ecstasy of my knot.

Flames, it'll feel good.

So. Fucking. Good.

The three of us start to let go, our control snapping as

Ailsa embraces what's happening to her, as our prey finally succumbs to being caught. Dominated. *Owned.*

It's the hottest fucking experience of my very long life.

I can feel Craze through the thin wall inside her. He's taking her ass with abandon, while I pump up into her pussy with the same savage vigor.

And Krolic… he's utterly lost to her mouth.

She's struggling to breathe, but if it's bothering her, she doesn't show it. She just revels in the moment, her tight little cunt squeezing the hell out of my dick.

Our Omega is going to come. *Hard.*

I circle her clit, pushing her closer and closer to the edge, needing to feel her channel tighten around me. Wanting her claim just as much as I want to claim her in kind.

"That's it, Miss Marvel," I tell her. "We caught you. Which means you're ours. Now show us what that means and come for us."

Craze roars, fucking her harder.

Krolic's grip on his knot looks almost painful.

All while our Omega writhes, taking us like she was made for this moment.

"Now, Ailsa," I command, pinching her clit. She jolts, then screams as I release it with the word *"Come."*

Her ecstasy is like a tidal wave of heat, her body strung tight and exploding between us. It's a beautiful fucking sight that instantly has my knot surging up from my shaft as my tattoos begin to swirl inside her, massaging her in the most intimate of ways.

Her eyes widen.

My lips curl.

"Hang on to me, Miss Marvel," I purr, my knot erupting as my seed pours into her. "You're about to see the stars."

Craze follows us over the edge next, his knot shooting into her ass and drawing a scream of shock from our Omega.

A scream that morphs into something else entirely as Krolic starts coming down her throat.

She starts to panic, her eyes wild, but a simple twist of my hips grounds her right back into her rapturous state.

"Swallow, Miss Marvel," I tell her, my thumb drawing a line down her throat. "Our king has a lot for you to take. Just keep swallowing until he's done."

Her nails bite into my shoulders as she clings to me, clearly overwhelmed. But as she gives in to the orgasmic spiral again, she loosens her grip and relaxes just like I've told her to do.

"Fuck, baby girl," Krolic whispers reverently as her throat works over and over again. "*Fuck.* I'm going to keep coming on her tits."

That part is for me, the warning a second before he pulls out of her mouth to stroke himself over her chest. I move my hand away from her neck at the same time, letting him claim her breasts while I continue to unload in her sweet cunt.

She's barely coherent, lost to the oblivion created by our joint efforts.

When Krolic puts his dick back at her mouth, she parts her lips and keeps drinking while he squeezes his knot. Then he lets his seed go down her throat and shoulders, marking her as his.

It's fucking exquisite.

The fiercest fuck of my life.

And we get to do it again as soon as we finish.

Knowing that has me pulling our Omega in for a kiss. She's drenched in Krolic's essence, but I don't fucking care. I need to worship this woman with my tongue. Tell her how much I appreciate this gift. This experience. This *everything*.

Craze is next, his fingers twining through her hair as he yanks her back to fuck her mouth with his tongue.

He drags his teeth along her lip, biting down in a way that will surely bruise, then kisses her again while filling her ass with his claim.

Krolic is last. But he doesn't take her with his mouth. Instead, he feeds her his dick again and says, "Don't swallow."

Her eyes fly open, confusion written in her features as he fills her mouth with his cum.

Then he tilts her head back to stare down at her. "Show me."

She parts her lips to reveal a mouth full of his seed.

"Such a good fucking mate," he tells her, his thumb tracing her mouth. "We're going to breed you now, Omega. Put our heir in your belly. Tell me you approve."

Ailsa doesn't immediately say anything at all, just holds his gaze.

Then she defiantly swallows.

"I approve," she says throatily. "Now give me more of your essence."

Krolic grins, leaning down to kiss her instead. "You're fucking perfect, Ailsa."

"A beautifully exquisite mate," I agree.

But it's Craze who says what needs to be said.

The words that ring with the utmost of truth.

Ones that will carry through the kingdom for everyone to hear.

Because our Omega has chosen us.

And we have chosen her.

All of which becomes perfectly clear as Craze says, "You're our Monsterland Queen."

AILSA

I'M FLOATING.

Or rather, I'm being carried.

But it feels like floating.

Like I'm high in the sky, existing in a beautiful place set in the clouds.

Fingers comb through my hair.

Lips meet my shoulder.

A deep voice murmurs in my ear.

It's all a blur. But I can smell my mates. Their distinctive aromas swirling around me, in me, through me.

I sigh, content to be engulfed in their warmth.

At least until a strange pang blossoms to life in my lower belly. I instantly clutch my abdomen, a hiss leaving my lips as I try to determine the cause of the pain.

"Shh," one of my mates hushes. *Krolic.* "Your heat is starting."

"Starting?" I echo, wincing as the agony grows.

We just experienced the most blissful event in the history of existence. And he says my heat is just now *starting*?

Oh, Gods...

These men already awoke a pleasure inside me unlike any other.

I don't think I can handle another round.

Not yet.

Not until I've come down from my high. Maybe had a bath. Eaten something. Had a glass of water, too, perhaps.

As though someone heard that request, a straw meets my lip. I suck without asking questions, earning me a deep groan from Craze. "Graves, you have the most incredible mouth, Ailsa. I can't wait to feel it wrapped around my cock again."

"I thought you wanted to share her pussy?" Catum asks, his words making my cheeks flame.

"That, too," Craze drawls. "I want it all."

The straw disappears and is replaced by Craze's tongue as he carries me somewhere. I'm no longer paying attention to our surroundings. I don't think I have been in quite some time, actually. Because we went through a portal. To where, I have no idea. However, it smells nice.

Like fire, cedar, and spice.

"You did a good job preparing the nest," Krolic says while Craze continues kissing me.

"It wasn't easy," Catum mutters. "Not with the escalated timetable. But I did my best."

"I think she'll love it, won't you, baby girl?" Krolic's fingers are suddenly in my hair, tilting my head toward him as he commands my attention.

I'm not really sure what he just asked, so I provide a lazy "Mm-hmm" in approval.

He chuckles. "You look exquisitely fucked, my love." His nose drags across my cheek. "I can smell myself all over you."

"Because you came all over her," Craze says.

"And I fully intend to do it again," Krolic returns before claiming my mouth.

That strange pulsing inside me—the one that's part

pain, part something else—springs to life again. I groan in response, both uncomfortable and turned on.

It's… a bizarre juxtaposition.

I don't understand it.

But then, I don't understand a lot of this.

I'm just embracing the absurdity. Reveling in life. Existing with my mates.

Gods, three Alphas.

All of them are mine.

I can feel it in my soul.

However, the bond isn't complete.

The kingdom needs an heir.

Krolic said something to me on the way here, something about how it doesn't matter who impregnates me first, just that it happens.

"So we're all going to breed you," he whispered against my ear. "All day and all night."

My thighs clench as I recall those words now.

I can't imagine doing this for hours, let alone days. I'm… I'm exhausted.

Yet I can feel the warmth growing inside me, the need stirring an intense sort of tension in my lower belly.

Krolic's tongue whispers across mine, deepening that yearning until I'm panting against him. "Mmm, you're almost ready," he says. "But I need you to eat something first, Ailsa."

He releases me to Catum, who presses something against my mouth. I part for him instinctually, then moan when I realize whatever he just gave me is cherry flavored.

"Beautiful," he praises. "You're fucking stunning, Miss Marvel."

I'm not sure how I find myself in his lap, but I do. He alternates between cherry treats and water, while Craze reaches over to feed me savory bites of cheese and meat.

The food doesn't seem to help the growing ache inside me, though.

When I tell Catum this, he replies, "That's because you're going into heat, Ailsa. The only thing that will satisfy you is a knot."

I shiver. "Is that why we'll be... fucking for days?" *Fucking* feels foreign on my lips. I rarely use that word. But it seems appropriate now.

And my mates seem to approve because they all grin at me in response.

"We'll be fucking you for days because we want to fuck you for days," Craze drawls. "We don't need you to be in heat for that."

"Pretty sure we're going to live inside you for the rest of our lives, baby girl," Krolic adds with a wink.

My cheeks flame in response. "That sounds..." I trail off, unable to fathom a reply.

"Sexy?" Craze offers. "Hot? Really fucking nice? Like a dream come true?"

Catum chuckles beneath me. "We'll let you shower, Ailsa. And rest. Sometimes."

My eyes widen. "*Sometimes?*"

He shrugs. "When the mood strikes."

Oh, Gods. "I don't think I can do this all the time."

"I'll remember that in about two hours when you're begging us to never stop knotting you," he murmurs, an amused look in his eyes. "But before we begin, is there anything you're truly afraid of?"

My brow furrows. "What do you mean?"

"Anything that you don't want done to you?" he rephrases. "You don't seem all that opposed to pain, which is good. We like mingling pain with pleasure. Not in a punishment kind of way, though. We're more into sensual play."

"Can you…?" I clear my throat. "Can you give me some examples?"

He looks at Krolic. "Can you get me the red candle?"

My frown deepens, confused by the subject change.

But Catum ignores me and starts clearing the table off in front of him.

When Krolic sets the candle down, Catum touches the wick, creating a flame with his fingertip. My gaze widens. "That's impressive."

He snorts. "Not nearly as impressive as the things I'm about to do to you, Miss Marvel." He picks up the candle and swirls it. "Now back to our discussion. I need to know if anything scares you. Like, say, fire." He brings it close, and I just blink at the flames.

"I… I don't want to be burned by it," I say slowly. "But it doesn't scare me."

He nods as Craze slides his chair closer, a knife twirling between his fingers. "What about blades?"

I stare at him. "Are you asking to stab me?"

He chuckles. "No, gorgeous. But I like blood. Just little knicks that create a sting." He holds out his palm. "Give me your hand and I'll show you."

I bite my cheek but do what he asks. He leans down to kiss my palm, his tongue tracing the pad and applying a subtle pressure that has my legs clenching again. I relax against Catum, liking this sensation.

Then yelp as Craze slices his blade across my skin. "*What…?*" I try to yank my hand away, but he seals his mouth over the wound—which I quickly realize is just a little scrape—and *sucks*.

My eyes widen.

Why…? Why does that… feel good?

His tongue runs along the shallow laceration, his eyes

holding mine the entire time. "Now imagine that on your breast," he murmurs, leaning back to look at my chest.

"Hmm, speaking of," Catum murmurs, the candle suddenly too close for comfort.

My lips part as he tilts the jar, causing some of the red liquid to pool.

"This is special wax," he tells me as it slowly leaks over the edge.

I jump as it lands right on my nipple, the sting of it eliciting a hiss from me.

"It cools quickly," he goes on, like he isn't torturing me. "And the process of removing it is… quite fun."

Another speck lands on my areola, and a third on my stiff peak.

All three men are transfixed by the sight, while I'm trying to decide if it hurts or feels good. The temporary pain distracted me from my overheated insides, but now those sensations seem to be burning with a renewed force.

Catum sets the candle aside—the spicy scent of it reminding me of Craze—and leans down to blow across my chest.

I shiver.

"Craze?" he murmurs.

The most mercurial one of my mates smiles and takes out his knife again, this time angling it toward my breast.

I hold my breath, both terrified and interested in whatever comes next.

He gently scrapes the wax from my skin, careful not to cut me. Which is a relief, and startling since he just mentioned wanting to use his knife on my chest.

But perhaps it's not knowing his intentions that creates the excitement. *Will he hurt me or please me?* I wonder, only to suddenly find my nipple in Catum's mouth.

A loud moan escapes me, the sensation of having his sensual attention after feeling the burn is… is… *amazing*.

The warmth inside me nearly combusts, my thighs instantly slick. *Oh, Gods…* I feel like I'm about to come.

Yet all too soon, the feeling is gone, and Craze is pressing another treat to my lips.

I'm trembling. "You're teasing me," I realize aloud.

"Testing your limits a little, yes," Catum replies with a devilish twinkle in his brown eyes. "You're about to give us your body for the next few days, and we want to make sure we care for it properly."

"We don't want to scare you," Krolic adds, his voice gruff. He's standing across from us, one shoulder propped against the wall, his cock fully erect.

Catum still has on his dress shirt and pants.

Craze is in jeans and nothing else.

And Krolic is as naked as me.

"Are you all right with being bound?" Catum asks me.

"She is," Craze answers for me, then sends me a wink. "We played with some vines, didn't we, gorgeous?"

I shiver, remembering his jump-rope routine that ended with me being tied up against him. "Yes," I whisper. I would definitely do that again.

"What about the idea of us double knotting your cunt?" Krolic asks, causing my eyes to widen. "The stretch will hurt. But the eventual pleasure… well." He smiles. "I think you'll enjoy that part."

I swallow, my insides suddenly on fire. "Okay," I tell him.

Because I'm crazy.

Insane, even.

But honestly, I trust these men to take care of me.

To protect me.

To keep me safe.

And I tell them that.

"There are no limits here," I conclude, meeting each of their gazes. "Because I know you'll never do anything to hurt me, and you'll always respect my choices."

They've more than proved that.

These men are my future.

My Alphas.

My mates.

I want to explore everything with them. Be their queen. Their Omega. And develop a new existence with them by my side.

This little realm of unordinary possibilities is my new normal. I accept that. I accept *them*.

Which means there's really only one thing left to do.

"Take me to bed," I tell them.

But Catum shakes his head. "No, sweet one." He lifts me into his arms. "We're going to take you to our *nest*."

I hold on to his shoulders as he moves, my gaze searching his. "Nest?"

He nods. "We prepared it just for you."

"Because we hoped you would accept our mating," Krolic adds.

"And agree to be brought here for your heat," Craze concludes.

I have no idea what he's talking about. And I'm no less confused when he sets me down on a large, beautiful mattress laden with silky sheets. "This is a bed," I tell him.

He smiles. "One you're going to turn into a nest."

"I don't understand."

"You will," he promises as he starts unbuttoning his shirt. "When your instincts kick in."

My eyes track across his sinewy muscles, enjoying the show of him stripping. "If you say so," I reply, my throat going dry.

"Nesting is what Omegas do once they're pregnant," Craze explains as he pulls me into his body in the center of the bed.

His hard cock lands against my thigh, making me gasp. I have no idea when he lost his pants, but he's very aroused now. And he proceeds to show me just how aroused by pushing me under him and settling between my splayed thighs.

He slides into me in a single thrust, sending electric shocks to every nerve ending in my body. "So fucking wet," he says, gliding in and out of me as Krolic and Catum settle onto the bed on either side of us. "So fucking *breedable*."

"Fertile," Krolic growls. "She's fertile."

"I know," Craze says, groaning as he begins to really move inside me. "Fuck, gorgeous, I'm going to need you to come around my dick."

I clutch his shoulders as he starts to fuck me even harder, his movements hitting me deep inside and igniting an inferno of need. I groan as dampness pools inside my sex, coating Craze's cock and spilling onto my thighs.

It's… it's something I don't fully understand. But ohhhh, it heightens the sensations.

Sensations that skyrocket even higher as Catum takes my mouth with his own. Krolic is next, his palm grabbing my breast and giving it a squeeze before taunting my nipple with his thumb.

Someone—Catum, I think—slides his hand between me and Craze, his thumb going straight to my clit. "You heard Craze," he says, his mouth near my ear. "He wants you to come all over his cock."

My thighs clench, drawing a groan from Craze. "So fucking tight." He slams into me even more, his grip on my hips bruising. But I don't care. It feels so good. I'm lifting my hips to meet him thrust for thrust.

And suddenly I'm spiraling, losing my mind, *screaming* with desire.

It hits me all at once.

Not an orgasm, but an unadulterated craving that takes my breath away. It fractures my mind. Alters my spirit.

I… I need so much more. This isn't enough. I… I'm on *fire*. Literal *fire*. Or maybe not literally. I don't know. I'm just a mess of need, the sensations so intense I can't stop screaming.

The men are all moving, their touch and mouths seeming to worship every inch of me at once.

But it's not enough.

I tell them this.

I beg.

I *demand*.

It hurts. It burns. It's too much.

"Breathe," Krolic says against my ear, his body behind mine.

I don't understand the request.

I'm too busy *screaming*.

And then I feel him enter my ass, his penetration momentarily grounding as pain shoots across my body. But the temporary reprieve soon dissipates as the fire reignites.

Craze is at my front, his hands massaging my breasts.

Catum is—

His cock thrusts into my mouth, going so deep that I choke. But it's a blissful action, one that helps me understand who I am and where I am.

However, like everything else, it's fleeting.

Suddenly, all I am is a ball of nerves. Of sensation. Of *need*.

And my Alphas are fucking me. Taking me. Giving me their seed.

I taste it in my mouth, feel it in my ass, and sigh as a knot locks inside my womb.

I don't care who is where, just that I'm full. Claimed. *Home*.

My world.
My chaos.
My own exquisite… happily-ever-after.

EPILOGUE

AILSA

SEVERAL DAYS LATER

"WHERE ARE WE?" I ask, staring out at the violet-colored evergreens. It's the first time I've really taken in our surroundings since my mates brought me here after the ritual.

I've spent most of my time in the nest.

Nest, I repeat to myself, giddy with excitement. I didn't understand that term at first, but I do now. I just put the finishing touches on it this morning after stealing a pair of Catum's boxer briefs.

He piled it high with linens.

I added their clothing.

Because my nest needs to smell like my mates.

A perfect midnight hike, I decide. *Cedar. Spice. And a hint of smoke.*

"The Violet Forest," Catum tells me from the kitchen. He's making a hot chocolate because I never tried the one in the Ice Planes, and he wants to rectify that. "This is where I'm from originally. So it's my favorite of the homes we own."

I smile. "I like it here, too."

He gives me an indulgent look. "After everything we've done to you here, you should like it, Ailsa."

My cheeks flame. I can still feel his and Krolic's knots pulsing inside me. They shared me this morning as I was coming out of my heat, their cocks stretching my sex so much that I'm surprised I can walk.

But one thing I'm quickly learning is that I'm no longer human.

I heal just like they do.

And from what I understand, all three men are very old.

Immortality exists in this world. My being an Omega has basically turned me immortal, too. Or maybe that's our mating. I'm not sure.

However, I'm thankful for the perks because it means pregnancy should be easier.

That's my hope, anyway.

I press a palm to my belly, aware that a little life is growing inside me now. I can't really sense it, but my mates can. They have no idea who the father is, and from what they've told me, it doesn't matter.

"We're all the father, baby girl," Krolic said earlier. "What matters is that you're both safe and protected." He kissed me on the forehead, then led me to the kitchen.

He's sitting at the bar now, scanning some sort of tablet.

And frowning.

"What's wrong?" I ask him as I slide onto the stool beside him.

"I forgot how much fun it is to be king," he grumbles. "The kingdom wants a coronation."

"So you can reclaim your throne?" I guess.

But he shakes his head. "No. So they can meet their new queen." His green eyes glance my way, his silver hair glinting in the sunlight streaming in from outside through the trees and glass. "I don't suppose you're up for a ball?"

"A ball?" I echo.

"We'll find you a dress that actually fits," Catum says as he sets the hot chocolate on the counter before me. "Shoes, too."

I snort. "Craze told me this morning that I'm not allowed to wear clothes ever again." He also said I will forever sleep with his knot inside me, because apparently we did that a few times over the last several days.

"I'll make an exception if the dress has a corset," he says as he enters the room, his dark hair dripping with water from his shower. "One I can cut off of you with a blade." He kisses my bare shoulder, then reaches around to tweak my nipple. "And good job obeying my rules, gorgeous."

I roll my eyes. "I chose not to wear clothes because I'm hot."

"That you are," he drawls. "That you are."

I ignore him and instead focus on Krolic. "What kind of ball?"

"A Monsterland-themed one," he replies, his lips curling. "Which means it'll be extraordinarily strange."

"Hmm," I hum. "I may actually enjoy that."

"You'll enjoy what we do to you afterward," Craze interjects. "That I can promise you." He grabs a ball from the platter on the counter and pops it into his mouth. "French toast bites are my favorite."

"I know," Catum says. "But I made them for our mate."

"I doubt she needs a hundred of them, Pillar."

"She's eating for two, de Hatte."

"And she can choose how many she wants," I interject,

grabbing one for myself before smiling at Catum. "Thank you, Catum."

"You're welcome, Ailsa." He looks at the hot chocolate. "Don't forget to try it."

"Why do I get the feeling there's something sexual about this drink?"

"Because you just spent five days exploring our knots," Krolic murmurs. "Sex is all any of us are thinking about right now."

"And balls," I point out, then giggle as I glance down at his lap. "Two kinds of balls now." I pop the French toast into my mouth, then frown. "Make that three."

Catum chuckles. "I think she's lust drunk."

"That just means we did our job," Craze murmurs, grabbing another bite. "So when are we hosting this coronation ball, K?"

He considers the three of us, then glances down at my belly. "Maybe in three weeks?" he suggests.

"Three weeks?" Craze sounds surprised. "I assumed you would want it to be sooner."

Krolic shakes his head. "We're on our babymoon."

"Babymoon?" I echo.

His alluring eyes slowly return to mine. "Omegas need a lot of attention when they're pregnant, baby girl. Almost as much as when they're in heat."

My legs tingle. "Oh."

"So obviously, we'll need to tend to your every need." He reaches out to drag my stool closer to him. "Ensure all of your desires are met." He leans into my space. "And thank you properly for being ours by worshipping every inch of your beautiful form."

"I… I think I like that," I whisper.

"Yeah?" He smiles. "I think we do, too." His lips brush

mine. "Now be a good girl and drink that hot chocolate. I think Catum may have added some special spices to it."

My brow furrows. "Special spices?"

"Try it and find out," he tells me.

I rotate in my chair to meet Catum's brown orbs. "Did you come in my drink?"

He bursts out laughing and shakes his head. "Only you would ask me that, Miss Marvel."

"That's not an answer, Master Pillar."

His lips curve upward as he shakes his head. "I'm not Craze."

I arch a brow. "That's still not an answer."

"I didn't come in your drink, Miss Marvel. If I wanted you to drink my cum, I would fuck your mouth." He leans over the counter, his gaze holding mine. "Which I now think I'm going to do as soon as you finish eating."

My nipples instantly harden, all signs of mirth dying between us.

These men do things to me. Good things.

I pick up the hot chocolate and take a sip, all while holding his gaze.

The flavor explodes across my tongue, eliciting a moan from deep within.

"You added cherries," I whisper.

"I added cherries," he confirms. "Now finish your glass so I can give you something else to drink."

I swallow.

This life is nothing like I dreamt it could be. It's better. *So. Much. Better.*

Because it's real.

Wonderful.

And perfectly... unordinary.

Thank you for reading *Monsterland Mayhem!*

MUSIC PLAYLIST

Circus Psycho - Diggy Graves
The Way That I Fiddle (3CHO Remix) - 3CHO & Clejan
Lets Go - Clejan
Pac Ave - Diggy Graves
Call Out - 3CHO & Clejan
Sad Reality (feat. Casey Cook) - Codeko
Shakedown - Clejan & West Coast Massive
Somebody Else - Bad Omens
A Little Bit Off - Five Finger Death Punch
Just Pretend - Bad Omens
Wolf Totem - The HU & Jacoby Shaddix
Take Me Back to Eden - Sleep Token
A Symptom of Being Human - Shinedown
Lose Control - Teddy Swims
Heavy Is The Crown - Daughtry
Evidence - Letdown
The Death is a Peace of mind - Bad Omens
Valhalla Calling - Miracle of Sound
Someday, Gone Forever - DSWL
Don't Look Back - Ludovico Moro
Distance Echoes - VXLLAIN, V0J & Narvent
On My Knees - Skeler
Fos - Amanati
Phelian - Fluidified
Stay With Me - Dreamer

USA Today Bestselling Author Lexi C. Foss loves to play in dark worlds, especially the ones that bite. She lives in Chapel Hill, North Carolina with her husband and their furry children. When not writing, she's busy crossing items off her travel bucket list, or chasing eclipses around the globe. She's quirky, consumes way too much coffee, and loves to swim.

Want access to the most up-to-date information for all of Lexi's books? Sign-up for her newsletter here.

Lexi also likes to hang out with readers on Facebook in her exclusive readers group - Join Here.

Where To Find Lexi:
www.LexiCFoss.com

ALSO BY LEXI C. FOSS

Blood Alliance Series - Dystopian Paranormal

Chastely Bitten

Royally Bitten

Regally Bitten

Rebel Bitten

Kingly Bitten

Cruelly Bitten

Blood Alliance Standalones - Dystopian Paranormal

Blood Day

Blood City

Crave Me

Frost Bitten

Dark Provenance Series - Paranormal Romance

Heiress of Bael (FREE!)

Daughter of Death

Son of Chaos

Paramour of Sin

Princess of Bael

Captive of Hell

Elemental Fae Academy - Reverse Harem

Book One

Book Two

Book Three

Elemental Fae Queen

Winter Fae Queen

Hell Fae - Reverse Harem

Hell Fae Captive

Hell Fae Warden

Hell Fae Commander

Hell Fae Prince

Hell Fae King

Immortal Curse Series - Paranormal Romance

Book One: Blood Laws

Book Two: Forbidden Bonds

Book Three: Blood Heart

Book Four: Blood Bonds

Book Five: Angel Bonds

Book Six: Blood Seeker

Book Seven: Wicked Bonds

Book Eight: Blood King

Immortal Curse World - Short Stories & Bonus Fun

Elder Bonds

Blood Burden

Assassin Bonds

Mershano Empire Series - Contemporary Romance

Book One: The Prince's Game

Book Two: The Charmer's Gambit

Book Three: The Rebel's Redemption

Midnight Fae Academy - Reverse Harem

Ella's Masquerade

Book One

Book Two

Book Three

Book Four

Netherworld Fae - Reverse Harem

Their Lethal Pet

Bride of Death

Noir Reformatory - Ménage Paranormal Romance

The Beginning

First Offense

Second Offense

Third Offense

Fourth Offense

Underworld Royals Series - Dark Paranormal Romance

Happily Ever Crowned

Happily Ever Bitten

X-Clan Series - Dystopian Paranormal

X-Clan: The Origin

Andorra Sector

X-Clan: The Experiment

Winter's Arrow

Bariloche Sector

Venom Island

V-Clan Series - Dystopian Paranormal

Blood Sector

Night Sector

Eclipse Sector

Kodiak Sector

Vampire Dynasty - Dark Paranormal

Violet Slays

Crossed Fates

Other Books

Scarlet Mark - Standalone Romantic Suspense

Rotanev - Standalone Poseidon Tale

Carnage Island - Standalone Reverse Harem Romance

Monsterland Mayhem - Standalone Reverse Harem Romance

Claim Me - Standalone Reverse Harem Romance